# SUNFAIL

BY

STEVEN
SAVILE

*Infamous*

Published by Akashic Books
©2015 Steven Savile

ISBN-13: 978-1-61775-406-7
Library of Congress Control Number: 2015933796

Printed in Canada

*Infamous Books*
www.infamousbooks.com

*Akashic Books*
Twitter: @AkashicBooks
Facebook: AkashicBooks
E-mail: info@akashicbooks.com
Website: www.akashicbooks.com

MIX
Paper from
responsible sources
FSC® C004071

## Also Available from Infamous Books

*H.N.I.C.*
by Albert "Prodigy" Johnson with Steven Savile

*The White House*
by JaQuavis Coleman

*Black Lotus*
by K'wan

*Swing*
by Miasha

*Caught Up*
by Shannon Holmes

*For Pat, a man of most excellent musical taste (meaning he's as lost to the eighties as I am) and my mortal enemy in fantasy football. Next year we shall rise—heed my warning and tremble . . . with laughter.*

# BEFORE THE END

I
T STARTED WITH THE DOGS HOWLING.
Their desperate barks mingled in the dark to become a single dangerous note. They prowled the streets, claws skittering across the blacktop. Their eyes glowed feverishly in the shadows as their growls echoed off the stone, brick, and concrete to fill the night. They were the creatures of nightmare, driven mad by some unseen force. They ran the avenues, hunting in packs.

News reports were already calling Manhattan "Dogland."

Above the skyscrapers and tenements storms brewed. The cloud formations were unlike anything that had been seen over the city before. It was more than just winter skies. They gathered, churning, swirling, swarming, promising the storm of the century. At first a flicker of wind would spring up, barely a breeze, but those flickers grew and grew until they were bullying people through the streets. As the wind raced through the canyons of the city it gathered in strength, feeding on the vitality of New York City as it whipped up the trash and yesterday's news lining the gutter and tossed both equally high in the air. From that little flicker of wind a maelstrom grew, strong enough to pull lovers' hands apart as they crossed Central Park, strong enough to panic horses and send their carriages careening across the six lanes of black-top, uprooting saplings.

And then the rains came.

They pelted the brownstones and office blocks alike with bullet-hard drops, the deluge deafening as it drowned the world in a gray blur.

The sky itself was tortured, bleeding purple, sometimes green, sometimes blue-black, shot through with veins of lightning that barely lit the damned dark long enough to cast forked shadows on the ground. It seemed that the storms were never going to end, as though the sun itself had failed them, and then as suddenly as they began, the storms ended with the clouds rolling back across the heavens, golden rays spearing down.

It was almost as if the city had been born again.

Evangelists took to the subways and the street corners, preaching a brand-new gospel. This time, they swore on their holy books, the end truly was nigh. They asked the question: "Have you made your peace with your god?" It didn't matter what creed or denomination, all of the gods old and new were ready for your confession, they promised. And why not? It was the end of the year, why not the end of the world as well?

They always talked about the end of the world, nuclear winter, mutually assured destruction, asteroids colliding with the earth, knocking Gaia off her axis, the sun imploding or burning out; there was always a cult somewhere in the city that believed all of these eventualities and more. As each year wound down, each decade ticked over, they'd crawl out of the woodwork to claim we were killing our planet. Fear is part of the cycle of life; it's as simple as that. Fear that tomorrow will be different. Fear that it won't. But with the storms and the dogs and everything else, so many portents everywhere you looked that couldn't be ignored, it felt different this time. They even had a hashtag for it on Twitter, *#sunfail*. It trended for six days. On the seventh day there was no Internet.

It was only natural that people panicked, that manners faded and the rules of polite society crumbled and slowly broke down. They were thinking about survival in terms of the fittest making it to the other side of the darkest days. People whispered their deepest fears: the earth was poised to strike back, to prove just how temporary we were as a species, motes in the eye of time. They barely dared to breathe the scariest thought of all: *We are the dinosaurs of our age, lumbering toward extinction.*

Tempers grew short, arguments were solved with fists, knives, and, more times than the stretched-thin law could cope with, guns.

A new culture thrived, not the old gangs of the seventies that the city had worked so hard to stamp out, not the old turf wars and tagging, but rather ordinary everyday people banding together, and more dangerous than any of those old gangs because they were fighting to protect their homes and livelihoods from looters and thieves. These "watches" coalesced in alleyways and vacant lots and abandoned buildings, putting down markers to divide the city into entirely new territories and claiming these places were protected. People drew comfort from their presence. The idea was simple: together we are strong.

Graffiti began to appear on walls and doors and mailboxes, old symbols that hadn't been used for centuries: the Eye of Horus, the Blood of Isis, the jackal head of Anubis. Other symbols joined them on the weeping bricks of the beaten city, strange unions of letters and images as though the alphabet had mated with a bestiary. The shapes couldn't easily be deciphered, but clearly carried meaning and significance, eerily beautiful and terrifying, and yet still somehow elegant. These weren't gang tags; they were devotions.

Yes, there was still beauty in the crumbling city.

It was just a different kind of beauty.

It didn't take long for the street-corner evangelists to drop their Bibles. The holy book didn't make a good shield. Morning, noon, and night, they clutched fetishes of feathers, scales, and tiny pots of blood, more like shamans and snake oil salesmen than Bible thumpers. They spoke of trials and warrior blood and hell on earth. The cops steered clear of them, not wanting to be tarred by the craziness. What did it matter if people bought a few protective talismans or had wardings inked into their flesh to fend off the evil spirits?

It didn't take long for people to start claiming they saw the dead walking the streets, pacing through the Bronx and Brooklyn, standing uncertainly on the sidewalks in Weehawken and Hoboken, lost, silently shaping words in Long Island City and Astoria. It was collective hysteria. Revenants couldn't return for justice denied them in life. That kind of talk was infectious though. Long-buried superstitions bubbled to the surface. The Day of the Dead wasn't just a holiday from south of the border now.

And yet not everything came to a standstill.

The subway trains still ran, even if cars clogged the streets, the highways, the tunnels. The good people of New York still went to work. Businesses still operated, even if reduced to a skeleton staff. Life went on. The city was bent but not broken. Bowed but not beaten. It was bleaker than before, but this was the city that never slept, this was the city where dreams were made. It had survived so much. It would survive so much more.

And then the birds began to fall from the sky.

Tiny feathered bodies plummeted to earth, their eyes wide and stunned, their wings flapping uselessly against gravity as they squawked and cried, sounding far too human in their fear as they fell. Even the pigeons, already street-dwelling scavengers, were completely grounded.

But worse was the silence that followed.

There wasn't a bird left in the sky above New York.

That was yesterday.

This is today.

The swimmer launched himself off the side of the boat, jumping high into the air, kicking and shrieking with laughter as he cannonballed through the surface. He disappeared beneath the spray, and then surged back to the surface, the ripples lapping around his shoulders, neck, and head. He slapped at the water, dived and resurfaced, shaking the surf out of his hair. There were good days, there were great days, and there were days like this. This was what life was all about.

The sun, high in the clear blue sky, was picture-postcard bright. He'd lit out and headed straight for the marina, knowing he'd find Pauline waiting. They'd set out the minute he was on board, and with the engine humming, he'd stripped out of the button-down shirt and vest and slacks while Pauline played the letch, enjoying the strip as he turned and bared his ass to her wolf whistles. He had the ocean to mask just how much he enjoyed his wife looking at him.

She joined him in the water. There wasn't anyone else for miles in any direction. He checked his mask, adjusted the mouthpiece of his tank, and then dove down, letting the water come together again over his head, the ocean swallowing him whole.

The quality of light changed down here; the sunlight filtered through in shafts of emerald and gold. Around those slanting paths were shadows, dim but clear. A school of vibrantly colored fish swam through the gold into the green before disappearing into darker water. They were captivating to watch. He ducked away from the light, his languid strokes carrying him slowly deeper as his eyes adjusted to the dark. Air bubbles rafted up beside his face. The steady inhale-exhale of the breathing apparatus was Darth Vader-loud in his ears. He glanced upward, seeing Pauline splashing about near the surface. He smiled around the ventilator. He was in the mood to go deep.

Kicking downward, he sent himself on a steady glide toward the ocean floor, kicking again every dozen or so feet deeper he went. It was only a couple of hundred feet to the seabed, and now that his eyes had become accustomed to the gloom he could see just fine. This aquatic world was in constant motion, schools of small fish darted past, surging around him, above him and below. As beautiful as it was, there was something in their rapid dart-twist-dive motion that kept him alert as he swam deeper. The fish were agitated. That wasn't a good thing. They weren't reacting to him as if he was a predator, but something had them skittish. It was dumb to ignore the fish. He wasn't dumb. Scanning the dark waters, he didn't see the telltale shadow of a shark or any of the ocean's more deadly swimmers.

He pushed on another fifty feet down, keeping his strokes

smooth and strong, enjoying the silence beyond the *dub-dub* of his pulse in his temples and the white noise of the bubbles he breathed out.

He loved it down here.

Part of him wished he could stay down here forever, swimming lazily above the beds of coral and watching the stands of seaweed and clusters of underwater flowers undulate beneath his shadow.

He watched as a tiny crab hustled along through the sand.

Then something caught his eye.

In the long sliding silence between breaths, he was sure it was the shadow of some huge marine hunter. His pulse quickened. To one side the ocean floor sloped away, the shallows dropping off a shelf and deepening into a wide trench. The light thickened long before he could make out just how deep it was.

That only piqued his curiosity.

He swam closer, turning on the small flashlight fitted into his goggles, and peered down into the dark shadows, each stroke taking him deeper.

He didn't trust his eyes, but he wasn't deep enough for the pressure to bring on any hallucinations. He wasn't drunk or high or just plain crazy, but what he saw didn't make any sense.

After staring for a minute, the swimmer kicked down hard, moving as close to the impossible landscape as he dared.

It was like nothing he'd ever seen.

A hidden world.

His first crazy thought was that he'd stumbled across Atlantis. He struggled to take in the sheer scope of the underwater city. In the distance he could barely make out the distinctive shape of pyramids towering above other drowned buildings. At the foot of them, a big, crouching sphinx guarded the place.

He checked his air. He was down to less than quarter of a tank. Nowhere near enough to explore the drowned city. So he made a judgment call and kicked for the surface. A minute later, his head broke through to open air.

He pulled the mask off and spat the mouthpiece out. The sunlight was blindingly bright; he squinted into it. He was no more than a hundred yards from the boat. He waved for his wife, shouting to get her attention. Pauline waved back. He didn't stop waving until she got the message. A few seconds later, the roar of the boat's engine echoed across the water as it glided toward him.

He trod water.

He didn't dare leave the spot until he could mark it. It wasn't like underwater cities turned up every day.

In the distance, he saw blue lights as thousands of ethereal, glasslike sea creatures were swept ashore by the wind.

It was hard not to think that there was something very wrong with the ocean.

Sitting in a darkened office that wasn't hers, staring blankly at a computer screen she shouldn't have had access to, Sophie Keane came to a decision.

What they were doing was wrong.

She'd known it for a while, suspected it for even longer, but confronted with the cold hard truth she knew she had to stop them or die trying. She owed the world that much, in expiation for the part she'd already played in this whole nightmarish mess.

But if she was really going to walk down this road she couldn't walk it alone.

She reached into her backpack for a still-boxed burner phone, and tore away the shrink wrap. She fitted the battery, slipped the back into place, and thumbed it on. A second later the small screen lit up.

She dialed the number. In this day and age of contact lists, this was one of the few numbers she still knew by heart even though she hadn't dialed it in years.

The call connected, the other end rang. And rang. And rang. Finally there was murmur, the voice warm and familiar. She'd missed hearing it. Getting his voicemail was good. She had a better chance of making it all the way through to the end of her apology without him interrupting her train of guilt.

"Jake," she said. She paused, licked her lips, and took a deep breath. "It's me." She closed her eyes, but that didn't help. She could see him, arms folded, giving her that *Are you really going to do this?* stare she remembered all too well. She opened her eyes, concentrating on the computer screen instead. The truth was there. She used it to gather the courage to continue. "Don't hang up. Please. I know it's been a long time, and I know you don't want to hear this, not now. It's too little, too late, but I need you to know I'm sorry. There are a lot of things I want to say to you, so many I don't even know where to start, and there's a clock ticking . . . I'm in trouble. I need help. I can't do this alone. You're the only person I can think of to call. Something is about to happen. Something bad. I'm not even sure how bad. No. I'm lying to you again. I know precisely how bad it's going to be."

Something clattered somewhere nearby, a small sound, but Sophie started, half-rose from her chair, eyes scanning the room. Nothing. The door was still shut, the lights in the hall still off. The only dim illumination came from the emergency strip-lighting out in the hall. Okay, deep breath. "Look, I'll call again, I promise. I'm sorry. I'm sorry for everything. You didn't deserve what happened. What I did to you . . . You're going to hear stuff about me. Bad stuff. I'm not who you think I am." She hung up before she said anything else. She was starting to unravel. She needed to focus. Stay strong.

She had lied to him again. He wasn't the only person she could turn to. She made a second call, reaching out to The Watchers. She knew they'd take her call. They'd been waiting for it ever since they approached her all those weeks ago and tried to turn her against her paymasters. It was a short call. She only said two words: "I'm in."

"Good," the voice on the other end of the line said, as if her participation had never been in doubt. "You know what you need to do. They won't remain hidden for long."

The line went dead.

Pocketing the phone, Sophie rose and moved soundlessly over to the door. She peered through its frosted glass, but didn't see any movement out there. She turned the knob carefully, willing it to stay silent as she opened the door a crack.

Still nothing.

A little more.

Nothing.

She waited, listening, then finally slipped out through the narrow gap into the hall. She pulled the door shut behind her rather than let the hydraulic arm close it automatically, making sure the catch didn't *click* as it dropped into place. When she was sure it was safe, Sophie turned away from the office and moved quickly for the fire escape and the stairs. It was all about speed. Now that she'd made that call, she felt better about her decision.

No looking back.

Sophie exited the building fast, disappearing into the city like ghost.

She wasn't the only ghost.

Once the Hidden's man was sure she was gone, he stepped out of the darkness.

"We were right," he said, seemingly speaking to the empty room. "She's turned. I'll take care of her." He raised a finger to his ear and terminated the call by pressing down on the earbud he wore, and followed Sophie out into the city.

She wouldn't get far.

# CHAPTER ONE

J ACOB CARTER IGNORED THE PHONE.

He was in the shower and he wasn't about to fumble around the wet room looking for it. If it was important they'd call back. He wasn't giving up the hot water—hard enough to get at the best of times, with the old building's antique pipes filled with rust and a boiler barely able to service the five apartments it contained. These certainly weren't the best of times. With the Dickensian rattle deep in the walls it wasn't much of a stretch to say they were slowly creeping toward the worst of times. But it was worse for others out there. The New York winter was brutal. He had a roof that didn't leak, and for a few more minutes at least, hot water on tap. There was food in the fridge, and, tucked away at the back, his Knicks bottle: an ice-cold bottle of Bud he'd been saving since 1999.

His dad had died the week before Latrell Sprewell broke the Knicks' hearts with the miss that would have taken the series back to San Antonio and at least made a contest out of it. He was glad his old man hadn't lived to see it. He died with hope in his heart, which is so much better than crushing disappointment. Jake had uncapped one of the two bottles and poured it out into the freshly turned soil, a commiseration beer, and made a promise to return with the last bottle to celebrate when the Knicks won the championship. One last drink with the old man. Maybe this would be the year? After all, hell might not exactly be freezing over—even if the city was—but some strange shit was happening out there. That had to mean something, right? He'd take any kind of sign he could get.

He savored the hard pelt of near-scalding water as it stung his scalp through his close-cropped hair, massaging the suds in and rinsing them out again. Water streamed down his slick brown body, clinging to the muscular contours of his abdominals. He gave himself one more minute of bliss then reached out, twisted the faucet, and let the noises of the real world seep back in to the little cocoon of his bathroom.

The first thing he heard was a gunshot.

It was always the same.

There'd be a siren too, soon, but the gap between the two was growing wider and wider these days.

There were other sounds: people down there looking to get ahead just like they always had, but not knowing what that really meant these days.

Jake toweled himself off, wrapped the wet towel around his waist, and moved to his bedroom. The phone was on the nightstand. The icons displayed one missed call and a message waiting.

He checked the message, and then he checked it again just to be sure he hadn't slipped and banged his head in the shower. Some people saw ghosts, Jake heard them. This one said, *"Jake . . . It's me."*

Sophie Keane? Seriously? After ten fucking years?

He couldn't remember the last time he'd thought about her, and even then when she'd crept into his head it had been bad news. But then, bad news had always been their MO. Bad news and good sex. The worse the news, the better the sex, like some sort of inverse-proportional relationship forged in the crucible of war.

They'd served together.

For a while that had been the thing that bound them, even after they'd left the battlefields of Afghanistan behind them it was there, ever-present.

They'd seen things, done things others couldn't understand.

They were the same, or so he'd thought.

They'd get through anything because they were fighters. Forget all that opposites-attract bullshit, there was nothing more powerful than fucking the female version of yourself. That kind of coming together was primal.

But sooner or later it would have blown them apart if she hadn't disappeared in the middle of the night. He'd been twenty-eight when she walked out the door. He'd never heard from her again, and never expected to.

*Something is about to happen?*

*Don't look for me?*

*I'm not who you think I am?*

Fuck it.

He tossed the phone onto the bed and turned to his dresser, ignoring the half-closed drawers for the clean clothes piled haphazardly on top of it. He picked out a pair of heavy jeans, a white T-shirt, and a dark sweatshirt. Five minutes later, leather jacket in hand, he was out the door, phone shoved into his pocket, wondering if the sex would be worth all the shit inviting Sophie Keane back into his life would bring.

It wasn't a question he'd ever thought he'd be asking himself, but then, these were the end of days, weren't they? Surely Sophie riding back into town upon her pale horse had to be one of the signs of the apocalypse.

A worn-down little Asian woman scrubbed at the steps of the tenement stoop opposite him. She looked up, stared daggers at him. He smiled at her craggy face. She grunted something and went back to scrubbing. The street smelled like stale cabbage and vinegar from the takeout place on the corner. Some things in Dogland, at least, didn't change.

An hour later, Jake glanced up from the junction box he was working on. There weren't a lot of jobs for people like him when they came out of the service. An ex had hooked him up with the gig at the MTA after he'd lost six months acclimating to life without people trying to kill him. He'd gotten a certain amount of skill with electrics, so it made sense. It wasn't hard work. Plus, it was that or private security, and standing around protecting some asshole banker from picking up his bonus wasn't exactly the kind of thing he wanted on his résumé.

The background chatter suddenly rose to a near-deafening explosion of white noise. Jake looked up and down the tunnel for the source. Seeing nothing but the looping coils of electrical cables overhead and the rails on the ground disappearing into the darkness, he gave the box one last scan before slapping the lid closed. He flipped the heavy locking mechanism along its side. He hated it down here. The darkness was oppressive. "Good to go on box one thirty-seven," he reported into the mic clipped to the front of his orange safety jacket. A second later a squawk and a scratchy, *Affirmative, board showing green,* came through to confirm the job was done.

Jake checked to make sure nothing was rumbling down the tracks before he moved quickly along the narrow center lane toward the platform. Gravel crunched beneath his feet, amplified by the tunnel's weird acoustics. There was something infinitely creepy about the subway tunnels, and not just the stories of the mole people who lived down here. It stemmed from the power pulsing through the third rail.

Jake emerged from the tunnel, reaching the platform edge well before the headlights announced the next train. He cut across the tracks and hauled himself up and onto the platform.

It might have been a decade since the last training ground drill or obstacle course, but he'd kept himself fit. Maybe not combat-ready, but he was in good shape. And the job was physical, lots of lifting and carrying and endless hiking through the miles and miles of tunnels.

He walked down the platform. His orange jacket and hard hat worked like commuter-repellent, clearing a path through the crowd.

Something was wrong.

People along the platform looked agitated.

There was a buzz moving through them like a swarm of angry bees. Jake checked out a couple of the guys closest to him as he passed them. There was an edge to them; they were tense. Up and down the platform he saw plenty of pale faces.

*Shock?* That was his first thought.

*Why?* That was his second.

He'd lived in the city long enough to know bad things happened. Who could forget that? This grim recollection led to a third thought, the bleakest of the three: *What's going on up there?*

He hadn't heard any announcements over the public address system, but that didn't mean something wasn't happening. He'd been a long way down the tunnel. He could
have missed the announcement, but surely the control center
would have given him a situation report?

Anxiety is contagious. He knew that. He'd been in combat situations often enough to know that fear spread like
wildfire, and once it was under your skin there was no shaking it.

He hurried toward the exit. A young guy in a hoodie
with his hands stuffed into the pouch pocket passed through
the turnstiles ahead of him. Jake caught his eye. "Hey, man,
what's going on?"

The man glanced up at him, startled, then saw the MTA
logo on his orange vest and relaxed, trusting that down here
he was one of the guys in charge. He shook his head as if he
couldn't quite believe what he was about to say. "Just came
over the news—Fort Hamilton. It's been hit."

"What?" Jake stared at the stranger. That couldn't be
right. Hit? No way would anyone assault Fort Hamilton.
That was insane. But he started to register fragments of
the conversations going on around him and realized he was
hearing the name Fort Hamilton over and over again.

"CNN had footage from their weather chopper, showed
the smoke. Not much else. But the place is burning. Fucking
terrorists."

"Jesus . . ." Jake crossed himself, muscle memory rather
than devotion. He now heard the beginning whisper-rumble
of an oncoming train, then spotted the headlights approaching around the bend. He was still trying to process what he'd
just heard. Fort Hamilton, gone? He couldn't get his head
around that. In some ways it was more shocking than the

Twin Towers. The old base had been there almost two hundred years in one form or another. It was a core part of the nation's defense, not some stockbroker's castle of commerce. Despite occasional calls to close the last active base in New York City, it was still home to a whole slew of reserve and National Guard units, and the North Atlantic Division headquarters for the US Army Corps of Engineers.

Jesus indeed.

A terror strike made a grim kind of sense, but to a man like him, trained in the turmoil of combat, a strike like that was never the endgame, it was just a move toward it. They—whoever *they* were—were cutting off an Army response to something else.

And then there was Sophie's message out of the blue: *Something is about to happen.*

Were the two related? They had to be, didn't they? And if they were, what the hell was she caught up in?

*Don't look for me.*

*I'm not who you think I am.*

He pushed his way against the flow of people rising up toward the street, and emerged into daylight, on some subconscious level expecting to see plumes of smoke. There were a lot of edgy people. He couldn't see any of the fuck-with-one-of-us-you-fuck-with-all-of-us bravado the post–9/11 movies had propagated. Most of these people were frightened they were about to go through hell all over again. Life had changed a lot in the last decade or so, and often not for the better. The years brought distance with them and a feeling of *It couldn't happen again* that was almost complacent. They'd willingly given up so many liberties to ensure it couldn't.

But it *could* happen again, no matter what anyone believed.

There were enemies within and without, and as far as Jake could tell they didn't need to be fundamentalists to want to see America humbled. That was the biggest change he'd recognized. He could still remember the anger he'd experienced firsthand when he rocked up to a bar in Paris during his leave. All he'd done was ask for a beer. The accent had been enough to earn a torrent of abuse about interference, being part of the world police, and other bullshit that made him turn around and walk right back out of the bar. He'd only wanted a fucking drink, not a lecture on the rights of man. It was worse than the crap he'd taken growing up because of his skin color. The world was black-and-white in so many different ways.

This wasn't an accident.

He knew it.

Even without seeing the smoke, he knew it.

Fort Hamilton was a strategic target.

The part of Jake Carter that would always be a soldier processed things in a logical fashion. Stage one: threat assessment. *What were they facing? Who was the enemy here? What is their endgame?* Stage two: intervention. *Become an obstacle between the enemy and their goal.*

He heard an old guy explaining to his daughter, "You hit Hamilton, you cripple the Army response to anything on land. Simple as that. Take out the tunnels and bridges and we're an island of sitting ducks. It ain't good, kid." The words carried easily despite the wind and the traffic. Jake stepped away from the stairs and onto the sidewalk beside the subway entrance. "Smart move if you want to inflict maximum damage." The guy was absolutely right.

Not far away, a young woman, an NYU student judging by her bohemian outfit and the hemp book bag slung over her shoulder, was a lot more alarmed. "What's next? We have to get out of here. First they take out the Army and the National Guard, what's next?" she wailed at her friend, clutching her arm tightly. Hysteria wasn't going to help anyone, natural or not. "They're gonna start herding us into little pens, like mice, and doing experiments on us! You watch! They hate us!"

He wanted to go over to her and explain that this was New York, not Auschwitz, and Josef Mengele was dead; if it was al-Qaeda they wouldn't be interested in turning her into a lab rat—but he didn't bother wasting his breath. Hell, he knew plenty of people who thought like that, and plenty more who'd argue that the Big Apple was already a major filth-ridden and rotten maze, complete with bits of cheese scattered throughout and a whole lot of panicked mice in business suits bouncing off each other every day of the fucking week.

Why Fort Hamilton?

If you were going to hit a major target, why not some place here in Midtown instead of down in Brooklyn?

He was getting ahead of himself.

He was thinking like it was a foregone conclusion that al-Qaeda, the Taliban, Hamas, Hezbollah, or even the Ku Klux fucking Klan was behind the panic. He didn't even know for sure what had happened, let alone who was behind it.

He thought about what the vet had said.

Which is when Jake realized that he was already working on stage two, figuring out the best way to put himself between the unknown enemy and their goals before he'd established who or what the threat was. It didn't matter that it wasn't his fight anymore. Once a warrior, always a warrior.

# CHAPTER TWO

S HE COULDN'T SEE ANYONE, BUT THAT DIDN'T MEAN there wasn't anyone watching.

Getting out had been too easy. She wasn't buying it. Too many years in combat situations and hot zones—and even more spent training others to cope with the demands of both—had drilled an almost preternatural awareness into Sophie Keane. She knew when she wasn't alone.

It wasn't just paranoia.

It was the middle of the afternoon. Paris was a *busy* city. Maybe not New York–busy, but it was always bustling with activity and beautiful people. The power brokers of commerce, big businesses, and big bank-balances dominated la Défense. Most of the people working in the neighborhood were inside, hidden away behind the anonymity of plate-glass windows. Even so, there were pedestrians, a mix of locals and tourists, cutting through the quieter streets on their way to livelier, more *Parisian* locations. Watching them was like seeing the physical laws of the universe played out on the streets. They moved in clusters, together or alone, everything at first seemingly random but ultimately following lines that provided order in the seeming chaos.

They weren't what had her on edge. That was something else. Someone else. Someone actively looking for her.

She'd been made. It wasn't like her to be sloppy.

She'd allowed herself to be spooked. And when spooked, she'd allowed herself to make mistakes. She'd been so fixated on just getting out of there that she'd forgotten the basics. She clenched her fist, painted nails digging into her palm. What's done was done. Her paymasters would send their killers after her to clean up the mess she'd made. Now she had no choice but to work around them.

She was good at that.

She was a survivor.

She checked left and right without turning around. Left, she used the reflection in a shop window; right, a car's passenger-side window. For behind, she used the windshield of a stalled Fiat stuck in the unmoving line of traffic. It was as if the entire street, everywhere around her, was filled with ghosts. They had no substance. Any one of them could have been watching her, but no one paid her obvious attention as she hit the sidewalk.

Sophie moved quickly down the boulevard. She didn't rush, but her native New Yorker's gait meant she moved with a purpose the Parisians didn't share. It was all about acting like you belonged there, giving no indication that you'd done anything wrong. A young French man strolled past, smiled, and nodded at her during that split second where they occupied each other's space, natural, flirtatious.

He was a good-looking kid and he knew it.

She offered a smile back. She didn't want him remembering her as the woman who was immune to his charms.

A young couple skirted her, moving up quickly from behind and then splitting apart to go around her on either side only to come together again a few steps ahead. They moved with the familiarity of lovers, barely acknowledging her presence as they swept past.

A bike messenger rushed by, bag slapping against his left leg as he pedaled furiously, weaving in and out of stalled traffic with the same death wish of bike messengers the world over. The streets were eerie these days, with the lined-up cars going nowhere. It had been like that for a few days now. Ironically, that stillness was the first sign that things were in motion.

She could *feel* her tail closing the distance between them.

She could run, but that turned survival into a game of chance.

She didn't know how fast her pursuer was, if they were working alone, or if a cordon was closing in around her.

She could run, but with no idea of who was chasing her she could never stop running. That was a problem.

La Défense wasn't some Parisian ghetto. It was one of the city's newer areas. It was less than sixty years old and had been revitalized in seventies, the eighties, and the nineties. Sidewalks were long and straight and clean with plenty of space for grass and flowers and low bushes between them and the buildings. The trees grew right along the edge of the avenues and boulevards, warring with the lines of cars for possession of the roads. The district was a wonderful place if modern living was your thing, but it was absolutely appalling for her current needs.

She scanned the area. Most of the buildings were new, functionalist, with wide, flat roofs. The architecture meant her hunter could have eyes up there too: a sniper with a high-powered rifle. They didn't need to be running and leaping from rooftop to rooftop like some kind of parkour freak. A skilled shooter with a decent sniper rifle could take out a target from a mile away with the high ground—even maintain a good hit probability from a mile and a half. She was a sitting duck down there in the wide street. Sophie resisted the urge to check for a red dot in the middle of her chest. If it was there, then it was too late do anything about it. Fatalistic, but 100 percent accurate.

She couldn't see anyone up there. That didn't mean they weren't there; the angles made it easy to hide. There was no telltale glint of sunlight on the sight to give them away. All she could do was keep moving.

Breathing slowly and steadily Sophie continued down the avenue. She had a finite time out here. She knew that. Her pursuer would grow tired of the game sooner rather than later and, if he was good, pick his moment to move in for the kill. She had to assume he was good. Better than her. That was the only way to stay alive. Underestimating the enemy was a good way to die young.

She needed to get off the street.

She scanned the rows of buildings and doorways as she moved, thinking how much easier it would have been a week ago to just jack one of the parked cars. It wasn't an option now. Even if she could get one of the engines started she couldn't move fast enough. The city was jammed hood to tail to hood. Any sudden moves would only escalate the problem faster than she wanted. She was already in enough trouble. She didn't need the gendarmerie hunting her as well; The Hidden's killers were more than enough to contend with.

She kept looking for another out.

A couple of minutes later, a possible solution moved

toward her: a small gang of students, male and female, all walking together, all chatting loudly and gesturing wildly. Deep in conversation, laughing, arguing, with all the passion of youth trying to one-up each other as they impressed their way into whichever pair of pants it was they had their eyes on. A couple carried small canvases and sketchbooks. They were budding Space Invaders and Zevs or whoever the new cool street artist du jour happened to be, on their way down to Montmartre. They took up the entire sidewalk—and were heading right for her.

She could use them.

Through the trees and buildings opposite her, Sophie noticed a brightly lit lantern beside an open doorway, the stairs down into the metro barely visible beyond the threshold.

Again, she could use them.

All she had to do was put the two together and she had the makings of a plan.

*Keep it simple*, she thought, and stumbled, deliberately colliding with one of the boys. She hit him with the force of a linebacker slamming into a test dummy and the pair of them hit the ground in a tangle of limbs. It wasn't graceful, but it was effective. The others reached down, trying to help them as Sophie waved them off and pulled herself to her feet.

"*Je suis bien,*" she said, straightening her clothes. A small crowd had already gathered, drawn by the commotion. Sophie needed to judge the moment carefully. As she turned, she deliberately knocked one of the student's sketchbooks with her hip. The artist's block was overflowing with loose sketches. As it fell out of the girl's hands, it opened and the loose leaves of paper teased up, flew into the air, and blew across the sidewalk.

"*Mes dessins!*" The sketchbook's owner—short, average

height, average weight, messy red-brown hair—scrambled about, trying desperately to rescue the pages before they were ruined. Her friends forgot all about Sophie and joined in the rush to gather up the pages.

Sophie ducked out of the group, careful to turn toward the metro entrance. She could only hope her watcher was having trouble following her through the chaos she'd just conjured. If luck was on her side, the students had blocked his view completely. If it wasn't she'd know soon enough.

She broke into a run, head down, arms and legs pumping furiously, straight for the metro. She ran ten miles a day, every day. Pounding the pavement helped her stay clear, helped her focus. Not that it would help if the watcher was going to take her down. She gritted her teeth expecting to feel the bite of the bullet.

Or maybe she wouldn't feel it if he was a good enough shot? Maybe her head would just explode and she'd cease to be between steps?

She didn't slow down.

Breathing hard, she raced down the steps two and three at a time, and hurdled the turnstile. She couldn't relax. Not yet. Evasive maneuvers. She needed to get on the next available train, double back, switch lines. She looked up at the security cameras as she rushed down the escalator to the platform just as a train rumbled out of the tunnel mouth ahead of her.

The doors hissed as they opened.

There were people all around her.

She took a seat in the corner, back to the metal wall, giving her a full view of the train car and making it impossible for anyone to sneak up on her. Never leave your back exposed.

She was safe, even if that safety was temporary.

The doors slammed after some unintelligible mumble from the public address system.

As much as she wanted to, she couldn't disappear.

Not yet. She needed to get to Jake.

And that meant stepping out of the shadows and into the light, both physically and metaphorically.

# CHAPTER THREE

"**FINN! WAIT UP!**"

Finlay Walsh sighed. She wasn't in the mood to deal with Tom. The guy was a creep. All hands and roving eyes, reveling in his thinly veiled misogynism, ludicrously attempting to hit on her with shitty one-liners. The last one had been the worst. He'd been drinking at the time. She could smell the whiskey sour on his breath, but even so that was no excuse: *The only reason I'd kick you out of bed would be to fuck you on the floor.* Classy. Yeah, the guy was a shoe-in for Boss of the Year with a mouth like that; in fact he *was* her boss, and that meant she couldn't ignore him as much as she'd like to, even if he was about to come out with another peach like, *Nice shoes, wanna fuck?*

She turned and waited for him to catch up to her.

Tom Campbell had been a good-looking guy, once upon a time. He hadn't aged with that George Clooney kind of salt-and-pepper grace, though, so the last of his youthful beauty lay in his blue-gray eyes. The years had turned the rest of him soft and rounded and left him with a dark Dracula peak of thinning hair, slicked back with gel to complete his seedy charm. His eyes were buried in a morass of wrinkles, bags, and extra flesh, which dimmed them. It was his father's face struggling to come out from behind his own, Finn thought. She'd met Thomas Sr. a few times, and the irascible old man was proof that the genetic apple didn't fall far from the tree. Maybe it was just a case of people becoming their jobs, because with his usual jeans, button-down shirt, and blazer, he looked every inch the department chair.

Scratch that, she thought as he approached, he looked every inch the alcoholic, sexist department chair. She didn't let any of this show in her face or her voice.

"What's up, Tom?" Polite. Friendly but in no way *too* friendly. She wasn't going to make the mistake of being shouted down as a cock tease the next time he was loaded.

"I just got off the phone with someone down in Cuba," he answered, and Finn's first thought was, *How does this get turned around into another attempt to sleep with me?* "A marine biologist. He's sitting on something pretty interesting, I think."

"On a scale of one to ten, just how interesting? I mean, we're not exactly the go-to team for marine biologists."

He considered this for a second. "I'd say this one goes all the way up to eleven."

She inclined her head doubtfully.

"We're not talking a new species of fish," he added.

"Don't make me drag it out of you."

"His team have found a city. Well, the ruins of one."

"Okay, you've got my attention. An underwater ruin off Cuba? That'd be, what, Olmec maybe? Did they make it down that far? Who else was in the area? How old is it? How extensive? What kind of shape is it in? Do we have images yet?" The questions came tumbling out. This was the sort of stuff she lived for. They all did. That's why they were here—Columbia University had one of the best archaeology departments in the country.

"Slow down," her boss told her, chuckling and managing to make those two words sound deeply condescending. She forced a smile. "We don't know much yet, but what *is* interesting is that whatever the nature of these ruins, they're covered in symbols. Could be decoration, could be writing, or both. That's where you come in. We all know how important the Rosetta stone was to our understanding of language. They've got funding to do a proper study. They need an archaeologist on-site, specifically one capable of deciphering those markings." He looked at her more closely, then offered that slightly uncomfortable grin of his that he thought was so charming. It took her a moment to realize he was beaming with pride. "I promised I'd put our very best on it. That'd be you."

She smiled genuinely now. No need to act humble. She really was the best when it came to ancient languages, ideograms, and pictograms. They all knew it—she had an entire wall of articles and presentation plaques and awards to prove she was an asset to the department. "Thanks. But . . . Cuba? I mean . . . *Cuba?*" It wasn't all cigars, smoky rooms, and danzón, mambo, and salsa. It was fine to say women's rights had progressed since the revolution, but it was still a country founded on machismo, domestic violence, and tourist-fueled prostitution. In other words, no country for a woman like her.

But Tom surprised her for the second time in as many minutes: "Yes and no. It's Cuba, obviously, but remember, this thing's underwater. They can't exactly drain the ocean. The only people actually on-site are going to be the divers.

They'll be shooting video the whole time, and taking digital images. They'll upload those to a shared server you'll have access to. You can work on the whole thing right from the comfort of your own office . . . Don't say I never do anything for you."

"I don't know what to say," and she really didn't. An undiscovered underwater ruin off the coast of Cuba? What an *incredible* find. It was the kind of thing immortality was built on. Everyone remembered Howard Carter's name. Something like this could see her name listed beside Arthur Evans, who uncovered the remains of the Minoan civilization, and Kathleen Kenyon, who excavated Jericho and proved it to be the oldest known continuously occupied human settlement. It could be that important.

Could be.

That was the thing.

She couldn't let herself get carried away before she'd had a chance to set eyes on those markings. They'd give her a clue to its history. But just hearing that it was there made it impossible not to wonder about who the inhabitants of this drowned city were, how it had got there in the first place, how civilization in that area had evolved and finally migrated as the ocean reclaimed their home.

"Try thanks, it's an all-purpose way of saying, *You did good, boss,* and I'll say it's my pleasure." He threw a meaty arm over her shoulder. "I know you'll do us proud, kiddo. Just think about it for a second. What a find . . ."

And then he had to go and ruin it.

He leaned in, and lowered his voice a little. Not exactly husky-sexy, but far from formal. "We should celebrate. How about dinner? Or at least a drink? Or maybe . . ." his voice dropped another half-octave, turning raspy as his arm tightened slightly around her shoulder. She couldn't help but think of it as a noose. "We should just skip the drinks?"

"We should definitely skip the drinks," Finn agreed, wriggling out from under his arm. She'd clenched her fist and was about to drive an elbow into his ribs as his arm slithered free. She stepped clear of him, a fake grin plastered across her face. "Thanks. Not for the invitation, for the project. The rest, that's so far over the line it might as well be in Mexico. Let's not go there."

"I never . . . that's not what . . ."

She turned and walked away, not bothering to listen to his denials.

She'd heard them all before. Tom Campbell didn't understand subtle hints or gentle brush-offs. He had the hide of a rhino. The only way to get through to him was ego-piercing bullets. Direct. Firm. No trying to ease the blow. He wouldn't take offense at a blatant refusal, she'd discovered. Unfortunately, he wouldn't take it to heart either, and soon enough they'd be doing this whole sexually inappropriate dance all over again.

# CHAPTER FOUR

THEY WERE ALMOST IN SIGHT OF THE TIMES SQUARE PLATFORM when the train died. The lights went out.

"Fucking trains," a fellow straphanger moaned, looking at Jake for affirmation that indeed the train cars were having a ten-minute conjugal coupling-uncoupling before pulling into the next stop. Jake just nodded. The nod meant: *That's life.* Nothing more profound than that. He eased his way forward, muttering an occasional "Excuse me," before shoving someone out of the way. It wasn't graceful, but it was effective. He was a big man. It wasn't exactly irresistible force meets immovable object. He worked his way to the front of the car.

"Hey!" He banged on the driver's door at the front of the packed car. A second later a flashlight shone in his face. It stayed there for a moment, blindingly bright. The glass door muffled the worst of the driver's cursing, then there was a moment of silence on the other side and the bolt ratcheted open. The flashlight lowered to settle on the MTA logo on Jake's vest. A second later the door opened.

"Need a hand?" Jake asked. Without the light in his face he could see the conductor was around his age, give or take a couple of years depending how hard he'd been living, Latino, missing out on muscles, with slicked-back hair and a neat Freddie Prinze mustache. There wasn't even a two-pack under his shirt.

He held out a callused hand. "Luis Trujillo, captain of this here sinking ship."

They clasped hands. "Jake Carter. Tunnel crew and all-round floatation expert."

He caught the other MTA employee's raised eyebrow. Working on the trains themselves was the top of the heap, the job everyone wanted. Handling platform trash and clearing track fires were the worst. But tunnel crew, that was some serious stuff—they did the actual repair work on the lines, skilled labor, and more often than not mission-critical. There were a lot of former Army engineers scouring the tunnels. It was good work.

"So, talk to me, Luis. Why are we sinking?"

Luis shook his head. "No idea, man. We were going along fine, then all of a sudden, no power. Nothing." He stepped back and opened the door wider. "You wanna take a look?"

"Sure." Jake slid into the tiny front booth beside him. He studied the small console. It looked fine, there were no obvious alarm bells. He pulled the voltmeter from his tool belt, and hooked its leads into a plug on the dash. He checked the meter's display with his own small Maglite. Nothing; the needle was flat. The train was as dead as Tupac and Biggie, and just as beyond resurrection.

"Zed's dead, baby," he agreed. Luis showed no sign of recognizing the Tarantino line, which knocked him down a peg or two in Jake's estimation. He packed away the volt-meter. "Let me call it in."

"Be my guest."

Jake pulled out his radio. The control room wasn't there. The only response he got was a burst of static.

"Mine's dead too. I was trying to call it in when you showed up."

"Makes no sense," Jake said, more to himself than the conductor. And it didn't. Even if something had cut the power to the subway, if there'd been some colossal clusterfuck in the control room or the entire grid had gone down, their radios should have been okay. They were battery-operated. He tried to think. Cell phone signals were mostly a myth down in the subway tunnels, but the MTA radios ran through transponders that were set up throughout the system. They were specifically designed to work down here. But what worried him most was that if the transponders weren't connecting then they had a much bigger problem than just a blown fuse.

"We can't sit here with our thumbs up our asses. We're going nowhere, so we've got to ship everyone out," Luis stated the obvious. Sometimes you had to help yourself. It was standard protocol for a stalled train, and they were almost at the next station anyway. Even so, it took balls to insist on evacuating the train and traipsing through the dark tunnel to the platform. No one was going to be happy.

"Right," Jake nodded. "I'll work my way back, let people know."

Luis followed him into the car's main compartment, pushing through the commuters to the first set of doors. He unlocked them manually. Jake helped him tug the doors open, then turned toward the far end, ready to do the same thing in the next car.

Behind him, he heard Luis call out above the miasma of grunts and complaints, "Okay, people, listen up! We're going to evacuate the train. I need everyone to proceed toward me in an orderly fashion, nice and steady. There's no rush, no one's in danger. We're maybe fifty feet from the platform. No need to push and shove. Just start walking toward me, take your time, and we'll all be out before you know it. Sorry for the inconvenience, but let's not make this any more difficult than it needs to be, okay?"

Jake left the other man to it, moving through the narrow connection point from one car to the next. When the subway was in motion there was a certain thrill to it, being literally outside the train while it was hurtling down the tracks. Now it was a lot less exciting, but considerably spookier with the lights off in both directions and no distant rumbles of other trains moving through the tunnels nearby. That was odd.

There was *always* noise down here.

The silence was the eeriest thing of all.

Jake entered the next car. A couple of cops were trying to keep everyone calm. He pushed his way through to them. It was already getting sweaty in there. Cramped bodies, uncomfortably hot conditions. "We're evacuating the train," he said. "If you guys could guide everybody through to the front car, we've got the first set of doors open. The conductor's leading the short walk to the Times Square platform."

"Got it," the shorter of the pair replied. He was a bull of a man with a notable absence of neck.

The taller cop, a woman with close-cropped blond hair and angular cheekbones, frowned as her radio picked up nothing but static on the airwaves. "Any idea what's up with the radios?" she asked.

"Your guess is as good as mine." The police radios

worked on the same transponders as the MTA's equipment, which should have made them rock-solid down here. "Someone will be working on it, though. They won't like us being incommunicado. People get antsy when they feel stranded down here."

The cops nodded.

Jake parted ways with them, continuing on down the length of the train.

He found another MTA worker, the secondary conductor, midway down, and another set of cops in the final car. Between the six of them they were able to get everyone moving in an orderly fashion and keep the panic down to a bare minimum. Most of the commuters, once they were told it was just an electrical problem, settled into the usual monotony of gripes about the MTA screwing up yet again. Jake was cool with that. Better to bitch and moan than panic in the confined space of the tunnels. What he didn't want was them putting two and two together (one of those twos being Fort Hamilton and the other being the words *terror attack*) and coming up with a disabling strike on the subway system. The thought had already crossed his mind. How could it not?

He'd seen the same thing the day of the big blackout, back in the summer of 2003—as soon as people realized it wasn't another terrorist attack, just a Con Ed issue, the atmosphere changed. The entire city relaxed. You could feel it ripple through the air. The fear dissipated. In its place there was mild annoyance and surprisingly open amusement at just how paranoid they'd all become.

He hoped the mood would hold. It'd be a lot easier to guide everyone out if they weren't jumping at every sound and shadow. Not that there were any sounds to jump at.

There were, however, plenty of shadows.

Jake brought up the rear, sweeping the beam of his Maglite back and forth to make sure he hadn't missed anyone. When he reached the front car again he saw Luis standing in the open doorway, waiting for him.

"Leave no man behind," the conductor said, slapping Jake on the back as he approached. He waved his key.

Jake stepped out, using the handholds to lower himself to the track. He moved to one side and hovered his light over the doors so Luis could lock them. The last thing they wanted was the power to come back on with an open and empty train waiting for some idiots to take it for a joy ride.

Once that was done the pair followed everyone else doing the zombie walk through the dark toward the platform. Its lights were out as well, adding to the overall sense of eeriness. There were MTA workers with emergency flares standing by the edge, waving people along.

"We're the last ones," Jake told them.

"Got it," the nearest flare-holder replied, and nodded sideways. "Go on. We were told to clear the station and stick around to guide any stray rats home."

Jake hauled himself up the ladder onto the service end of the platform.

He pushed through the *MTA Employees Only* barrier to the public area. A few people still milled about, making their way slowly toward the tunnels and unmoving escalators that would eventually lead up to the fresh air. Most of the commuters had already cleared out, leaving this whole underground world with an unfamiliar feeling of abandonment.

As Jake waited for Luis to catch up he caught movement off to one side and aimed his Maglite beam that way. The light picked out a pair of guys lurking near the exit stairs.

They were dressed all in black. One of them had something shiny in his hand. A paint can?

Fresh paint adorned the yellow tiles beside the stairs. It was some sort of scrawl, one of those weird old Egyptian hieroglyphs that had started appearing across the city. It wasn't a gang tag. At least he didn't think it was.

As Jake focused on them, both men twisted their heads away from his light. But not before he caught a glint of green. It was something he'd seen way too often, back in the service. He recognized it instantly. They were wearing NODs—night optical devices. What the fucking fuck? NODs?

Two thoughts rushed through his mind: *The only reason you'd have NODs on hand was if you knew there was going to be a blackout. And the only way you'd know was if you'd caused it.*

"Hey! You! What the fuck do you think you're doing!" Jake shouted at their backs, then took off after them.

They were already scrambling up stairs worn down by the relentless trudge of city life and broken dreams, sure-footed as they ducked around the last lingering people. Their night-vision goggles gave them an advantage over Jake's flashlight, but he was fast. He closed the gap quickly, moving others out of his way with his bulk and strength. He offered a litany of apologies as he pushed through the crowd, never once looking away from the two black-clad men in front of him.

Halfway up the stairs he saw another mark, much like the first: big and swirling and more like a picture than writing. There was another, this one a weird cross between the two, at the top of the stairs from the N/Q/R platform. It was like some hidden communication was being scrawled out across the city, messages hidden in plain sight. What were they? A call to arms? A warning?

He checked left first, but didn't see them.

Glancing right, heading for the stairs up to the S shuttle, the two men bolted up the final few steps and cut left, toward the 1 train.

Jake raced after them, caught out as they bypassed the stairs down to the trains and headed for the turnstiles instead. "*Fuck*," he cursed, gritting his teeth, and picked up the pace. If they made it through those turnstiles, they'd be in Times Square in a few seconds and there was no way he'd find them in the busiest couple hundred yards in the world.

He pushed himself hard, powering on through the pain as he chased the pair of terrorists. That's what they were, he realized. That's what the night-vision goggles meant.

It hit him then.

*Holy fucking Christ, what if they've left something down there?* And then once it was in his head, it wouldn't get out. *Saran, maybe. Letting off something like that here . . . it'd take out thousands of people . . . and the trains would spread it far and wide. Fuck. Just fuck.* Jake crossed himself, hoping to every god, devil, and deity he could think of right then that he was wrong about that.

"Stop them!" he yelled to everyone and no one.

Nobody paid the least bit of attention.

He slammed into the turnstile, pushing through it.

The two men were already beyond the ticket booth and the banks of machines, a couple of steps from the base of the stairs that led out, when the world exploded behind him.

The force of the blast threw Jake forward, taking him off his feet. He flew onto the backs of two women who went sprawling across the ground.

Lots of people were down.

There was no smoke, so it hadn't been a bomb, or if it

had been it had been so far down the smoke hadn't risen yet. Still, the blast had been forceful enough to shake the foundations of the old station.

What the fuck was going on?

Jake couldn't hear anything. His head rang with the aftershocks of the explosion. His vision was blurry. His breath came in jagged gasps. He looked down at his hands. They were shaking. But he was still breathing. That was all that mattered. His hearing would return, the shakes would stop, and his sight would sharpen.

He stumbled forward, trying to see his quarry within the chaos, but they were gone. Ghosts with concussion grenades. He'd run head-on into the blast as they dropped them over their shoulders.

Night-vision goggles, concussion grenades. This was a military maneuver.

Jake hauled himself up the stairs and out onto 42nd Street. He stopped and stared.

The two big theaters, the E-walk and the Empire 25, were just down the street to his right. On the far side of the square, NASDAQ covered in screens and displays. Bright lights, big city—yet for one of the brightest places on the planet, constant lights and motion that was enough to blind most people, it was utterly dark. There were no garish ads, no commercials, no scrolling movie trailers. There were no flashing lights at all.

All the lights in Times Square were dead.

It was all connected, wasn't it?

It had to be.

Fort Hamilton, the subway tunnels, the blackout.

It had to be.

He heard a shout off to his left. It was the first thing he'd heard since the grenade. It came to him through a fuzz of distortion: "Where are the warriors?"

He couldn't be sure he'd heard it right until the answer came from somewhere within the press of frightened people: "*We* are the warriors!"

He moved toward the source of the shouts, trying to figure out what the fuck was going on.

# CHAPTER FIVE

"IT HAS BEGUN, MR. ALOM."

"Are our pieces in place, Miss Kinch Ahau?"

"They are. And the children are playing their part, adding to the confusion, as you predicted."

"Money well spent."

"Indeed. Paying the cattle to cause a stampede—genius. The iconography, particularly, I thought was a nice touch."

"It gives the illusion of some greater force at work, older superstitions coming to play, which is exactly what we want."

"Feed their anxieties."

"They can never have enough to worry about. Even with the polar shift causing havoc with the earth's magnetic fields, we have a very limited window of opportunity. The stars are aligned, so to speak, and now we must act. Has there been word from our man in Paris?"

"The assassin, Cabrakan, has matters in hand, Mr. Alom. Sophie Keane—" She no longer used the operative's call sign. She was burned. Dead to them. Now she was merely an obstacle. "Rest assured, our friend will not be allowed to interfere with our plans."

"See that she doesn't. Perhaps it would be wise to dispatch Ah Puch," he invoked the name of the god of death, "to make sure the job is done?"

"Xbalanque is in Berlin. She is closer."

"And she's good?"

"Very."

"Then make the call. Miss Keane's hours among us are spent. I will not tolerate her betrayal. An example needs to be made of her."

"And it will be."

"Has Hunhau made contact?" The prince of the devils was in Manhattan, downtown, overseeing the crew infiltrating the finance district. It was a delicate dance, this rite of theirs. So many intricate strands of cause-and-effect that needed to be teased out and pulled very gently if they were going to succeed. But the rewards went beyond wealth. They went to the very root of society. Everything that had been lost was there to be won again. And now was the time. It was foretold.

"His team is in place."

"And he knows what he has to do?"

"He knows."

"Ixtab, Kauil, Cum Hau, and Huracan?"

"All teams are in place, Mr. Alom."

"We have been hidden for a long time, Miss Kinch Ahau," he said, invoking the old goddess' name again.

"Yes, yes we have."

"Now it is time to reveal ourselves."

"We shall be hidden no more," she agreed. "We shall rise."

"Into the light," Mr. Alom said, as though making a toast.

# CHAPTER SIX

**S**OPHIE DIDN'T SEE ANYONE.

She didn't have much time.

She'd caught sight of the assassin. She recognized him: Cabrakan. The assassin was one of the new generation of killers she'd trained. That put him at an advantage, in that he knew her, how she moved and thought. She'd instilled her patterns in him. But she had no idea how he'd changed them to match his own personality. Every killer was unique. She could safely assume that if he didn't have them already, he'd soon know her address, bank details, card numbers, passport, and every other bit of her life that was out in the public domain, and all her secrets a matter of hours after that. She needed to get out of the city. She should already be gone, dust in the Parisian wind, but she'd made a mistake. She hadn't planned her exit strategy carefully enough. So she was stuck in the 10th arrondissement, back against the wall, watching the door to her apartment building through the glass of a patisserie window across the street, thinking about doing something really dumb.

Everything looked quiet, but if anyone knew looks could be deceptive, it was Sophie.

She returned her Vélib' bike to the same corner rack she always used—she was a creature of habit, not necessarily wise for an assassin, she knew—then ducked around the corner. She stayed close to the little patisserie, her face turned toward its plate-glass windows. Anyone watching from across the street would have a hard time identifying her.

She made it to her building's front door without being hit, slipped her key into the lock, and eased it open.

Looking back over her shoulder, Sophie stepped gratefully into the cool shadows inside. The inner door required a different key. That extra layer of French paranoia was one of the things that had attracted her to the old building. It would buy her a few extra seconds if someone came in after her.

She closed the door securely behind her.

Every second counted. Simple as that.

A rickety old wire-cage elevator in the center of the marble foyer serviced the building. She never used it.

There was a wide staircase that wrapped around the elevator shaft. She took the steps three at a time, running all the way up to the fourth floor.

Her apartment door was closed. Sunlight crept beneath its bottom edge.

Sophie waited outside the door, watching the line of light. It remained unbroken. If anyone was in there, they knew better than to pace impatiently in front of the door. Hopefully, though, she'd beaten them here. She wasn't about to assume anything. Assumptions didn't make an ass out of you, they got you killed.

She drew her knife from the sheath at her calf, reversing the hilt so it pointed down.

Given a choice she'd rather have a gun, but France didn't allow civilians automatic firearms. A concealed carry just wasn't worth the risk.

She held the blade flat against her forearm as she eased her key into the lock, then turned it. The lock was oiled. It was an old habit. She wanted it to turn silently.

The tumblers glided into place with a soft *click*. Again, she waited a second. Nothing changed behind the door: no footfalls, no shadows, no sounds.

She threw the heavy door open and surged through, rolling to come up several feet beyond the threshold, back to the wall, knife in hand ready to cut out the heart of any lurking threat.

Nothing.

Heart hammering, she scanned the lounge/bedroom and the adjoining kitchen for intruders, quickly marking off the areas before finally checking that the tiny bathroom was clear.

The only advantage of living in a five-hundred-square-foot apartment was that it was easy to search. It only took her a few seconds to be sure the place was empty.

Sophie kicked the door shut again. Locking it wouldn't slow anyone down, it wasn't a heavy-duty security door like some of her neighbors had. Leaving it open might, conversely, buy her an extra second or two if they assumed it was locked.

She headed into the bathroom. The toilet was an antique gravity-flush model with a porcelain tank overhead. She stood on the toilet seat and reached up, pushing back the tank's lid. A strap had been taped to its underside. Yanking on the strap, she pulled a watertight bag out of the tank. She eased the lid back into place.

She stepped back onto the tiled floor, and checked the bag's contents.

It was her escape kit: passport, cards, money, and most importantly, weapon. Keeping a "go bag" ready was a throwback to her military days. Back then, it would have included staples like power bars and water, a change of clothes, anything she might need for deployment. This was different. She'd been burned. When she left this apartment the woman who had been Sophie Keane would be dead.

Assuming she survived long enough, she'd be born again as Monica Guerra. That was the name on the passport and cards.

It was going to be hard to say goodbye to Sophie. She liked who she was. But it was better to be born again than simply die.

Slinging the bag over her shoulder, Sophie headed for the door.

She stopped on the threshold.

She didn't know how close behind her they were, but she had to assume Cabrakan was near. She needed to change the most obvious things about her appearance to throw him off. No point in making it easy for the assassin. She kicked off her trainers, and shoved her feet into her hiking boots, lacing them tight. Better. Her leather jacket hung in the closet beside the bathroom. She shrugged into it.

Next she went for her computer. This was the part she didn't have time for, but it needed to be done. She grabbed the thumb drive sticking out of the computer's USB port and pocketed it, then picked up what looked like a car alarm remote sitting beside it and hit the *Lock* button.

There was a small pop from the computer, followed by a flash of smoke. She'd detonated a small charge inside the case, mangling the hard drive.

It was crude but effective. They wouldn't learn anything

from the machine. The acrid scent of burning wire and metal fused with the curls of smoke.

Turning to go, Sophie saw the only thing in the entire apartment she'd truly miss: a picture hanging on the lounge wall. It was a beautiful landscape, an Impressionist-style watercolor of Notre Dame at sunset, painted on a hand-woven paper scroll. She'd picked it up from a stall on the Brocante des Abbesses the day after she'd landed in Paris.

On a whim, she stepped over to it and lifted it from the hook, broke the glass frame, and pulled it out. Sophie rolled the scroll up and tied it with the attached ribbon before thrusting it into her go bag. It was a silly thing to cling onto, and those couple of seconds of sentimentality cost her.

As she turned back toward the door, she heard a faint scuff.

Cabrakan had caught up with her.

Sophie flattened herself against the wall so her shadow wouldn't reach the door. She'd sheathed the knife when she'd gone for the go bag. Close quarters a knife was better than a gun, though she had no intention of sticking around to fight.

One of the things that had drawn her to this apartment was the way it invited the warm sunlight in through the glass double doors that dominated the lounge's outer wall. The doors led out onto a small balcony, just big enough for a tiny round table and two folding chairs surrounded by a cluster of bright potted plants. In nice weather it was somewhere to relax, sip strong black coffee, and eat a pastry from the shop across the street while she watched the people down below. Today it was her way out.

She opened the doors, looking back over her shoulder as she stepped out. This was going to be fun.

Without thinking about what she was doing, Sophie

gathered herself and leaped from the balcony. Misjudge it by a couple of inches and it was suicide.

She threw herself to the left and for one sickening second thought she was going to miss the top of the iron rails of her neighbor's balcony and cannon back off them. She slammed into the rusty iron, kicking out and scrabbling for purchase fifty feet above the Parisian walkway.

For another long sickening second she thought her boots wouldn't find anything to grip onto, then the steel toecap caught between two of the railings and gave her just enough traction to haul herself up. She folded over the railings and dropped down onto the worn tiles of the balcony.

Behind her, she heard the impact of her apartment door being thrown open, hard.

Her apartment was in the middle of the building. The balcony ran around the entire span of the apartment, giving it a beautiful double-aspect. It also meant that in five steps Sophie was out of sight—unless they had eyes below.

She grabbed the wrought-iron railing and swung herself over the edge, grasping the rails with her other hand as she lowered herself. The iron bars had vertical beams for hanging lanterns and clinging vines. Those beams were as good as a ladder down to the balcony below. The decorative curls of the wrought iron made easy hand- and footholds.

Sophie descended quickly, jumping the last few feet to the ground. Looking back up, she saw the assassin's dark figure leaning over her balcony, scanning the streets. She couldn't make out any signal between Cabrakan and someone down on the ground, meaning he was almost certainly alone. That was all that mattered. She ran for the Vélib' rack, intending to grab another bike and lose herself in the crowds on the Boulevard de Magenta, but stopped short.

There was a motorbike parked outside her apartment building, a beautiful beast of red and chrome: a classic Swiss Egli-Vincent. It hadn't been there when she'd gone inside. No one in her building owned one.

It was the assassin's.

Never one to look a gift horse in the burning chrome, Sophie stepped up to the bike. It *was* an Egli-Vincent, but it was brand new, not just beautifully maintained. It looked *exactly* like the original model, complete with analog gauges. No circuitry.

Throwing her leg over the chassis, she straddled the machine. The ignition key was missing, but that wasn't a problem. It took her half a second to pull the multitool from the outside pocket of her bag and jab the narrow screwdriver blade into the ignition. With a twist the makeshift key worked just fine.

A tug on the throttle, and the motorcycle's engine roared to life beneath her. Sophie flipped up the kickstand, gave the bike some gas, and then she was gone, weaving through the logjam of unmoving traffic. She saw men in the cars, trying to make sense of why they weren't moving.

She started humming, *It's the end of the world as we know it (and I feel fine)* . . .

And it was. It really was.

# CHAPTER SEVEN

JAKE COULDN'T FIND THE MEN IN THE CROWD. Out in the open, night-vision goggles gone, the self-proclaimed warriors blended in. That was the trick: looking like anyone meant you looked like everyone. It was midmorning but the winter sun offered no warmth. The cold hit him hard and fast with its punishing kiss. His breath corkscrewed in front of his face.

He gave up and walked away from the dead square and the milling people before the shouting died down.

He tried calling in again, but his radio was dead. All he heard was cold empty static.

He listened to it for longer than was healthy, trying to make out anything in the white noise, a voice, a hint, a shred of hope. There was nothing.

A couple of cops tried to maintain some semblance of order, barking out commands, telling people to back off, to go home. It was the same message over and over. He heard it clearly as he approached. They didn't know what was going on either. The best course of action was simply to stay safe, go home, batten down the hatches, and wait it out. Some even listened.

Jake walked, trying to take it all in.

The city was strange. He hardly recognized it. So much had changed in the few months since the dogs went feral and turned the island into Dogland. Something very fucking weird was going on. Yes, it was still his city, but for all it had been battered by storms and the tremors and everything else, it had changed more starkly in the last few hours than all of those weeks combined. He wasn't a superstitious guy, not really, he had enough trouble dealing with real-world prejudices in a time when being black meant shit like *Stand your ground!* could get a brother killed and fear could see a six-year-old girl Tasered by trigger-happy cops. Sure, life wasn't all *Driving Miss Daisy*, *Roots*, and *My name is Kunta Kinte.* Not while rappers like Jay-Z and Kanye hooked up with all that celebrity pussy and gave the average black kid in America something to aspire to: being a fucking Kardashian. Talk about the ninth circle of hell.

Somewhere behind him, he heard a busker singing the ghetto anthem "Hard Knock Life," and couldn't help but smile. You could turn the lights out and the world on its head, but some aspects of the city would never change. The guy was banging out the rhythms on an upturned bucket.

Everywhere there should have been a spark of power there was nothing. It didn't take a genius to realize something had taken out the electronics, transforming New Yorkers into a shuffling horde cut off from the constant stream of life and social media that was their lifeblood.

The cell towers were down.

But it was more than just that.

The traffic lights were dead. Radios dead. The bank of TVs in the Best Buy's windows, dead.

It was the same with the cars. They were all stopped along the streets, cars and buses and even motorcycles. He saw drivers pounding on the wheel like they were trying to give their vehicles CPR even as they flatlined. He saw men hunched over engines, trying to make sense of what wasn't going on under the hood.

Most of the abandoned cars were newer makes and models, all of them with onboard computers and electronic ignitions. He'd seen an ancient Ford Torino, brown as dirt and twice as battered, that was boxed in by dead engines, its own still rumbling even if it couldn't go anywhere.

He saw a couple of bike messengers weaving through the congestion, heads down, pedaling hard. They rode with the same death wish they'd always ridden with, but without the fear of fast-moving traffic and distracted drivers to slow them down.

Jake saw an old man who looked dead on the side of the road. He'd simply fallen where he stood. Jake's first thought was that his pacemaker had failed along with all the other electronics in the city. A woman was on her knees beside him, pushing at his chest. She looked up at Jake with tears in her eyes.

There was nothing he could do, so he kept on walking. No one else stopped to help her.

There were more than eight million people in the city. Many thousands kept alive by pacemakers regulating their heartbeat. He didn't want to imagine how many times this scene was being played out across Manhattan.

The shuffling, disconnected zombie horde made walking difficult, though Jake wasn't in a hurry. He was walking without real purpose. He'd given up on the idea of heading out to Fort Hamilton. Without the subway running it would take hours to get out there and there was nothing he could do. He knew the protocols. Hamilton would be cordoned off while they waited for the military to send reinforcements—and that would be a serious operation. They couldn't just drop-ship troops in if the blackout was down to an EMP—electromagnetic pulse—or something like that. Maybe by sailboat, or a diesel engine, something without any computer parts or circuits driving it. The military were smart; they would find a way. It would only be a matter of time.

He was young. He was strong. Military training. There was stuff he could do here before panic genuinely took hold. The longer the blackout, the worse it was going to get. He knew that much.

In the perpetual quest for status, the brightest, the shiniest, and the newest, New Yorkers had bought themselves into helplessness.

Jake was still thinking about the irony of it all as he reached a break in the buildings to his left. He glanced around, surprised to discover an entire block that was nothing but steps and benches and a few scattered trees. He recognized it, but didn't understand how he'd wound up all the way down by Zuccotti Park. The natives still crowded the benches, but there were other groups in the park this afternoon, just as there had been for weeks now, people gathered together for comfort and support.

He spotted one cluster with their heads bowed and hands linked. The sight both warmed and disgusted him. A prayer group? Now? What the fuck did they think was going to happen? Maybe their god would give them a holy miracle to make everything all right? Well, God had given them light once before, Jake figured bleakly, so maybe he'd turn the lights back on.

As he stood in judgment over them, Jake noticed a man walking down the opposite side of Trinity Place, moving parallel to him. On a normal day he wouldn't have paid him the slightest attention, even though the guy moved with real purpose. But all New Yorkers moved with real purpose; it was only the tourists who walked with their heads up, looking around, trying to take it all in before someone lifted their money roll in a big old fuck you from the Big Apple.

The walker took long, solid strides, eyes focused straight ahead. He didn't deviate from his path once in the minute that Jake watched him, causing people to get out of his way. That single-mindedness was quintessentially New York. But today he was the only person Jake had seen who looked like he knew where he was going, and that included the cops he'd come across trying to keep order.

That made the guy interesting.

Jake wanted to know what the guy was up to. He followed him, keeping his distance as the walker headed down Trinity Place. He stayed on the opposite side of the street.

The guy was shorter than Jake, but a bull of a man, dressed in faded black jeans and a black leather jacket. Jake checked out his shoes. They were Timberlands or a generic copy, solid and practical, common enough not to draw attention but comfortable enough for real use.

They passed under the footbridge to Trinity Church. Then the guy changed tack, crossing the street toward Jake.

He thought about slowing his pace, but that would only make it obvious he was tailing the guy, so instead he stretched his stride. It was just as easy to follow someone from the front if you knew what you were doing. It was a basic maneuver, but surprisingly effective because most people don't pick up on it.

The entrance to the Rector Street R stop was right in front of him. Jake darted down the steps, disappearing into the subway.

Like most stations, Rector Street had two separate entrances, both on the same side of the street, a few dozen feet apart and facing in opposite directions. Jake didn't venture down into the station proper—he crossed the landing and emerged from the other side, on the corner of Trinity Place and Rector Street.

He unclipped his radio from his safety vest, pulled the orange top over his head, rolled it up, and shoved it in a trash can along with his tool belt. It was a small change, but a very visual one, hopefully enough to throw him off if the guy hadn't gotten a close look at his face.

Jake emerged as the man cut left on Rector.

Rector dead-ended at Broadway, offering a fork in the road. He chose left. At the next corner, he turned right onto Wall Street. Cement pylons meant the street was closed to cars. Not that there were any trying to get in.

The man headed straight down the center of the street, walking along the white line.

Jake stayed off to one side, hugging the Bank of New York's towering walls, and turned again, this time going left.

The walker slowed as he rounded the corner, then stopped.

Jake lingered half a block back. He could observe the man freely now.

The Federal Hall building was across the street, but the guy was looking down Broad Street at a massive white stone building. The structure had enormous columns running from the middle of the third floor up to an impressive cornice. Stone rails ringed the building in place of gutters. Below the columns was a row of balconies brooding over wide double doors. To the side of them, a single set of glass double doors with golden latticework above them and a black band that would normally scroll company abbreviations and stock prices over and over until they made no sense to the common man.

The New York Stock Exchange.

It was one of the many iconic buildings in Manhattan, and in the age of the psychopath, the very heart of the city. Even one of the most powerful financial centers in the world wasn't immune to the blackout. Though of course it had generators and contingencies, it couldn't be allowed to go offline.

A group of men filed in through that solitary set of glass doors. They weren't dressed like stockbrokers.

Their faces were covered and they moved with the grim efficiency of military men, at pace, in tight formation.

*The fuck?*

One guy held the door. He was the lookout, scanning the street for signs of trouble. Trouble walked toward him in the form of the stranger Jake had been tailing.

The guy stepped back into the shadows and watched.

Jake tried to process what he was seeing. The walker hadn't come down to rendezvous with the crew, but he clearly knew they would be there. That posed its own set of questions, not least of which was still his identity: Who was he? FBI? Homeland Security? If he was either, he was here without backup. He was armed, though. Jake could make out the telltale bulge of a holstered gun at the small of his back. The leather jacket did a good job concealing it if you didn't know what you were looking for. Jake did; his training ran deep.

He heard the gunshots before the last member of the group stepped inside, letting the door swing shut after him.

The walker rushed out of the shadows, catching the door before it fully closed.

Jake was already moving. He wasn't thinking, it was all instinct. Once a warrior . . .

He stepped through into total darkness, with no idea what he was getting himself into.

# CHAPTER EIGHT

**A** FEW HOURS AGO THE NYSE'S LABYRINTHINE CORRIDORS were bright, garishly lit by the sleek fluorescent panels running along the wall's length.

Now everything beyond the door was pitch black.

One wall was tiled while the other was mirrored. He only knew that because he'd seen through the open door. With the outside world locked away, he might as well have stepped through into *nothing*.

Supposedly the loss of one sense would heighten the remaining ones, but that was bullshit. The darkness just meant he heard the blood of his pulse in his ears louder, not that he was more attuned to the sounds of the dark.

Soft footsteps echoed up ahead. Jake could just make out the slumped shadows of dead guards. He knelt to check for a pulse: nothing. Same at the second and the third. No survivors. He picked a path through the dead.

Jake closed his eyes, counting through eleven Mississippis, then blinked and started after the footfalls. It wasn't foolproof, but the short count had given his eyes a few more precious seconds to adjust to the dark. Not that he wanted to see more than he already could. There was a faint light at his back that added definition to it now.

He kept one hand on the wall and moved forward until he reached a glass door. It opened with the slightest touch, which felt inherently wrong. Security should have been airtight. Without power, though, and without the computer systems online, nothing was working. And that meant there was nothing to stop him from walking right down to the trading floor. Not that anyone was trading.

The place was a mausoleum to money. Jake crept forward until he reached a pair of steps. Beyond them, the hallway split, running left and right to ring the floor.

He peered down the left-side passage. He saw nothing as it disappeared into absolute darkness. To the right, though, he caught the tiniest glint of something shifting through the blackness of the corridor. He tried to focus on the shape as it resolved into the shadow of a man. Ahead of both of them came the sudden, shocking detonation of concussion grenades. There was no alarm—which meant they had to be inside the system as well as the building. This was rapidly escalating from really bad to a whole new plane of existential torment.

Jake didn't move. Fumbling in the dark was going to make noise, and even after the concussion grenades, noise was going to bring trouble. The *only* smart thing to do was turn around and get the fuck out of there. But the smart choice was a coward's choice. He wasn't a coward. He could handle himself, even if the only thing he had in common with any of the action heroes of the world was that he was expendable. He wasn't walking away, not now. Not ever. The fact that he was a black man breaking into the still heart of capitalism didn't pass him by either. His would be an easy death to explain on the evening news if things went south.

His one advantage was that no one was expecting him to crash the party. His only tool, the mini-Maglite, wasn't the kind of thing he could use to break a few skulls, and lighting up the trading floor wasn't an option. This was an advance recon. Simple as that. Do not engage the enemy, soldier.

The corridors crossed and crossed again, offering what felt like hundreds of choices. He moved slowly, trailing his fingers against the wall. It would be easy to get lost in here with no recognizable landmarks. Every shadow and dark shape looked exactly the same, save for the structure damage caused by the explosives.

He reached a stairwell whose door was closing as he approached. Jake slipped his hand into the crack and caught it, listening for the soft footfalls ascending. He counted them before he pushed the door slowly open, wincing as it sighed on the hydraulic arm.

Time was the one commodity not being traded here.

Jake started climbing as quickly and quietly as he could. The sounds of the other man's careful footsteps stopped. A door opened then closed, the rasp of it settling back into the frame echoing in the silence. Then the clatter of running feet filled the stairwell. The guy had thrown caution to the wind and was moving fast. That meant Jake needed to move faster. He could only hope the din would swallow the sound of his own ascent.

He charged up the stairs, taking them three at a time, hand on the rail for balance in the darkness, breathing hard before he was around the fourth landing.

More gunshots came as the last defenders of this financial Camelot fell.

He saw a chink of light up above him, on the next landing. A door opening.

It wasn't natural light. A flashlight?

Jake slowed down. He didn't want his own steps emerging as the other man's faded. A bead of sweat broke and ran from his temple, trailing slowly down his cheek before it was absorbed into his neck. Nostrils flared, he fought to regulate his breathing. Everything was suddenly quiet. He didn't like that.

Who the fuck brought a flashlight to a gunfight?

He rose up a single step, listening for the telltale signs of trouble. He clenched and unclenched his fist at his side. He banged it against his thigh, using the impact to mark time: another eleven count. Jake always added one for luck. That's just the way he was.

On the count of eleven he moved, reaching for the door. He found the handle. What it opened onto was breathtaking.

Jake had never set foot inside the New York Stock Exchange before, never mind the trading floor; even so, he knew he was looking into the very heart of the building. It was an iconic sight, like the Empire State Building or the rectangle of Central Park seen from above. You didn't need to have been inside to have seen it; the trading floor was on the news every day.

The room was *enormous*.

The ceilings were easily sixty feet high, with an array of overhead beams supporting lights and wires and cameras as if it were a concert stage, which, given the kinds of performance art that played out here, wasn't a completely inappropriate analogy.

One wall was almost entirely green glass. Despite the fact that they were nearly opaque, the windows let in enough light for him to see the trading floor. There were nine dead men sprawled out in the center of it. Several large clusters of computers, workstations, and screens, built in a circle facing inward, dominated it. The walls were lined with more work-stations with stools and chairs spaced haphazardly along them. Several massive screens hung from the ceiling at vari-ous points around the room, all dark now.

An enormous American flag dominated one wall. NYSE banners hung on either side of the flag.

It was an amazing place.

Jake could only imagine what it looked like normally, full of life, hundreds of people running, shouting buy and sell or-ders, waving frantically to relay information. There were no day traders barking orders. There was no stock ticker count-ing down the fiscal apocalypse. Suit jackets had been tossed carelessly over the backs of chairs, papers still piled on desks. He saw several Coke and Mountain Dew cans and takeout containers beside silent computers.

The corpses weren't the only people on the trading floor. He saw the man he'd been following, and beyond him, the team he'd come here to intercept. The soft buzz of voices came from the room's far side, directly beneath one of the big scrolling boards. They moved with grim efficiency. There were more computers there, hulking units that kept the back end of the system up and running so the traders could do their work up front.

The crew, some sort of paramilitary unit, gathered around the banks of machines as a computer screen lit up. What the hell? There was no juice in the place and it seemed pretty obvious an EMP or something equally toxic to electron-ics had wiped out every system in the city, but these guys just happened to have found the one working network in New York?

He watched the team move down the row, doing something to each machine in turn. Before they moved on to the next, the terminal powered up, lighting the room with its cool digital glow. The backup generators must have been fucked up beyond repair by whatever it was that had brought the systems down citywide.

This was big.

Important.

Whatever had happened today, just like the graffiti artists on the subway, these guys were *prepared*.

*Where are the warriors?* he thought, remembering the line they'd shouted.

But who—or what—were they at war with? He didn't have any answers.

The man he'd followed to the trading floor slipped into a booth, using the shadows from its curving partition for cover.

*Smart,* Jake thought, but the only similar place he could see for himself was across the floor. He couldn't risk crossing that kind of killing ground. He stayed where he was and watched from the shadows, gambling that no one was going to follow him in through the door.

It didn't take long to see there was one guy on the team who was the alpha dog; he barked out rapid-fire instructions and no one argued with him. His guys sat at their row of reactivated computers. Six terminals, six men.

Almost as one they began typing.

*Okay,* he thought, *this is some sort of high-tech heist.* It made sense, kind of, but even if the terminals were working, they had to be offline, surely? With the systems down the trades wouldn't register. And when the system came back online it'd reboot from backups, wiping out anything they'd done.

But the men kept typing.

Jake almost missed the sound of the stairwell door opening behind him. He barely had time to duck down as a new figure strode calmly toward the trading floor.

He was older. He moved with confidence that bordered on arrogance, like he owned the place. The gray in his cropped hair caught the screens' backlight. Average height, stocky, and dressed in the same nondescript black jeans– dark jacket combo of the guy Jake had followed. He walked straight up to the team leader.

A nod passed between them.

The newcomer walked along the bank of machines, talking quietly. Jake could just make out the sound of their replies, but not the actual words.

The man nodded several times, and moved in closer to study one of the screens.

Jake could see his face: blunt, with harsh features like he'd been chipped from rock, all the rough edges left untouched. Native American, maybe, possibly Latino. It was difficult to tell in the ambient glow of the computer screen.

The man nodded again and stepped back, pulling a pistol from under his coat, and abruptly shot them in the back of the head one after another. The silencer, visible along the barrel, kept the noise to a soft whisper of displaced air.

None of the men at the terminals had the time to save themselves. They barely had the time to make a sound as they slumped and fell out of their chairs.

Jake had seen violence before. He'd experienced death. But not like this. Not this rapid-fire, cold-blooded murder. What the fuck had he got himself wrapped up in? Hit teams? Deadly assassins?

The killer checked each body in turn, holding a finger at the thick vein in their necks to be sure there was no pulse.

Satisfied, he rose and tucked the pistol back away in its holster at the base of his spine. He crossed the trading floor, walking slowly up the ramp toward the doors where Jake was hiding.

Jake didn't move. He didn't dare to so much as breathe.

There was no sign of the man he'd followed in here. Either he was hiding or he'd already taken off when the shooting went down. It didn't matter. He wasn't Jake's focus.

The mission directive had changed. He'd gathered his recon, and at the heart of it found a killer. He might have come in here thinking this wasn't his fight, but it certainly was now.

He was a simple man. People didn't get away with cold-blooded murder in Jake Carter's world. It was that black-and-white.

*Where are the warriors?* he thought. *Right here. I am a fucking warrior.*

# CHAPTER NINE

I̲T WAS BRAVADO.
This wasn't Kabul. He wasn't packing. All thoughts of taking the killer down vanished as survival instinct kicked in. That was good. Nine times out of ten, pulling dumb shit like that was suicide. A different time. A different place. Yes. But not here. Not now. When the killer had real skill, which this guy had in spades, it nixed even that slim 10 percent element of chance—luck—that *might* have gone in his favor.

Jake had seen firsthand just how well the guy knew his way around a gun: six men picked off in half as many seconds, head shots all around. Lethal.

Size and strength didn't matter against that kind of precision. One misstep and he'd be left having a religious experience he wasn't ready for. All he could do was let the man walk out. It wasn't cowardice. It was basic combat stuff. Priority one: stay alive.

Jake waited a few tense seconds, not daring to breathe. The stairwell door eased shut on its hydraulic arm. He didn't move.

I
N
F
A
M
O
U
S

He gave the killer time to descend before he slipped through the door after him. Instead of following right behind the man, Jake ran down across the trading floor, avoiding the dead, to the banks of computer screens. He had no idea what he could learn from the terminals, but he had one shot here. Right now he knew nothing. Anything he could learn would be a start.

Jake guessed he didn't have much time before the NYSE security apparatus noticed its team was missing, so he didn't linger as he stepped over the split skull of a dead man to get to his terminal. The screen filled with scrawling numbers and code that moved too quickly for him to fix on any of the command lines being executed by the machine. He wasn't a programmer. He couldn't scan the streams of code, and unfortunately there was no handy *Press Enter to Destroy Western Civilization* icon on the screen to make sense of it all.

Whatever they'd come here to do was done. Nothing he could do to stop that, apart from maybe yank out a cable. His technical know-how only stretched that far. Done, he turned his attention to the corpse.

It was a mess. The entry wound was clean, though the exit wound was anything but. It had opened a hole in the man's forehead the size of Jake's fist. Some sort of hollow-point ammo designed to cause maximum damage on the way out.

Jake rolled the dead man over. His arm fell uselessly at his side, smearing the blood across the outer edge of the trading floor. The smell of death was already beginning to gather around the room; it began with blood and shit as the bowels emptied. No one ever talked about that. It wasn't like in the movies. When the guy went down, hole in his head, the hole in his ass opened, the last and most brutal humiliation of murder leaving the victim to rot in his own shit.

Jake hunkered down beside the dead man and went through his pockets. There were no wallet or other clues to his identity. No distinguishing features or marks. He was, quite literally, a dead end.

Jake looked up, scanning the vast room for movement. The quiet was getting to him. He tried another corpse, which had likewise been stripped. It was the same for the others.

If someone came in now there'd be no way he could talk his way out of this. He was alone in a room with a lot of dead men and most likely the only working computers in the city. *Forget being black, this doesn't look good on any planet,* Jake thought, giving up on them.

He killed the other terminals before he headed back to the stairs, knowing it was a risk, and not sure it would make the slightest bit of difference. He needed to get out of there. The cops would show up soon; he didn't want to be around when they did.

He nudged the door open a crack, then pushed it slowly wider, slipped through, and eased it closed behind him. He'd given the killer a full minute and more of a head start.

Jake couldn't hear any sounds of the man's descent, and assumed he'd already made it to the bottom. *Don't be waiting.* Part thought, part prayer.

He followed him down, fast, making up the ground. By the time he reached the bottom and emerged from the stairwell into the short, dark corridor, Jake was less than thirty seconds behind him, and gaining.

Which was good *and* bad.

Good, because he'd come this far. Bad, because there was no turning back now. Not with the body count very much in the house. He was in for the long haul. This had become his fight. Whatever—and whoever—the fuck he was fighting.

He wasn't the kind of guy who could just turn and walk away.

Sometimes he wished he was. It would have saved him a lot of grief over the years. But the dead needed a voice, whatever their crimes. No one deserved to die like that. And for a minute, an hour, a day, or however long it took for some semblance of normality to return to the city and its stock exchange, only three men knew they were dead—their killer and the two men who had watched them die.

He couldn't walk away from that.

Up ahead, the beam of the flashlight disappeared.

For a second he thought the killer had turned it off, but then he saw the diffuse blur of light again and realized he'd turned down not one but two cross-corners in the labyrinthine structure.

Jake followed the beam, moving quicker. Three turns and he was no more than fifteen seconds behind the killer, close enough to hear the dull echo of his footsteps in the dark corridor. He tried to time his footsteps to match those of the killer.

The place was cold. His skin prickled. There should have been all sorts of sensors and silent alarms protecting the place. Nothing was happening. He could hear his breathing as his nostrils flared. There was no such thing as silence, not true silence, not in the dark. He clenched his fist, then realized what he was doing and tried to relax, but that just caused every other muscle in his body to tense up.

The light stopped moving.

The killer had reached a door.

Jake froze, caught in no-man's-land. He didn't know the

building, didn't know where he was, but as light streamed in, he realized the killer had found another exit. The plain metal fire door opened out the back of the building, onto New Street.

Backlit, the man looked like a giant, his silhouette filling the doorway. He stood on the threshold, seemingly to take it all in, the city at his feet.

Jake heard singing. It took him a second to realize that's what it was. Singing. One voice, stark, distinctive. The killer was no Mick Jagger, but hearing the haunting refrain of "Gimme Shelter" in the aftermath of what he'd just witnessed was chilling. The man was *enjoying* himself.

He walked down the block, back toward Wall Street, singing to himself every step of the way.

Jake followed him out of the darkness into the cold day, keeping close to the walls of the stock exchange. The killer's voice echoed down the empty side street. Between the uncertainty, the darkness, and the cold, Jake imagined that most of the population was already seeking shelter indoors. Anyone who had somewhere to go would get there fast. The coming night would be brutal without power. How many old and vulnerable people would it claim?

The old building didn't offer much in terms of cover. If the guy turned around he was fucked. There was no way Jake was a good enough actor to pull off innocence or ignorance, not after what he'd just seen.

At the corner another set of cement pylons kept stray traffic at bay. Not that it was a problem today.

Leaning against one of them was an old Honda motorcycle with a heavy chain looped around it. The bike was all gleaming chrome and black enamel, like new, but it lacked the sleek lines of modern bikes. There was something about its solidity and the power of its clean lines that was unasham-edly masculine, and meant to appeal to boys across the world.

Jake was still half a block back as the killer knelt beside the bike and unhooked the chain.

Jake was trapped in that moment, staring at the killer as he straddled the bike and stamped down hard on the kick starter, revving the engine as he settled onto the black leather seat.

The killer stared right at him.

He'd been made.

The man's lip curled slowly into a mocking smile. He raised two fingers to touch his temple, either giving Jake an ironic salute or miming blowing his brains out, and pulled away from the pylon, burning rubber and roaring back up Wall Street toward Broadway, where refugees of the black-out bundled up against the elements and continued their long walks home.

Once he hit the expanse of Broadway, the killer would open up the throttle and disappear into New York City and that would be it. There'd be no justice for the dead back there, and nothing to stop the man from finishing whatever it was he'd started.

Jake was stubborn. It wasn't his most endearing trait, but it kept him going long after others would have admitted de-feat. He ran after the killer—it was all he could do.

He dodged around an old woman burdened under bulg-ing shopping bags overfilled with the bare necessities of life. Unable to stop himself, he slammed into a kid crossing the mouth of the street, and sent the boy sprawling.

He didn't have time to feel guilty. He ran on three more staggering steps, hands almost dragging across the blacktop, be-fore he righted himself and cast about, searching for the killer.

He could hear the bike, the rider mocking him by revving the engine as he let every one of those horses loose.

What he saw was another one of those damned bike messengers peddling toward him like the devil was on his tail. Jake stood his ground, meeting the rider head on. There was a moment when their eyes met and the rider realized what Jake intended, but by then it was too late, he was falling. The back wheel skidded out beneath the messenger as he clawed at the air, desperately trying to catch ahold of something to stop him from going down.

Jake stepped aside, avoiding the tangle of man and machine, then stooped to grab the bike's handlebars and was running and mounting it before the fallen biker could yell "Asshole!" at his back.

His height gave him an advantage, as did the bike's smaller, lighter frame, but it wasn't much of an advantage once they hit the open road. As long as there were people—lost and looking for leadership—the messenger bike was more maneuverable, which made up for the motorcycle's greater speed.

In the distance a pack of dogs howled, the chorus reminding him they faced another night in Dogland. Snow couldn't be far away.

The killer reached the end of the block. There were cars there, all at a standstill, most long since abandoned.

The killer looked back over his shoulder, almost as if he were making sure Jake was following, then eased his motorcycle into a gap in the snake of traffic that was barely there, between a yellow cab and an SUV, before accelerating the wrong way up Broadway.

Gritting his teeth, Jake stood on the pedals. His weight put more force behind his movements. He pedaled as hard and as fast as he could, the wind battering his face and hair, but no matter how furiously he pumped, the killer was getting away. Jake forced more speed out of his burning thighs, every muscle tense, quivering, as the bike's frame veered violently beneath him.

Mercifully, for the length of Broadway, past the back of Zuccotti Park, across Cortlandt and Dey and Fulton, right past where the new Fulton Street station was still going up, *nothing* was moving.

There was a lattice of scaffolding before the cement barricades cut the street down to two lanes. Jake didn't slow, but the killer did, needing to weave a way around abandoned vehicles.

Then the street widened beyond the barricades as City Hall came in sight. The killer leaned into the curve, making Jake think he'd swing right, but at the last moment he straightened and stayed on Broadway.

The wide avenue made it easier for Jake to keep the killer in sight. The guy slowed up slightly under the flags of City Hall, crossing Chambers, as if playing with Jake.

Jake's legs were on fire. Every muscle burned. There was no way he could maintain this pace and they both knew it. But the killer wasn't opening up the throttle and leaving him flailing around behind him, he was enjoying the chase too much.

As long as the Honda had gas in its tank he *could* disappear off into the distance. Jake had a finite amount of strength left, and the gradual rise was burning it up fast. Somehow he was going to have to force the guy off his bike.

The killer crossed Duane.

Jake was still half a minute behind him, and weaving between pedestrians was no easy task.

The street was lost in the shadows of the two buildings on either side of the road.

The killer twisted around in his seat. He had his gun in his hand. The real one this time, not his fingers. The man's bike veered left, unbalanced as he leaned back. This was all that saved Jake's life.

Jake hunched down over his handlebars trying to make himself small. The move slowed him. He felt rather than heard the shot as the killer fired at him.

The crack of the gunshot was dislocated by the sounds of the city, at once unique, at once terrible, and yet almost negligible in terms of the actual noise it made. But then, how much noise was a life worth? That one solid muffled sound of the bullet piercing the skin? The deathly quiet whisper of air and lead through the silencer? The rush of displaced air the second before sound catches up with the agony of impact?

There was no pain beyond the sting—like a wasp, angry, unexpected—as the bullet tore through his jacket sleeve, digging into the tense muscle of his bicep. The sudden flare of pain was intense and almost toppled him from the bike as he reared back. A second shot missed, the killer overcompensating and firing wide to the right. Jake heard the *crump* of it tearing into the side of one of the abandoned cars behind him.

They were just coming up on the New York Public Records building when the killer angled his motorcycle to the right, hard, hopping the curb and going back onto one wheel as he ploughed across the wide, plaza-like sidewalk in front of the building. As his front wheel came down, he braked hard. The back wheel slewed out beneath him when he planted his foot, bringing the bike around.

He faced Jake, engine idling, and raised the gun. This time he took the time to aim.

Jake didn't even think about it; he threw himself off the bike, hitting the deck hard and rolling across the asphalt as three quick shots tore into the blacktop inches from his face. He pushed himself up and hurled his body sideways, putting a truck between himself and the shooter, only to hear another succession of bullets drill holes in the metal panel above his head.

*Fuck.*

Jake crawled forward another couple of feet and heard the engine revving. The killer was moving to get a better angle to take him out.

He was effectively trapped behind the truck. He couldn't move—not unless he wanted a bullet in the head for his troubles. All he could do was listen to the throaty grumble of the Honda's engine.

Someone screamed.

That sound reinforced the fact that he wasn't alone out here. There were innocent people standing in line to become collateral damage in this showdown. It was like something out of *The Godfather*: that fucked-up scene where Sonny's car gets riddled with bullets while he's sitting inside it, blood and glass everywhere.

"Get down!" he yelled, like they needed telling.

Another shot and it was pandemonium, people running without thinking, anywhere away from the sound of gunfire spitting their way.

And when the shooting stopped, there was only the sound of panic.

He couldn't hear the Honda's deep-throated rumble anymore. It was gone.

He rose slowly to his hands and knees, and crept along to the edge of the truck, risking a glance into the plaza. The killer was nowhere to be seen. Rising to his feet, Jake slammed his fist on the truck's hood, hard enough to dent the metal.

"Fuck, fuck, fuck, fuck, *fuck!*"

# CHAPTER TEN

OQUELLES, A TINY COMMUNITY WITHIN PAS-DE-CALAIS, on L'Européene autoroute, was two hours north of Paris.

It took Sophie ninety minutes to make the drive on the stolen bike.

The highway was full of stranded cars and desperate people. It was likc riding through some Hollyweird version of a postapocalyptic landscape. Coquelles comprised a few hotels and a shopping center. It was also where the French side of the Channel Tunnel descended beneath the sea.

The terminal building was dark.

London was her only logical destination.

She could have gone deeper into Europe, through Luxembourg into Germany, and looked to hide out in the Alps, but that wouldn't help. She knew what was going on. She was one of the few people on the planet who did. It also meant she knew that there were several places being adjusted—that was what her paymasters had called it, *adjusted*, such a bland word for what was taking place—just as Paris had been. The two prime targets in this hemisphere were now London and

New York. Knowledge in this case was dangerous for her health.

Yesterday flying would have been faster—less than an hour in the air to Heathrow—but with all the electronics going down there was no way she was boarding a plane, even if they could get one airborne. Going home to New York was out of the question. Thanks to the tunnel, London wasn't.

Not that it would be easy.

The journey from Gare du Nord in the heart of Paris to St. Pancras should have been about the same as the drive to the Eurostar terminal, a couple of hours, but without the trains she was being forced to improvise. The people out to get her were too, so it wasn't all bad.

At the top of the hill, Sophie pulled off the rue du Moulin and braked, stopping along the hard shoulder. It was quiet here, mostly because the trains weren't running, but it wasn't deserted. She watched a guard pace along the black lines of the tracks as they disappeared into the tunnel entrance.

One man.

Was he really alone? The one man guarding the last frontier? It felt too easy. She didn't know what she'd expected, really, a line of armed soldiers standing at the mouth of the Channel Tunnel ready to turn back the screaming hordes?

Unlikely, to say the least.

Well, unlikely until the powers-that-be worked out just what the hell was happening, and by then the military response would be so far behind the curve it'd be too late to make a damned bit of difference.

Sophie wheeled the bike around and walked it back away from the edge, then dismounted and stretched, working the kinks out of her spine and getting the blood flowing again. It was a sign of age, even if she didn't *feel* old. There was of course a psychology to it; ten years ago she could have run the fifty kilometers through the tunnel in a respectable marathon time, now the thought of another couple of hours in the saddle felt like cruel and unusual punishment.

Thinking about the old days made her think of Jake Carter.

She would have paid a lot of money to be a fly on the wall when he picked up her message. It was hard not to wonder what he thought of the whole *I'm not who you think I am* line. It had been deliberate. She knew what he was like when tugging at the threads of a mystery: he wouldn't rest. She could have just said, *Hey, Jake, it's me. I need to talk to you,* but that wouldn't have been half as effective. It was a cheap trick, but she didn't feel bad about manipulating him.

She knew where he was. She had known for a while now. It was part of the job after all—she monitored people. She gathered intel on who might or might not prove useful in the grand scheme of things, and Jake Carter had a skill set which made him worth watching. His choice of post-Army career was fitting in more ways than one, but there was no escaping the irony that he'd wound up back in New York, right where she needed him to be. The breakup hadn't been good. She hoped he'd eventually put two and two together and find the link between her and the redefining of the city. With the networks down, there was nothing else she could do but trust that he was still the same stubborn bastard he'd always been, and gamble that he wouldn't walk away from trouble when it found him.

Because that was the point of her call: to make sure trouble found him.

He was the one person she knew was clean. That meant

he was the only person she could trust. The grim reality was that she wasn't getting out of this, now that she'd made a stand against them. She knew that, but she didn't want to face it on their terms. It had to be on her terms. That meant she needed to get her ducks in a row, make sure the contingencies were in place, and then wait for the ride to stop. It was only a matter of time, and somewhere along the line she would get off. But until then she was determined to be the biggest fucking pain in their ass as possible, and that meant getting the fuck out of Paris.

Of course, they'd expect her to go to London. That couldn't be helped.

The rest would be up to Jake. She just hoped he was big enough and ugly enough to take care of himself.

Instinctively, she looked over her shoulder. The road was clear so she clambered back onto the bike.

The road ran just above the tunnel entrance, no more than a hundred feet from the edge where the hill abruptly cut off, its side planed away by a sheer concrete wall. Below that, twenty-five feet down, was a wide concrete service road, and then another drop, closer to forty feet this time. To the side was an incline, grassed over, but man-made, complete with a sidewalk at the far side. The incline ended beside the train tracks.

Sophie gunned the engine and raced the bike straight toward the edge. It was a long way down. She'd gotten the Egli-Vincent up to sixty when the ground disappeared from beneath it and she surged over the edge.

There was a breathless moment where there was nothing between her and seventy feet of drop, then a bone-jarring impact that traveled all the way up the ladder of her spine, rattling her teeth, as she hit the grass incline. The Egli-

Vincent's wheels kicked up dirt and grass, biting deep as she wheeled it around, then raced down the incline, covering the distance to the tracks in seconds.

There was a low chain-link fence between her and the tunnel proper. She didn't have time for finesse.

The guard had seen her. He shouted something into his radio, then broke off and raised the rifle at his side. She had no way of knowing if his call would bring help or if his radio was as dead as the rest of the world's electronics. It didn't matter. She barreled right through the chain-link fence, hitting it head-on. The bike's speed tore the fence down, and the Egli-Vincent drove straight over the barrier. She pivoted again, taking the bike off the concrete lip and kicking out the back wheel to twist midair. The bike landed on the tracks facing the dark, gaping hole that was the Channel Tunnel's entrance.

"*Arrête!*" the guard shouted, running toward her. He fired a warning shot. "*Arrête!*"

Sophie didn't need warning. She hunkered down over the handlebars and gunned the engine instead. The Egli-Vincent roared, tires spitting gravel, and powered forward, the sheer force of the engine unleashed over the short distance between her and the terrified guard. He couldn't stand his ground without being mowed down.

Self-preservation kicked in; he hurled himself out of the way and Sophie disappeared into the dark mouth of a world beneath the sea.

It wasn't completely dark, and it didn't much feel like a tunnel. It felt more like a vast nuclear bunker.

Emergency lights ran at ceiling height along one side of the cylindrical concrete tube, offering enough illumination to see the tracks stretching out ahead of her as well the walls closing in around the vanishing point.

The tunnel was wide enough to accommodate two trains passing, and had offshoots for emergency vehicles and maintenance workers. The dark smears where water seeped slowly through the concrete were unnerving. The roar of the engine intensified, amplified by the peculiar acoustics of the tunnel.

Thirty-one miles under the incredible press of water.

She looked at the speedometer, running the numbers in her head. At current speed she'd reach the other side in a little less than half an hour. The question was what would be waiting for her when she got there.

There wasn't much one French border guard could do to stop her. The tunnel didn't have blast doors they could seal to prevent her from getting off sovereign French soil, but if their radios were shielded, they could get word to their British counterparts in Folkestone. She was going to be coming out of the tunnel hot.

But she had a thirty-one-mile drive to think about what she'd do at the other end, more than enough time to run through her options and come up with a plan. It wouldn't be a good plan, but it was better than no plan.

The tunnel was straight, the center of the track reasonably level, but the sleepers every few feet promised a jarring ride, so she hopped the rails and followed the flat gravel track running alongside the rails until she reached a branch in the tunnel which took her through to a second, much smaller tube.

She could almost reach out with her hands and touch both sides at once as she roared down the flat surface of the maintenance tunnel. It was an alien landscape, harsh, new, clean, with acoustics that meant the engine's roar swelled to deafening levels, folding in on itself as the echoes reverberated through the cramped confines.

Sophie was armed: she had her pistol and her knife. She could do a lot of damage with either of them if she had to. One-on-one she'd hold her own in any fight. Two-on-one the odds were still stacked in her favor. Three-on-one things would set a little hairier, but she had nothing to lose. That meant she wasn't afraid of getting hurt. That, in turn, meant she was much more dangerous than any men who might be waiting for her at the other end of the tunnel, because they had wives and children and things they didn't want to lose weighing them down. Yet she didn't want to kill anyone else unless she really had to.

Unfortunately, she might not have a say in it.

Sophie put her head down and drove, thundering through the tunnel so fast the emergency strip lights blurred into pulsing lines on either side of her head.

Twenty minutes later, the brand-new Egli-Vincent burst out of the Channel Tunnel entrance like a runaway train, engine racing, wheels a blur as it hit the open air like a flame.

Six guards were waiting for her.

Not enough, no matter how good they thought they were.

She was better.

The bike's sudden appearance caught them off-guard, even though they'd braced themselves, taunted by its roar for minutes before it finally appeared.

She deliberately steered for the biggest and ugliest of the men in front of her, standing point with a submachine gun leveled at her. The gambit was a simple—and desperate—one: she had to assume he wanted to stay alive.

He had less than twenty feet to decide. Not enough time for rational thought to take over. He was operating purely on instinct as he squeezed off a burst of gunfire. The bullets tore up the road in front of her because, as she'd hoped, he had no intention of killing a defenseless woman.

She didn't so much as veer an inch from her path. She needed him to know she had no such qualms as she surged forward.

He bought the gambit and hurled himself out of the motorcycle's path, leaving a gaping hole right at the front of their line.

She raced through the center of the line, taking the Egli-Vincent's speed into the red zone. There was nothing between her and London.

# CHAPTER ELEVEN

"WE HAVE A PROBLEM, MR. ALOM."

"Then fix it. That is what we pay you for."

"It's not as easy as that."

"It is. You might like to think it is more difficult, but in reality things are only as difficult as you make them. This is business. Nothing more, nothing less. And in business you strategize, you prepare, and you capitalize, and then, if you are lucky, you make a killing. We aren't trying to win friends here. There is nothing to be gained in being cautious. We must be bulls. If there is a problem, you deal with it. That is what you do. There is no room for doubt. The plan is solid; we have at our disposal information none of the competing factors are party to. Today is all about follow-through. Today, with the grace of the old gods, we become kings of the world."

"There's a problem," the assassin began again.

"Then find a solution, or die trying."

"Yes, Mr. Alom."

"Better. I take it you encountered resistance at Wall Street?"

"Very little. None of our friends made themselves known,

though we picked up an audience."

"And judging by your 'problem,' I assume you failed to deal with it at the time?"

"The priority was getting out of there."

"No, the priority was doing the job you were paid to do, Mr. Cabrakan. You disappoint me. There can be no witnesses. Do you understand?"

"I do." The words were delivered like a marriage vow.

"Good. Do not disappoint me twice in one day or we shall have to consider liquidating our assets." There was no misunderstanding the threat. "I take it the operation itself was a success?"

For a moment there were only the sounds of the city on the line, and even those were muted by the absence of traffic with just the one engine revving quietly beneath him, then the assassin took a deep breath and finished his report: "The adjustment was successful."

He explained that the programmers infiltrated the system and inlaid a real-time delay, allowing their systems precious milliseconds to react upon the trades before they actually happened on the stock exchange servers. It was barely perceptible, not visible to the human eye, but given the hundredths and millionths of a second it took these machines to react, it was almost a lifetime in terms of cold hard calculating time—as good as being clairvoyant, allowing them to make all the right trades, grab stocks a moment before their share prices hiked, and dump them before the bottom fell out of the market. Fractions of a second were all it took for the machine to make a killing, and once the worm was embedded, no simple reboot was going to cleanse the system, no matter how clever the SYSOPs believed their system was. Pulling the plug wouldn't change a thing.

They were in.

It was only the start. He wasn't party to the myriad strands of the plan. He was only a pawn in this game, with Alom and his kind the kings and queens. He knew that. He knew that he was disposable. He'd be a fool to think otherwise. But if he played his part and didn't let Alom down, he could walk away from this richer than any god. The prospect was almost worth dying for.

"Send word, we need more foot soldiers. Let the youth rise up and feel useful." It was a simple enough plan to keep the Watchers busy so that they wouldn't know where the true threat lay. With the city already on edge, masked kids with spray cans were every bit as frightening as an armed jihadist. Anarchy on the streets had always been the best alternative when it came to distracting law enforcement. And it was so much better to use disenfranchised youth than it was to risk any of their own men. "There is still so much to do before we emerge from the shadows, Mr. Cabrakan. You know what you must do. Very simply put, give them hell."

Or, in the case of the gate-crasher who'd stumbled into the party back on Wall Street, open the gates and push him through with a bullet in the face, the assassin thought grimly.

He had no intention of failing Mr. Alom.

He knew better than that.

# CHAPTER TWELVE

"HOLY FUCK . . . I MEAN . . . JUST . . . LOOK AT IT . . . *look* at it." Finn Walsh couldn't take her eyes off the screen. It was astounding. Breathtaking. She was quite literally lost for words. She shook her head. She knew she was grinning like a kid, but she didn't care. It *was* incredible. It was everything she'd dreamed it would be and so much more.

An underwater image dominated the screen. It had been taken with some sort of night-vision lens, making it bright and clear, but heavily tinted to a pale blue-green. It was like looking down on an alien civilization in some distant world.

There was a row of buildings, or more accurately foundations, clearly squared and far too precise to be artificial. Beside that row was a second row. This one was far more than just rectangular bases and broken foundations, with three complete structures. Each of the three submerged buildings' four walls sloped inward to form a rough pyramidal point. The first and last of the three structures had smooth sides, but the middle one was broken into squared rings, each one narrower than the one below it. Stair steps. She was looking at a stepped pyramid through the green filter of the sea. The two ruins flanking it were regular smooth-sided pyramids.

These three buildings made this underwater ruin an incredible discovery. A life-changing one.

It was the very first image of the ruin the divers had found. They'd included it and all of their early seismographic readings on the server so she could get up to speed on the project. A husband-and-wife team who'd first stumbled upon the area, and then returned to survey the ruins on behalf of the Cuban government, had taken the shots. The area in question, in the Pinar del Río province, was right on the edge of the Bermuda Triangle and was rife with shipwrecks, so the motivation behind the first dives, she assumed, had almost certainly been salvage related.

Instead, they'd stumbled on something so much more important than lost treasure.

The pair, Pauline Zalitzki and Paul Weinzweig, had shown the images around, drawing a great deal of interest very quickly, including from *National Geographic*. But the economic truth was these ruins were over two thousand feet beneath the surface, both difficult and costly to examine. The fact that standard oceanography suggested the area would have taken almost fifty thousand years to sink to that depth, significantly predating any recorded civilization, didn't help, though it really should have been the thing that had the moneymen the most excited. They were dealing with so many anomalies. The first Egyptian pyramids had been built roughly five thousand years ago. The numbers just didn't add up, financially or historically. There was no way the couple's discovery could be ten times the age of the pyramids of Giza. It wasn't possible. Unless the area had somehow sunk suddenly, due to fractures around it, perhaps? A break in the plates?

But that didn't stop Finn from being stunned that it had taken so long—over a decade from the first sighting of the ruin—to fund a proper exploration.

Government approval? Jurisdiction on the find was probably a nightmare with it falling between Cuba's and the United States' governance. The two countries had had plenty of issues. And, of course, the initial discovery had been right before 9/11. Everything had stopped after that, with the obsession over Homeland Insecurity taking precedence. Who cared about looking at old underwater ruins, especially near Cuba, when there were civil rights to infringe upon in the name of national security?

Their loss was her gain.

Technology had marched on significantly during the last decade, so the timing was good in that regard too. They were capable of closer scrutiny, with significantly more clarity, at much less cost. And back in 2001 there was no way she'd have been involved without being on-site—innovations in global communication and file-sharing had changed the world in ways it was still hard to comprehend. To quote Walt Disney, it really was a small world after all.

It was also one in which the university employed ancient backup generators, otherwise it would have been as dead in here as it was out there. Sometimes it was good to linger in the technological dark ages, she thought wryly. The hard-science division eggheads were always playing around with miniature cyclotrons and god only knows what else, everything they touched capable of generating massive power surges capable of bringing down the network—so all of the computers on campus were shielded, and isolated from the city's electrical grid. The grid had been out for six hours now. It was probably their fault. Her network connection kept dropping, but other than that mild annoyance, her system seemed okay even if it had taken about five times longer than necessary to download the initial batch of files to her local hard drive to access whenever she needed.

But there was no getting around the fact that things were weird outside Columbia's walls. An ounce of imagination was a very bad thing.

At first it had been a cacophony of honking and blaring horns following the unmistakable screech of tires and squeal of brakes and the sharp, tearing sound of metal upon metal. Quickly it had transformed into the chaos of crunching impacts and so much else, but those had been overtaken by the proper sounds of chaos. Voices first. People screaming, initially in fear, then at each other. Eerie silence had slowly taken over, and that was worse than all of the noise put together.

Finn hadn't dared leave the university's protection to see what was left out there. In her mind the world beyond the campus limits had taken on a complete *Escape From New York* vibe. The problem was, she was no Snake Plissken. She didn't want to venture out in case it turned out there was nothing but a wasteland beyond the campus gates. She couldn't help it. Once her mind had gone down that track all she could imagine was a barren *Mad Max*esque ruin that had once been one of the busiest cities in the world.

*Give it enough time and there'll be primitive tribes out there, people hunkering down behind makeshift forts and attacking each other with whatever weapons they can bring to hand*, she thought. All that was needed for wide-scale panic to kick in was someone realizing the lights weren't coming back on—then they'd lead a revolution straight to the nearest grocery store, slaughtering anyone who tried to take the food from their hungry mouths.

It was basic psychology.

It had been drummed into the American psyche ever since the Y2K hype. The whole notion that the computers would just suddenly stop and everything they knew and trusted and built their lives around would come to a juddering halt was ingrained now. The first hint of trouble, of a tornado or even a storm warning, and the lines at the groceries stores were a mile long with people lining up for toilet rolls and stockpiling batteries and canned foods, anything with a long life, anything that wouldn't go off and stink the place up. Then they'd go back and turn their homes into bunkers and batten down the hatches. That was the reality of America today, and it wasn't just the rednecks.

Given all of the portents over the last few months—the dogs, the birds—Christ, last week there was talk of the animals fleeing Yellowstone and other woodland parks, heading for the high ground—all of it just made everyone even edgier. They were living day-to-day, expecting the worst, some of them even wanting it to happen, she was sure. She'd seen the doom patrol out there preaching their end-of-the-world gospel, bless their hearts.

Six hours.

A lot could happen in six hours.

She didn't want to find out exactly what. Not yet.

For now she just wanted to immerse herself in the wonder that was scientific discovery. She had lost worlds to explore, digitally at least. It was a gift that put her on the autism spectrum, she knew, but like a lot of obsessives she could forget the world even existed when she wanted to, especially when confronted by the unknown.

It was more than mere intellectual curiosity, it was compulsive, like she needed to turn the lights out five times before leaving a room or knock on any closed door three times to announce her presence. She liked to think of it as a quirk, the kind of thing that made the Sheldons of this world adorable, but that need was what made her good at what she did.

She studied the latest geological tests.

The geophysics suggested that the entire area was made up of granite: close to twelve square miles of granite bedrock. That was several times the size of Central Park. It was difficult to adjust her thinking to account for something on that scale. If she was right, it meant they were talking about something on par with a city, not a couple of ruined buildings, which really was beyond her wildest dreams. And ever since that first image had come in she'd been dreaming big.

She was banking on that making her job easier as opposed to looking for the proverbial linguistic needle in this very wet haystack. She was more likely to encounter writings on a larger site, and the more samples she had, no matter how eroded or unclear, the easier it would be to run comparisons on them.

Her primary aim was to identify the language. Her secondary one, to build a lexicon.

Anything that could add to the greater knowledge pool of ancient languages, offering some new understanding, some new glimpse at the way things might have been back then, was better than gold, even if it was something as mundane as Jesus' shopping list. *Not that any self-respecting messiah did his own shopping*, she thought, grinning as her train of thought derailed.

A lot of it was about joining the dots.

The raw data was out there just waiting for someone to interpret it. Sure, it wasn't all ones and zeroes of strings of hex or whatever it was the guys in the computer labs were using today, but it was there, every bit as concrete—or in this case granite—as the mathematical strings they used when it came to examining the building blocks of the world.

There shouldn't be any granite in the region, it was as simple as that. The sheet rock was anomalous. Cuba was mostly limestone, so the granite had to have been brought in by whoever built the city beneath the sea.

The exploratory team had only taken a few preliminary photos and videos of the find so there wasn't a whole lot for her to look at yet, but it was obvious that time and tide had worked their damage, with entire levels of the pyramidal structures missing and whole sides of what may have been temples collapsed.

On the plus side, granite was a hard stone, capable of withstanding the battery of the elements, and even after all this time lost to the sea the granite had survived the worst of the erosion virtually unscathed. That meant the few symbols she could make out in the images were sharp. They'd been carved deep into the stone blocks, and even though the top layer of strata had worn—or broken—away, the remainder was still chisel-clean.

She had no difficulty transcribing the symbols. Pulling up a graphics package, Finn began the painstaking process of tracing the first one, saving it as a clean layer so that she could study it independent of its surroundings.

*Peculiar*, she thought, and not for the first time. The pyramids suggested an Egyptian influence, that much was obvious, but the thinking was highly suspect. The Olmecs and Mayans had constructed pyramids, and theirs were often stair-stepped like the central one in this image.

But that presented its own set of time line problems: Olmecs hadn't started erecting pyramids until circa 1200 BCE (Before Central Event, which was exactly the same as Before Christ for the non-Christians of the world); the Mayans were an even younger civilization, their pyramids built closer to 1000 BCE, only three thousand years ago—so neither of those fit her flood-basin time line. There were the ziggurats of Mesopotamia, they were old enough to correspond with the estimated age of their discovery, but that civilization was half a world away in the cradle of humanity, Iran and Iraq, and with no evidence of Mesopotamian society having ventured as far as Europe, never mind the Americas, and even if the Great Ziggurat of Ur dated back to the twenty-first century BCE, most of the ziggurats were actually from the same time period as the Olmecs and the Mayans.

She removed the overlay to study the first symbol. It definitely wasn't an Egyptian hieroglyph. There was no denying the similarity, certainly: it appeared to be a flower, definitely representational rather than phonetic, showing something instead of sounding something out. But Egyptian markings were more finely crafted than this. The hieroglyph for *owl*, for example, was a likeness of an owl, complete with beak, talons, and feathers. This icon was cruder. In a lot of ways it was closer to an Olmec representation, though it didn't exactly match their more stylized symbols.

The fact that she didn't recognize the language right away was exciting. Had it simply been Egyptian or Olmec or some other known variant, her job would have been a simple case of translating a few symbols. If they'd just uncovered a lost language, possibly even the oldest extant example of a written language, her job was only just beginning. She'd be the first to study it, to document it, and to try her hand at translating it. That didn't happen more than once in half a dozen lifetimes in her world. It was beyond being career-defining. It was life-changing.

She knew she was grinning like a lunatic. She didn't care.

She saved the first symbol, eager to see what else the underwater world had to show her. Turning back to the original photo, she selected the next symbol, created a new layer, and began tracing it. It was going to take awhile to get through all of the symbols, but she wasn't in a hurry to go outside. She had heat, light, and quiet in here, what else did she need? Power bars and Coke? Check. There was an ample supply of both in the vending machine across the hall. There were spare clothes in her office closet, along with a few blankets.

She had everything she needed in here to survive a mini-apocalypse.

# CHAPTER THIRTEEN

FOR A MINUTE, AT LEAST, HE'D FORGOTTEN about Sophie's enigmatic message.

That was something. But in the grand scheme of things, not a whole fuck of a lot, really.

Jake grabbed the messenger bike and hauled it up off the ground where he'd abandoned it. He didn't get on it. Anger, frustration, impotence welled up inside him and he hurled it away, hard. The handlebars hit the asphalt, but the back wheel kept spinning after the bike slammed into the door of a nearby truck. People were staring at him. He didn't care. He was so thoroughly pissed off he wanted to break more things. A pipe or bat would make a fine weapon, but even sans weapon he was happy to start bashing the fuck out of things with his bare fists and boots—windshields, headlights, and roofs, it didn't matter. The only thing that would appease his anger right now was watching glass fly and hearing metal squeal like a pig.

But he wasn't going to get any satisfaction. It didn't matter how much he raged, how many things he hit, he couldn't vent on the one guy who deserved it.

He'd blown it. He'd just let a guy get away with shooting a bunch of people dead while he watched. He could have made a difference, he could have done something. He should have, but he'd blown it.

*Fuck. Shit. Fuck.*

Jake stormed over to the battered messenger bike, lifted it up again, climbed on, and ignoring the people trying to help him, cranked the pedals hard, no particular destination in mind. He just wanted to be away from there.

He needed to think smart. The cops might be swamped, but they wouldn't ignore a shooting, even if Joe Public couldn't call it in on their cells. He wasn't going to try to explain what the fuck was going on, mainly because he didn't have a clue.

Yet.

That was a powerful word.

Yet.

It suggested he would have the answers at some point down the line.

He lived and died by that word. It meant there was a way to change things, even if he didn't know what he was dealing with right now.

Angling down a side street, Jake swung over to the curb. In the shadow of tall trees, he pulled over, still straddling the bike, and pulled out his cell phone. He had two reasons to hope it would have survived the wipeout. One, he'd been underground—a long way down—when the blast hit, assuming it was a blast of some sort. The other, ever since mustering out of the service, he'd been paranoid about being cut off and paid good money for a satellite phone. As long as the hundreds of feet of bedrock shielded the phone's electronics, it should still be able to receive a signal from one of several satellites in low earth orbit. He didn't want to think about the fact that they had taken out the relay towers. He deserved a bit of luck.

He thumbed down the green call icon. There was no dial tone to tell him if it was alive or not. The only way he'd know if there was a connection to the satellite uplink was if it held the call.

He dialed quickly. It was a number he knew by heart. He hadn't programmed it in—the guy he was calling was paranoid about people from the past catching up with him. Jake couldn't blame him.

There were plenty of people lining up to do bad things to Ryan Johnson. Russian mafia, Serbian goons, Latvians, Lithuanians, all along the entire bloc. He wasn't a popular man. Jake wasn't exactly sure what he'd done, something related to computers and fire walls and making a lot of money for a lot of mean people and then upsetting them. Badly.

Ryan was also the only person Jake knew who was paranoid enough to shield his home electronics *and* carry a sat phone.

The phone rang twice before it was answered.

"Yo." That was it, just the one syllable.

Jake grinned with relief. "Ryan. It's Jake."

"Jake?" There was a moment's silence. "Long time." The tone was a little less guarded, yet despite the words, Ryan was obviously *not* happy to hear from him. But that was Ryan. Jake didn't even know his real name, despite the fact he'd known the guy most of his adult life. Some people liked to keep their secrets. He didn't know what had gone down with Ryan, and he didn't want to. Right now, Ryan was the only person he could think of who had the skill set to help.

Jake got right to it: "You busy?"

That earned a chuckle. Ryan had sworn he'd turned his life around when he'd returned to New York a few months back, done with freelancing, as he put it, done with chasing the big-money score and being some bastard's puppet; now he was just looking to keep his head down.

Jake believed him, but unfortunately that wasn't enough to stop him from saying, "I need a favor."

"Everyone who calls does. So what do you think I can do you for?"

"To be honest, I'm not really sure."

"My favorite kind of favor."

"Okay, here's what's just happened . . . I just walked into the middle of a shit storm on Wall Street. A bunch of guys were messing around with the computers on the trading floor, and now they're dead. I need to know what they were doing, and why."

"One question before we get into this."

"Shoot."

"Did you do the killing?" There was no judgment in the question. Ryan had a history of violence. It was simply part of the world he'd grown up in.

"No. But I saw who did, and I couldn't stop it from happening. That's why I want to know what was worth their lives."

"Yeah, all right, man, I can see that. Taking on the troubles of the world. I'm cool with that. The networks are fried since this whole sunfail thing, so I can't do it from here, but I can bounce down there and work my magic. In and out before anyone notices."

"Thanks, man. You know the drill: don't leave any trace, and don't get caught. I really don't want to have to explain what I've got you involved in to Von."

Ryan laughed. "Almost worth getting busted for that conversation. I'll call when I'm done."

"I owe you. And do me a second favor while you're on it: give my love to that gorgeous cousin of mine." Blood ran deep in this life. It didn't matter if you'd taken the road from the projects into the military or into and out of gang life, blood was blood. You didn't fuck with blood.

Yvonne, Ryan's partner, was blood.

Jake knew that was the only reason he'd been the one they'd called when they hit town rather than just keeping their heads down. He'd read the stuff in the papers about Ryan's crew out in Russia damn near triggering an international incident. They were private contractors. Mercenaries by another name. Ryan wasn't muscle, he was the brains. There was a guy called Markham who was basically a grunt. Jake had heard stories: how he'd been suspected of rape and a bunch of other crimes against the locals, and turned up lynched by the same locals who'd had enough of his shit. The only reference in the press back home was to a businessman by the same name who had died while working out there—no mention of a memorial service or anything of the sort. But that was all parallel-world stuff for Jake. He'd been an enlisted man. There was a proper way of doing things, and you didn't fuck with the locals, not when you were out there to keep the peace.

"Will do." The connection dropped.

Jake tucked the phone back into his pocket. He felt a little better now—a problem shared and all that. He trusted Ryan. The guy had too much to lose to be a dick. And he knew computers better than anyone Jake had ever met. He could make them dance and sing. He'd come up with the goods.

The next question, Jake thought as he hopped off the bike and started walking it down the street to keep moving, was a big-picture one: *How does all of this fit together?*

There was a pattern here and he wasn't seeing it. First it had been Fort Hamilton, then the subway, the power grid, finally the stock exchange. So how did it all connect?

Despite hitting Fort Hamilton first, that attack didn't jive with what he'd witnessed at Wall Street. It was violent. Bloody. Lethal. But it was intimate too. Not like 9/11, which was about spreading the fear. Not just the murders, but the fact that the killer had been riding one of the few working engines in the city. It was like one of those damned finger puzzles, those little Chinese torture devices, where the more you worried at them the harder they clung to your fingers.

He had little pieces of the puzzle, things he could extrapolate from, like how the killer had known in advance the power would go out, just like the guys spray-painting the words of their prophets on the subway walls had known the lights were going out. Did that mean they were in this together?

Back in the Army they'd used hardened batteries that were designed to keep working even in the event of an EMP. It wasn't inconceivable the motorcycle had been shielded in the same way; logically then, the team *could* have been utilizing a shielded battery to power up the computers. Lots of ifs and coulds and shoulds in there, but realistically, there was always going to be a logical solution to each stage of the chaos they'd unleashed. The problem wasn't working it out so much as working back from the effect to find the cause, and right now, the best he could do was stick with the assumption that the killer knew what was happening. The way the victims deferred to him before he'd put bullets in their heads suggested he was the big man.

But that didn't mean he wasn't just a foot soldier answering to a bigger man, because every revolution needed men on the ground who could handle the killing.

Jake reached the corner where Varick angled off West Broadway, leaving a narrow little wedge of brown grass and stunted shrubs. A single row of trees wilted in the middle. The "square" wasn't big enough to warrant a park bench.

This was usually a quiet spot, depressingly so. The streets were wide, the buildings light-industrial complexes housing utility companies and small manufacturing plants. There were a couple of tech companies and an art academy had moved into one of the old factory units. And, of course, fancy converted lofts for multimillionaires

But not today.

It was so crowded that Jake stopped in his tracks, stunned by the wave of noise that rolled over him. A wall of people blocked his way. The noise was inhuman.

It took him a moment to realize what he was hearing, then the first in a pack of dogs went racing past. They were a mixed bunch—terriers, retrievers, Labradors, mongrels, and fighting dogs. They darted through the crowd, finding gaps in the gathered people that hadn't been there seconds before, breaching the wall of flesh, howling as they ran. Their voices rose in a loud, mournful wail. It made the hair on the nape of Jake's neck prickle as a shiver ran down his spine.

Fear gripped the crowd, adding to the cacophony. Some were wailing, others muttering or shouting, with little sense to any of the sound.

They weren't staring at the dogs, he realized, as the pack moved on. Everyone was looking at the ground around their feet.

Jake pushed his way forward, unwilling to relinquish his grip on the bike.

The grass was littered with small, broken, feathered bodies.

Birds.

Thousands upon thousands of birds, birds of every shape and size—pigeons, usually ground grubbers, made up maybe half of them, along with starlings, crows, magpies, and more brightly colored finches and thrushes.

And all of them were dead. Every single one of them, though some of the carcasses still twitched, clinging to the last shreds of life as their nervous systems shut down.

Jake looked at the sky. There wasn't a single bird up there.

There were more fallen birds on the sidewalk, turning it into a path of black feathers. Even more lay in the streets around him, the littered bodies spreading far beyond the boundaries of the little park.

Apparently all of the birds across the city had fallen out of the sky. So many of them.

Someone beside him turned, deathly white, and gripped his arm. "It's happening, isn't it?" she said. "It's the end of the world . . . we're all going to die, aren't we?"

Beside her someone else asked, "Have you made your peace with God, because if you haven't you're going to hell."

And that terror spread like wildfire.

Jake wasn't listening, he was thinking.

Birds flew on air currents. Their brains adjusted in order to read the wind. But it wasn't just the wind, was it? They flew according to magnetic fields. Without magnetic fields to follow they couldn't fly right. If something had interfered with the magnetic fields across New York, every bird in the sky would have fallen.

I
N
F
A
M
O
U
S

There was science behind this end-of-the-world horror.

An EMP would've overridden the magnetic field, like when you skipped a stone across a still pond. The waves rippled out, affecting the whole surface. It made sense. He liked when things made sense.

It fit with the notion that the killer had been forewarned. It wasn't supernatural bullshit. This supported his first guess: an EMP or something like that had hit the city, and the killer knew exactly where and when it was going to be set off. That was why he was on the old motorcycle; it wasn't reliant upon the kind of circuitry that would have been fried by an electromagnetic pulse.

This might also explain why his sat phone had survived while he was deep underground.

A burst of static caused him to turn around. Across the street, right by the Franklin Street station's stairs, he saw a group of college-age kids clustered around a working radio. He could hear the crackle, and as he closed the distance between them, the voice of the newscaster: ". . . *similar outages have been reported in Los Angeles, Boston, Dallas, and Atlanta so far. We'll keep you up to date with all developments when news comes in, but we now understand that most of the United States has been affected, with unconfirmed reports of trouble in London, Paris, and Berlin as well . . .*"

Everything he thought he knew was wrong. It couldn't be an EMP. Not on that kind of scale. It was impossible.

An EMP could perhaps take out a city, but not an entire country. There was just no way. And reports of London, Paris, and Berlin being hit? It couldn't be an EMP.

Not unless it was some sort of concerted terror effort, hitting strategic locations, triggered remotely. But the kind of planning and precision that would require? Occam's razor came into play, surely. Sometimes the easiest possible answer was the right answer and the rest were all just conspiracy theories. It was hard to believe anyone could pull off something that big without attracting the attention of the NSA, Homeland Security, the FBI, the CIA, or any of the other law-enforcement acronyms out there. No. This was something else. It had to be.

A glassy-eyed little man hoisted up his *End of Days* placard.

Jake wasn't laughing.

Was it? Were all the whackos finally right? *Even a stopped clock's right twice a day*, he thought, unhelpfully.

Maybe it *was* the end of the world and God had kicked things off by cutting the electricity first. *Go fuck yourself*, he thought bitterly, not buying the whole apocalypse crap. It didn't work. For one thing, if it was divine, surely the air would be fucked, the sun black or something a bit more . . . Hollywood? The biggest threat now was snow as day faded into evening. As raptures went, it was pretty lame.

And if it really *was* the end of the world, why had that guy hit the stock exchange? It's not like he could take stocks and bonds with him into the afterlife. Which meant something else had to be going on. Something much more mundane, that could be explained with good old-fashioned science, with the same two things at its root, money and power.

Jake wasn't a scientist, he was a soldier. He had the basic skill sets of an engineer, more than enough to get him the job with the MTA, and a decent understanding of the stuff he needed to know, but when it got into the realms of hard science, quantum entanglement, dark matter, string theory, and all of the other buzz words of the day, there were better men than him to talk to. Men like Dr. Harry Kane, who was pretty much the smartest person in the room, no matter what room he happened to be in.

He'd met Harry when his unit had been paired with a British team for a joint exercise. Harry was old money. His family owned a castle somewhere in the highlands of Scotland. His pet theory was how everyone misunderstood Time's Arrow, how it was all about nature trying to find equilibrium rather than flowing in a direction of past to future. He explained it using a coffee cup he'd watch gradually go from steaming hot to tepid to cold. The molecules in the liquid weren't in a pure state. They were affected by their environment, just like people were—people living in the projects found a different equilibrium to those living in the high-rises of Manhattan, it was all about the choices life presented and the levels it offered—trying to find a state of equilibrium with the world around them.

Harry had mustered his way out a couple of years after Jake, moving over to the States for work and switching from applied engineering to chemical engineering research. He'd been teaching up at Columbia since then, though he traveled across the world.

They'd celebrated his appointment the last time they were together. Hard. Jake had very few memories of that particular weekend beyond the fact he'd woken up with someone, feeling like shit, dazed and confused and looking to get out before she woke up, which was always a classy move. Still, no point crying over some one-night stand. She'd live. He'd live. It was all about perspective. They were both consenting adults, they'd had a good time, and he'd saved her the walk of shame.

He didn't need to be a scientist to know he shouldn't be wasting his time thinking about a one-night stand. First and foremost, he needed to work out what was going on, what it meant, and how long it was going to last. Without those three pieces of information there was no way he'd be able to counteract it.

And there was one more nagging question he couldn't shake: *Where does Sophie Keane fit into all of this?*

*I'm not who you think I am.*

Jake shouldered his way through the crowd and mounted up again. It was going to be a long ride up to Columbia and he had a lot to think about on the way.

# CHAPTER FOURTEEN

CIVILIZATION TEETERED ON THE BRINK. The only conceivable positive was that priorities had changed overnight. Values shifted. Value itself shifted away from Xboxes and PlayStations, designer labels, and all that other stuff the ad men told us to crave. If it wasn't food or some other life-giving necessity, it was losing value fast. Things hadn't quite degenerated to the point that gold, diamonds, and paper money were worthless, but as people slowly began to realize what was happening around them the obsession with wealth changed beyond all recognition.

It had only just begun, but that tidal shift wouldn't be long in coming.

She knew how they'd react, she'd been trained to think the same way and act differently: protect the important stuff of life; after food and shelter it was medicine—ibuprofen, aspirin, insulin, inhalers, things people needed to survive. Company databases were a long way down the list of essentials. And when a cataclysmic event had rendered said company databases nothing more than a bank of inert computer hard drives, the natural thought was: *Why bother when there are other more immediate concerns?*

That's what she was banking on.

The difference between Sophie Keane and just about everyone else out there came down to a single fact: she knew how temporary the blackout was. Knowing that, she understood just how useful it could be to gain access to things like those corporate databases before the systems came back online.

Money and power. It always came back to one or the other, or a mixture of both.

This was no different. Money and power.

Which was why Sophie was contemplating infiltrating the London Stock Exchange as she rested in the back of an SUV outside London.

The drive from Paris, through the Channel Tunnel and then up from Folkestone to London, had been grueling. As the crow flies it was only a two-hundred-mile journey, but with the gridlock of dying Paris and London on either side it meant weaving in and out of abandoned vehicles, looking for the points of least resistance along the hard shoulder, and tearing along the dotted white line in the middle of the road where she could. Two hundred miles meant scavenging gas not once, but twice along the way. Neither time had been easy, but on the English side of the border they already had a makeshift home guard in place trying to protect the pumps. They made a fight of it. It was almost a pity to have to hurt them, but she was good enough not to have to kill them. Had they known what they were up against they would have realized just how lucky there were to be breathing.

She drove away hard, not listening to their cries for help. They weren't her problem. They wouldn't bleed out unless they were very unlucky. And if they were that unlucky, then maybe it was just their time.

She had to concentrate. Focus. A single pothole in the road could become the difference between making it out alive and not. That level of focus for such a prolonged time was exhausting. She had wanted to keep going, but that would have been a dumb move. It would have left her open to mistakes, and she couldn't afford to make a single one. Not now. Too much was at stake. So, she pulled over before reaching the city proper and stashed the bike, taking refuge in a small parking lot half-filled with abandoned cars. With minimal fuss she broke the passenger-side window of a Range Rover because the backseat was big enough for her to stretch out in, set her internal alarm clock to two hours, curled up under a checkered blanket, and fell asleep.

# CHAPTER FIFTEEN

I T FELT LIKE A LIFETIME SINCE HE'D BEEN ON THE CAMPUS.
In truth it had been barely even a year since Harry dragged
him to that party. A lot could happen in twelve months.
*Like the end of the world*, he thought, not appreciating his own
gallows humor.

Columbia always made Jake think of a medieval for-
tress with its tall stone buildings ringed all around the central
square. An optical illusion gave the impression of a continu-
ous wall guarding the rarified academy within.

Jake hefted the bike up onto his shoulder and started
across the sidewalk and then between the two front-most
buildings, following the walk onto the wide grassy expanse
of the South Field beyond. The campus was much as he
remembered it, students wandering around, kids huddled
on the lawn despite the cold, still interested in being cool.
*Where's the panic? Where's the confusion? Why's everyone so calm?*
Why, in other words, was it all so . . . normal?

He glanced over his shoulder without even thinking
about it, looking back there for proof of everything he'd

been experiencing so far that day. Beyond the same gap he'd just walked through Jake saw a pair of parked cars, and past them a stalled taxi bumper to bumper with a tiny Smart car. There was no one on the street. In a few days it would be buried under a foot of snow. He didn't want to think about what that would mean for the already damaged city.

In front of him life carried on as if nothing had happened; behind him it was a different world. He had to shake his head; it was the living proof that the academics had their heads up their asses in their ivory towers.

He crossed the green, and then cut across campus in front of Low Library. How would these pampered few react when the first food trucks failed to show up? How would they cope when the temperature inevitably dropped and none of the electric ignitions worked on the furnaces? It would be a rude awakening.

Jake followed a path that ran alongside the grand University Hall toward the back of the campus. On the other side of it the real world waited impatiently to intrude upon this idyllic academic solitude. He ignored it in favor of a hideous redbrick building, all sharp angles and odd cutouts that didn't match the stately edifices around it. It appeared to have been constructed using Lego. Seeley W. Mudd Building, home of the School of Engineering and Applied Sciences. Jake headed for the front door.

There was a bike rack right outside it, under the shadow of the exterior stairs leading up to the second floor. He inevitably dropped the messenger bike there. He didn't have a lock; if someone stole it, he'd just have to snatch another one. Not exactly the circle of life, but there was definitely a life lesson in there somewhere.

The Applied Physics and Applied Mathematics department was on the second floor. He heard a strangely familiar noise: the chime of an elevator door opening. It was the last thing he'd expected to hear. On the far side of the lobby he saw the silver doors open. There was only one guy inside. His brain was still trying to process why the elevator was working as the doors slid shut, leaving him staring at them.

The lights were on. He hadn't noticed them at first because they were such a natural part of his surroundings. The elevator working, the lights on? It was like he'd stepped into some bizarro *Twilight Zone* world where everything was *normal*.

He took the stairs.

"Can I help you?" a woman asked as he stepped into room 200, the department office. There were a handful of desks arranged along the side wall, a big table facing a row of mailboxes along the nearest wall, and twin photocopiers, ancient relics of the nineties, taking up most of the back wall. The woman, apparently one of the departmental secretaries, didn't break from sorting the mail into the slots.

"I hope so," Jake replied, putting on his friendliest you-really-do-want-to-help-me face. "I'm looking for Harry—" He caught himself. "Sorry, Dr. Kane. Do you know if he's teaching right now or in his office?" If he remembered correctly, Harry's office had been up on the eighth floor.

"I'm sorry, *Professor* Kane isn't here right now."

"Any idea when he'll be back?"

This time she did look at him, half with annoyance, half something else—frustration? Confusion? Concern? "He was supposed to be back already—winter break will be over in a few days. But," she glanced out the window, "the airports are shut."

"The airports?"

"He went home for a few days," the secretary said. She stopped what she was doing long enough to look Jake up and down, his clothing and skin dirty and sweaty from the ride. "I don't mean to be rude, but who did you say you were?"

"I didn't. Jake Carter. I'm an old friend of Harry's."

"I'm sorry, I can't help you, Mr. Carter. Given what's happening out there we just don't know when he'll be back." She turned her back on Jake.

He was about to walk out, defeated, when he remembered there was someone else he knew on campus. Even if he wasn't 100 percent on her details, he knew her name. He leaned over the desk, grabbing the faculty catalog from the counter, and left before the secretary realized what he'd done.

It only took a couple of minutes skimming the mug shots in the catalog to find Finn Walsh's picture, her department, building, office, and extension. Hopefully she'd have Harry's number, but whether she'd be any more forthcoming with it than the secretary, given the way they'd left things, was open for debate. He'd have to rely on his good old Carter boy charm. Grinning to himself, he realized just how screwed he was.

Jake headed back down to the lobby and out, taking a side door that opened to a small quad. He checked his reflection in the glass doors of the next building as he pushed them open. The best he could say was he looked like shit, and that was being generous.

He took the elevator up to six. The Art History and Archaeology department's office was a dead ringer for the Applied Physics and Applied Mathematics one; even the secretary behind the desk could have been the same. Maybe they cloned them, Jake thought as he walked past the open door. He didn't need directions. All the doors were numbered. 612. He found it easily enough.

He knocked twice on the closed door and saw a shadow move into view through the frosted glass. The door opened.

"Yes?" Finn Walsh said, before she recognized her visitor.

She was prettier than he remembered, with that whole sexy-librarian thing going on. She was pale from all those hours in the classroom, dark blond hair mussed with strands coming loose from a ponytail. He saw the dark circles under her eyes. She wasn't wearing any makeup, which made the contrast starker. She looked like she'd lost weight, but he wasn't about to say so. It was her eyes, though, blue-gray, with flecks like ice in the irises, that hinted at who she could have been in another life: the sultry Italian model masquerading as a washed-out academic.

"Hey," he said, resisting the temptation to add, *Remember me?*

It was obvious from her reaction that now she did. Those flecks of ice turned glacial. She lifted one hand to the doorframe, blocking the entrance with her body.

Jake wasn't exactly skilled in the ways of women and body language, but even he could tell she wasn't pleased to see him. "What're you doing here?"

So much for pleasantries. "Sorry, look, I know it wasn't . . . great."

"That's an understatement."

"I wouldn't have come here, but I need to get in touch with Harry."

"Ah, your pimp."

Jake made a face. "He's been called many things, but that's probably a first," Jake said, doing his best to make light of it. "I need to get in touch with him."

"And you thought, *Oh, I know, I'll go talk to that woman I boned and bailed on.* What on earth made you think that was a good idea?"

"Desperate times," he said, gaze drifting over her shoulder. Did she have a clue what was happening outside? "Anyway, as much as I dig a good old-fashioned reunion, do you have his home number?"

She frowned, clearly thinking. "Home? He's not home . . . Oh, you mean back in Scotland? He should be back by now. He was only supposed to be gone for a week."

"The airports are closed."

"Really? Why? What's going on?"

That made him laugh. Short, sharp. "Haven't you been outside?" He gestured past her, toward her office window.

"Of course I have. I'm not an idiot. Why do you think I'm holed up in here?" Jake now caught sight of a cot pushed up in one corner of the office behind her. Given the fact the building had power, it was probably the best place in the city to crash. He approved.

She turned away from him, heading for her computer. Since she hadn't closed the door behind her, Jake followed her.

She hunched over the desk, opened her e-mail, and tapped in the first couple of letters of Harry's name. She typed something else in, then scrolled again until she found what she was looking for. "Here you go," she said, waving Jake toward the screen. It was an auto-response where he'd left his contact number for the week he'd be out of the country. She gestured at the phone on the corner of the desk. "We've got a really good long-distance plan." She actually smiled a little when she said that. Was the glacier thawing?

There was something odd about being in the same room as someone you'd slept with, and the oddness multiplied a thousandfold when they almost certainly hated your guts for sneaking out instead of cuddling up and whispering the right sweet nothings. He could have offered a thousand excuses, but the truth of the matter was they were both adults, and if it hadn't been him sneaking out it would have been her. That was just the way of the world. Still, he was happy for her to play the injured party if that was what she needed.

Jake nodded. "Thanks." He dialed in the number. There were a few quick clicks and then the line went dead. He hung up and tried again. Same response: the call hit the international pipe and died. "No joy. Maybe I'm doing something wrong?"

She took the phone from him and duplicated the process. Her frown deepened. "Maybe his line's down?"

"Then we'd be getting a canned response, one of those *We're sorry, but the number you have dialed is not in service* things. This just isn't going through. It's hitting a block somewhere along the line." If it had been cell phones rather than landlines, he'd have guessed that a tower was down somewhere. With landlines the signals ran through the transatlantic trunk lines. They had a dial tone, so they were hooked in at this end.

"Maybe one of the trunk lines is down?"

*Could an EMP do that?* He thought about it. How could something like that even happen? Those things were buried deep down in the ocean, and they were completely shielded. An EMP wouldn't even scratch the surface. But even a trunk line went through relay stations, which *could* be interfered with.

He was finally starting to think clearly: if these guys could resurrect the stock exchange computers they could certainly manipulate a relay station, effectively isolating a city or a country or even a continent, if that's what they needed to happen.

The penny dropped. Jake knew where the relay station was on this end: back down near the South Street Seaport, not far from Wall Street and the stock exchange.

He was already heading toward the door when Finn said, "At least say thank you before you ditch me again. Way to make a girl feel special."

"Thank you. Seriously, thank you. I'll explain later," he said without turning around. "I need to be somewhere. I'll be back."

# CHAPTER SIXTEEN

Fuck Jake Carter. Just . . . fuck him.

She couldn't believe he could turn up on her doorstep expecting her to help him. The arrogant son of a bitch. Finn paced around her cramped office. She wanted to break something. Preferably his face, but he'd disappeared again. She'd barely even thought about him for the best part of a year. It wasn't like she was some desperate schoolgirl who drew his name in a heart on her notebook, or that he was the only notch she'd carved on the bedpost, but there was something about the guy that just got under her skin.

It wasn't like he was so fucking gorgeous or anything. He wasn't all rugged lines with a six-pack of muscles.

So why had his appearance completely thrown her off her game?

She couldn't concentrate on finishing off cataloging the images and annotating all the symbols she'd found within them. Instead, she kept thinking about what it had felt like when he was inside her, and how, given the chance to make the same mistake twice, even now, she'd happily do it again.

She'd always had a thing for tall, dark, and damaged. She wasn't that struck on golden skin or the whole narcissistic metrosexual look that had overtaken the campus. There was something odd about dating guys who were prettier than her, and used more product than she did. She liked a bit of intelligence. She liked a bit of charm. A dangerous grin. Something that stood out from the preppy boys who haunted the campus. He definitely did that, even if it was all a bit too much GI Joe for the usual boyfriend material.

She wasn't surprised she'd taken him home—and it had been all her doing. It had been a combination of circumstances and the fact that she'd spent a long day fending off Tom Campbell's handsy advances, which only grew worse as the drink flowed. Jake had been her knight in not-so-shining armor for a couple of hours. He'd been interesting, engaging, attentive with her, and most importantly not connected to the university in any way, shape, or form—all rarities in her limited social circle. Which was why she'd given in to temptation. And that was fine, two grown-ups enjoying each other's bodies. There was no crime in it.

So what if he'd skipped out before dawn, without waking her, no note, no goodbye kiss on the forehead while she dozed, nothing remotely intimate? Some people weren't good with that, putting up walls as quickly as they pulled up their pants. He was one of them. Hardly surprising, given the life he'd led out in Afghanistan, fighting just to stay alive. It still left her feeling dirty, though, no matter how understandable it was.

She wasn't going to let him get to her. He was an idiot. Instead she started to think about the call he'd tried to make to Harry.

Everything she'd seen suggested that electronics had

gone haywire all over the world. There'd been plenty of speculation about terrorism, but there was no way one EMP was responsible. You'd have been talking dozens and dozens of detonations, spread out around the globe, happening simultaneously. The coordination that would have demanded was damn near impossible, and it couldn't have taken out the trunk lines. The science didn't work like that.

She shook her head. And what was Jake Carter's role in all this? Did Harry have the answer? Was that why he'd risked her ire?

She forced herself to concentrate on the intellectual problem the failure of the trunk lines implied: What was capable of taking out global communication? Of sabotaging electronic devices across the world near simultaneously? And, of course, the natural follow-up question: Why was it happening now?

She needed to think about it all logically, and that meant starting with the core concepts. What did she know? The power had gone out, not the power grid, but power everywhere, in everything. No. Not everything, in everything new and unshielded. Older electronics weren't all disabled, and shielded equipment like her computer was fine. Which of course explained the leap of logic that led to thinking about EMPs, disregarding the scale of detonation that would have demanded. The effect of a pulse was terminal; the detonation burned out the electronics in question. But she'd seen people around the campus using their cell phones—meaning this was temporary, not terminal.

*It isn't just the campus, or even the city,* she reminded herself. It was worldwide. Which meant surely it had to be natural, didn't it? Some kind of global phenomenon?

Something stirred at the back of Finn's mind; something

she'd heard at a lecture a few years back. She sat with her head in her hands, trying to dredge through the memory. It had been a symposium on historical events and how they shaped language and other aspects of our culture. One of the speakers had been talking about significant natural events, things like the biblical flood and the formation of the Grand Canyon. She couldn't remember his name, or the title of his talk, she wasn't even sure of the name of the symposium, which didn't help, but she knew where and when it had been held, give or take a month or two.

It was a place to start. Turning to her computer, Finn typed in search terms. If she could identify the symposium she could dig up a full program, and then narrow it down from there until she'd identified the speaker. Assuming he wasn't some whack job, she was willing to bet his talk, or the foundation of it at least, would be available in an academic journal somewhere. Everything was online somewhere. That was the modern world.

She scanned the results her search returned, following a few of the links to dig deeper. It gave her something to focus on—a distraction from the man who'd just walked back into her life and then turned around and ran right back out of it as if his ass was on fire.

*Fuck you, Jake Carter . . . just . . . fuck you . . .*

# CHAPTER SEVENTEEN

JAKE REACHED THE CORNER.

There was absolutely nothing remarkable about the building in front of him. It was a typical New York red-brick with retail space on the first floor and apartments up above. There was some stone at its base, offsetting the red brickwork, and art deco detailing around the windows, all stylized blades and notches and waves. The building stood away from others on the block. The view from here was mainly office buildings with very few vantage points high enough to look out over everything onto the water.

Looks could be deceptive.

When the Atlantic Telegraph Company installed their operation, they'd wanted something that looked dignified and prestigious, with plenty of space. Over the following century, Manhattan real estate would come at a premium. The land around the building had been bought and sold for ever-increasing profits over the years, but the relay station had remained.

Part of his job with the MTA involved keeping track of

underground tunnels and old access points. There were still a lot of fiber-optic transatlantic trunk lines that ran into the city. When they'd gone in, the companies—and the government—had recognized the need to monitor them, converting some of the old cow tunnels and other preexisting tunnels that weren't part of the burgeoning subway network into maintenance tunnels so they could keep an eye on things. Since the old relay station had been in good shape at the time, they'd simply added to its functionality, coupling it into the labyrinth of tunnels beneath the city. It made financial sense: why build a whole new office to do the same thing when you already had one available?

The shadow of the stock exchange didn't quite stretch this far, but it came close, creeping up the blacktop. If the trunk lines had been sabotaged, this was where it had happened.

Jake froze in the middle of dismounting the stolen messenger bike: the relay center's front door swung open and a group of men emerged. They were less than two hundred feet away. They hadn't noticed him, and he wasn't sticking around until they did. He ducked back out of direct line of sight. He counted nine men, all dressed in black. He couldn't make out any details beyond the fact that they appeared to be carrying briefcases. No, he realized, not briefcases, toolboxes.

They moved with the same kind of military precision as the group he'd seen entering the stock exchange. *Not just entering, they died in the stock exchange,* he amended, reminding himself of the stakes. There was no way he was ever going to forget those few cold-blooded seconds that had snuffed out their lives.

The team walked in the opposite direction, away from him. Jake spat out a curse. He'd been right, but being right was no consolation prize; they'd beaten him here and done whatever it was they had to do. He was always at least one step behind them. Or three or four steps if he was being honest with himself.

There was a pattern here, a grand scheme of things they were working toward, but all he could see were a couple of threads that he kept pulling at. They'd hit the stock exchange network and the relay station. There had to be a connection between the two. What did they stand to gain by disabling the trunk lines? How did that fit in with the financial exchanges? Time and money.

The men turned and headed into the parking lot alongside the building. Jake rolled quickly down the sidewalk after them, stopping just shy of the portico that ran all the way to the building's edge. He had a view of the parking lot. It wasn't perfect, but it reduced the chance of them seeing him. Any closer and the risk of being spotted rose exponentially.

The team clambered into the rear of a gray minivan parked on the outermost edge of the lot, next to a lamppost. The engine rumbled to life—obviously shielded just like the killer's motorcycle had been. Two of the team held back, ushering the others inside. One of the two turned slightly, looking his way. Jake didn't dare so much as flinch, knowing that any kind of movement would only draw the guy's eye. There was a glint of metal on the guy's shoulder, right near the collar. It was too far away to make out any kind of detail. The second guy shifted, following the direction of his partner's stare.

Jake tensed. There was no mistaking the killer's face, even from a distance. He had his connection.

Jake watched the man pull a pistol from a sheath behind his back tucked under his coat. He knew what was coming.

The man beside him did the same. Both guns had the long silhouette of silencers on their barrels. They nodded to each other, finishing their visual sweep of the surrounding street, and turned as if to duck into the van with their team.

The noise barely carried.

Jake didn't need to hear the suppressed shots, he heard the slump of bodies against the panels of the minivan, and the grunts of the dead as their lives were brutally silenced.

It took two seconds flat to finish shooting and close the doors on the corpses.

There was nothing Jake could have done to save any of them—and it wasn't his place to. He wasn't naïve enough to think the dead men were angels. They'd gone into the relay center with their eyes open, no doubt promised riches in return for their expertise. If they believed, maybe they'd get their reward in heaven.

Jake tasted the bile in the back of his throat. He hunkered down, unable to look away, but not dumb enough to risk drawing attention to himself. At least not yet.

Watching people being executed was becoming a bad habit. He was one guy, unarmed, against two killers. He'd bleed out in the street before he made it halfway across the no-man's-land between the relay station and the minivan. Besides, there was no point in being a hero for a bunch of dead men.

That was the cold hard truth.

They were dead; Jake joining them wouldn't help anyone. The only thing he could do now was watch. Whatever these guys were up to, it was worth killing their own people for. That made it something Jake *wanted* to know all about. He was contrary like that.

The first man turned, and for a second he and Jake

locked gazes. He could tell by the way the killer's eyes widened then narrowed that he recognized Jake.

The killer raised his gun.

Jake spun back behind the building's edge as brick chips spat from the wall.

Three shots. Not that he was counting. He was too busy trying to stay alive.

He heard running feet—the two shooters covering the parking lot in seconds. He didn't have a lot of choices, or time to make a plan. He couldn't retreat, the block was too long and he'd be offering them his back. The only thing he could do was tackle them head-on and hope the stupidity of it saved his life. Speed and surprise were the only things he had going for him.

Jake powered out of the alcove, pedaling frantically, eyes straight ahead, desperate to get to the other side of the street and disappear between the buildings before the devil knew he was dead. He passed within a few feet of the men, but the gamble paid off: they hadn't counted on him being stupid enough to turn on them.

They fired again. He didn't feel anything so he didn't slow down. It was as simple as that. If the bullet wasn't punching him out of the saddle he wasn't getting off the bike. He gritted his teeth and kept on pedaling hard, expecting a bullet to slam into his spine any second.

It didn't.

He couldn't hear them coming after him. Jake turned left, swerving around a half-parked UPS truck, then swiveled around to put himself between it and an abandoned station wagon, dismounting and ducking down to stay out of sight. He waited.

It only took a couple of seconds, but then he heard it: the

one sound that up until this morning was so ubiquitous with city life it was simply background noise, part of the lifeblood of New York like the steam venting from the sidewalk drains, but now stood out as brutally as a gunshot—the roar of a car engine.

A small sports car turned into the street. It couldn't go very fast because of the other vehicles littering the road like blood clots in the arteries of Manhattan.

They were hunting him.

Jake edged back a couple of steps as the car's hood came into view opposite him, retreating behind the UPS truck. He kept the high-sided vehicle between him and the killers as he walked the bike around the back of the truck, which put him behind enemy lines.

The absence of gunfire meant they hadn't seen him.

He was under no illusion as to how it would go down. No questions. He was a loose end, even if he didn't know anything. He'd been seen at two of their engagements, which was enough to make it *seem* like he knew what the fuck was going on. Under the rules of engagement that was pretty much a death sentence.

The noise of the engine grew gradually fainter as their search took them farther along Water Street.

He was in the clear.

A flash of light saved his life.

The glint reflected off the UPS truck's side mirror. It was all the warning he needed.

Jake threw himself off the bike, hitting the ground hard as the bullet that had been meant for his head shattered the mirror instead, detonating in a spray of metal and glass.

He scrambled forward and looked up to see the killer

from the stock exchange astride his motorbike. They'd faked him out. His partner in the sports car was nothing more than a decoy to lure him out as it passed. And he'd fallen for it.

Jake abandoned all thoughts of the bike and dashed back around the corner of the truck, using it as a shield.

He tried the door, praying it was unlocked. There was nothing obvious inside he could use as a weapon or a shield. There was an umbrella, a metal lunch box—admittedly built like a brick—and a handheld scanner the UPS guys used to record signatures. It wasn't much, but Jake grabbed all three.

The windshield shattered above him, raining glass down across his back. Jake pulled back out of the truck but there was nowhere to turn.

The killer was there, waiting for him, the cold dead eye of his gun aimed squarely at his face.

Instinctively, Jake hurled the scanner as hard as he could. It arced high, spinning in the air. It was a distraction, the sudden movement drawing the killer's eyes for a split second. But the gun never wavered; so much for the fake-out.

Jake threw the lunch box. It caught the gunman square in the forehead just as his eyes darted back to Jake. He staggered backward a single step but didn't drop the gun.

Jake stood there, a dead man, waiting for the hammer to fall.

The gunman fired twice, blood in his eyes . . . and somehow missed.

He heard the car turning, drawn by the gunfire.

Two against one, without a pot to piss in, he wasn't exactly writing himself a glowing epitaph. Still, there were worse ways to die.

He faced his killer.

Ready.

"Do it," he challenged the man. "Kill me. Because if you don't I *will* kill you." They were hollow words from a hollow man.

"If you insist," the man said, taking his time to aim square at the center of Jake's chest.

He fired again. The trigger clicked on an empty clip as he squeezed it again and again.

"Looks like it's your lucky day," the killer said, reaching into his pocket for a spare ammo clip.

Jake grabbed the handlebar of his messenger bike and whipped it around, straddling it. Head down, he pedaled away fast, heart slamming against his chest. He couldn't believe he was still alive—even as another shot tore into the bodywork of the car beside him. Whatever gods, devils, or angels saddled with watching over him were working overtime. He wasn't about to make their job any harder than it already was. He wove between the stalled cars, keeping as much metal between him and the killer as he could.

There was a towering office building across the street, one of those metal-and-glass monstrosities, with a huge portico that left the sidewalk completely in shadow. The portico was supported by a dozen pillars. Jake aimed for them, jumping off the bike just before it slammed into the glass doors, then ditched it where it wouldn't be immediately noticeable from the street. He hunkered down and hid behind one of the wide metal pillars, expecting to hear the killer's voice goad, *Come out, come out, wherever you are.*

He barely dared to breathe in the silence. He hated that the city was so utterly bereft of life. Even the slightest sound would betray his hiding place.

The car drove past a few seconds later, moving at full speed this time. There were two men in the front seats.

He wasn't falling for the same trick twice. *Fool me once, shame on me, fool me twice and I'm as dumb a fuck as George Dubya.*

He didn't move. A minute passed. Two. Three. Four. Time was dragging desperately slowly. Five. And he still hadn't heard a sound. He risked a glance around the pillar. There was no sign of either of them.

He stepped out of the shadows, looking back down the street, and saw the gleam of the killer's abandoned motorcycle lying in the middle of the road. It confirmed what he knew—the killers were in the car. Whether they were hunting him or not, he didn't know. Right now, he didn't care. He needed to keep operating under the assumption that they were. Which meant moving fast, thinking two, maybe three steps ahead if he could.

The old motorcycle was a step up from the bike, and given the complete clusterfuck that was modern electronics right now, the odds of them having GPS or some other tracking device on it were next to none. He walked across to the motorcycle, lifting it upright, ready to kick-start it, only to change his mind. *Do unto them as they would do unto you,* he thought, grinning for the first time in he couldn't remember how long.

He had a plan. It was a stupid plan, which meant it might just work.

He wheeled the motorcycle toward the relay station's doors.

The killers would assume he'd run. It was the obvious thing to do. What wasn't obvious was breaking into the relay station they'd just abandoned. It was counterintuitive. Instead of running away from trouble he was running into the heart of it. Sure, they'd done whatever it was they'd set out to do in there, just like they had in the stock exchange, and they'd murdered their team to make sure there was no gingerbread trail for anyone to follow, but that didn't mean there wasn't something back there that would help him make sense out of what was happening.

There was safety in the unexpected. Given that he was onto his second life now, he didn't want to waste it by being predictable.

They hadn't bothered locking the door behind them. That was the kind of arrogance these people were operating with. It was a solid steel fire door, no windows or panels of any sort. If they'd taken a second to be sure it had latched behind them he'd have been shit out of luck.

He wheeled the motorcycle inside, hoping its absence would complete the illusion, and closed the door behind him. If they thought he'd taken it they would assume he was miles away by now, even if they hadn't heard its engine roar. The brain would make its own connections, buying into the smoke and mirrors.

He had no idea what to expect inside, but it couldn't be any worse than what was outside—seven dead men in the back of a minivan—could it?

# CHAPTER EIGHTEEN

F INN STRETCHED. HER MUSCLES PROTESTED, each vertebrae cracking audibly as she arched her back. She'd lost track of how long she'd been hunched over the computer. She always ended up working in the same unnaturally cramped position with her legs curled up under the chair and crossed at the ankles, leaning so far forward her breath could have fogged the monitor if it got any colder in the office.

She pushed herself up out of the chair and made her way toward the door. It was still daylight, but not for much longer. She was hungry. She hadn't realized just how hungry until she'd stopped working. She got like that when she went into the zone, obsessed with what she was doing. She'd only stopped now because her head was banging and her vision was starting to blur with that premigraine darkening around the edges. She needed to eat, so she ventured down to the break room.

One of her colleagues was fiddling with coffee pods when she walked in.

"Hey, you. The rumor is you landed some cushy new gig.

Did I hear scuba diving?" Elise Bennington handled early Mesopotamian research for the department. She was ferociously intelligent and wore Velma glasses to hide the fact that she was a definite Daphne on the Scooby scale of hotness. She was, of course, Tom's favorite, mainly because she humored him and played the game every bit as well as he did when it came to inappropriate comments in the workplace.

"Me and water, can you imagine?"

"Bikini all packed then?"

Finn barked out a short laugh. She went over the fridge and pulled out a cold Coke Zero, then grabbed a banana and an apple from the ever-full fruit basket. It was almost a nutritious meal. It certainly covered at least one of the basic food groups. "It's not as adventurous as it sounds," she told Elise. "I'm analyzing a bunch of symbols marking ruins they found just off the coast of Cuba. It's all video chat stuff."

Elise saluted her with a stiff black coffee. "Nice. A dig you don't even have to leave your office for. Like I said, cushy." She took a sip, then smirked. Finn knew that look. It was the same one a predator wore as it homed in on hapless prey. "And speaking of your office, who, pray tell, was that absolutely fucking gorgeous man you were entertaining? I almost felt my womb contract and I was fifty feet away. That's one dangerous man."

"He's all yours," Finn replied, looking anywhere but at Elise, which of course just encouraged her to tease some more. Jake was still a sore spot. Unsurprisingly, he hadn't called back. She couldn't believe she'd actually thought he might. But that was her all over: gullible. "He's a friend of a friend. No one special. We met at the holiday party last year."

She watched Elise's eyes widen as she got the reference.

"Oh, fuck me, he's *that* one? Well Jesus Christ, woman, if that's the guy who got your panties unbunched, all I can say is good fucking taste, girlie. I'd be all over that thing like a dose of chlamydia."

"Elise!" Finn laughed.

"Tell me you disagree. I mean, you went there, not me, I'm just giving you the Elise Bennington seal of approval. So what did he want? Round two? You can't tell me he just stopped by to chat, I'm not buying that. I want the gossip. Make it juicy. I need to live vicariously through your slutiness," Elise rambled on. "And you know me, I'm a dog with a boner—and yes, I went there. So make it good."

"He wasn't here for me," Finn told her.

"Well that's a disappointment."

"You know what? Whatever. It doesn't matter."

"Best way to get over a bad one-night stand is to get under a good one-night stand," Elise said, grinning. "Fuck him. Or, you know, don't. Alas, I must love you and leave you, which is rather apropos, given the whole tall, dark, and handsome thing. I'll catch you later, okay? You, me, a big old tub of Ben & Jerry's and we'll set the world straight."

"It's a date," Finn agreed. "Now get out of here before Tom turns up."

"Laters, babe," Elise said, and was gone. That woman was a phenomenon. Finn stopped short of calling her a natural disaster, though she often left a trail of devastation in her wake.

As Finn peeled the skin from her banana, a shadow crossed her vision. She glanced up expecting to see Tom there. It wasn't Tom.

A man walked down the hall toward her. He'd just turned the corner that led back to her office, one of only three down there.

It wasn't exam or term paper time, so there was no reason for any undergrads to visit her. She didn't recognize him. Tall, slim, moved like an athlete, easy and graceful. Not exactly good-looking, certainly not in the world according to Elise Bennington, but distinctive. He had *arresting* features. That was the only word she could think of to describe him. Strong and sharp bones, dusky skin, and dark hair that looked almost brassy in strip lights, like burnished metal. Central American, maybe Salvadoran. He was too old to be a student, at least an undergrad, and wasn't wearing the obligatory man-bag/backpack they all wore these days. He wasn't dressed like a student either. His clothes were tailored. Actually, he looked like he belonged in an ad for a casino or some fancy ski resort. He certainly didn't look at home in the dank halls of academia.

"Can I help you?" Finn asked as he approached, thinking that maybe he had something to do with the research project. He looked the part, projecting an aura of wealth.

He looked up with a dark, intense gaze, then brushed right by her, picking up speed as he hit the stairwell.

"Hey! You! Wait a minute!" Finn started to follow him, but he was already through the door.

*Aren't I just Miss Fucking Popular today. First Jake and now this one. I see a good-looking guy, he sees me, and he bolts.*

Shaking her head and laughing at her own grim humor, she headed back to her office. The door was ajar.

She'd locked it. She knew she had, it was habitual. She didn't want to set foot inside, expecting to find that it had been trashed like in some cheesy movie, papers everywhere, desk overturned, her chair lying on its side, her computer a smoking heap.

But paranoia aside, everything looked fine so she left the

door open behind her. Finn put the Coke Zero on her desk and sank back into her chair ready to finish her feast.

It took her a moment to realize the angle of the monitor was off. It had been moved. It was only a few degrees, but it meant too much light reflected on the screen. She readjusted the monitor.

Her first thought, and not a very comforting one, was that the guy had been in here rooting around for something. What could he want with her or her computer? There was nothing exactly espionage-worthy about the new gig, but who knew what got into the heads of otherwise sensible people? Money made people do strange things.

Maybe he was some kind of treasure hunter who'd got wind of the dive and wanted to take a look at the photographs?

One stranger in the hall and a door that hadn't latched properly and she was envisioning all sorts of grand conspiracies playing out like something from *Tomb Raider*, only she was no Lara Croft, and as far as excitement went this would make a pretty tame level in the game.

# CHAPTER NINETEEN

W hen she awoke, the thought of checking in to one of the roadside hotels for a shower had crossed her mind, but they were all full of commuters who hadn't been able to make it home for the night. Even if there had been a spare room, there were too many people who might remember her. She didn't like being remembered.

Instead, she stole a candy bar from the parking lot's nonfunctional vending machine and got back on the road.

And now here she stood in the heart of Paternoster Square, looking up at the eight-story building that housed the London Stock Exchange. Though it was a clear and unseasonably warm night, with soft moonlight blanketing the square, it was completely quiet. This place wasn't a shortcut to anywhere. There was no reason for people to pass through on their way to somewhere else, especially at night. There was no crowd of protective camouflage for her to hide within.

There were guards, of course, and an array of security measures that slammed down into place the moment a threat materialized.

She figured she'd just have to ride her luck.

Sophie had learned a long time ago that the best way to gain entrance anywhere you didn't belong was to act like you did. People were inherently trusting. They expected you to be who you appeared to be.

If you tried to skulk along, head down, clinging to shadows, you were basically telegraphing a subliminal message to everyone who did see you: *I don't belong here, remember me.* Her primary concern right now though was that the wrong people had beaten her here. She didn't have a choice. She needed to get inside.

Sophie strode across the plaza, past the column with its gold flame–filled copper urn.

The stock exchange's first floor was two stories tall and jutted out from the rest of the building. There was a colonnaded overhang dwarfing its arched windows and doors.

Sophie moved through the shadows without anyone shouting at or shooting her. So far so good. That didn't mean they weren't watching.

The wide glass doors were locked, but she'd come prepared. She pulled a lockpick gun from her go bag and inserted the muzzle into the bottom set of locks, then mirrored the move with the top locks. The gun made short work of the standard key locks by pushing different picks forward until they hit the right combination to trip the tumblers. It wasn't rocket science. The locks were an antiquated deterrent; the real security was the sophisticated alarm system, which on any other day would have taken a team of master thieves to beat. Today, the same sophisticated alarm system had been rendered impotent by the blackout, leaving the place vulnerable. It was all part of Alom's master plan, and better than mass murder, which was a very real alternative.

She pushed through the door. The sheer scale of the lobby was daunting, all glass and steel. A single open foyer led all the way up to skylights that made the glass-globe sculpture that hung in the open space above her shimmer in the moonlight. Normally the sculpture, called *The Source*, shifted and moved each day, the glass spheres changing position to create new and interesting shapes, including words. Now the component parts hung motionless.

Unlike the New York Stock Exchange, London had moved from an open-outcry system—which required a public trading floor—to a purely electronic method of trading several decades ago.

There wasn't a single centralized space for traders now. Which was very useful, as it meant that any office inside the complex would suffice for what she intended; they were all tied into the same central computer system.

Sophie moved quickly, but again without rushing. She did her best to take in all of her surroundings without lingering. It was another layer of appearing like she belonged there. She didn't want some security guard thinking she was an intruder, even if she had just forced her way in. She headed for the stairwell, climbing to the third floor; low enough to get out in a hurry, high enough to have a decent vantage of the plaza below while at the same time minimizing the risk of someone stumbling upon her. It was all basic probability, really.

She picked an office at random. The door locks were electronic, jammed shut during the outage. They didn't pose much of an obstacle. Her entry was so simple it was almost embarrassing considering the kind of secrets she hoped the room would offer up; two microscrews anchored the doorplate, then it was just a case of tripping the lock mechanism with her fingernail.

She pushed the door open, then stepped inside. It was a blandly corporate space, a company logo she didn't recognize emblazoned on the wall behind the receptionist's desk, comfortable couches that worked hard to look like classic Eames designs to the side so guests could wait in relative comfort for their escort to take them through the single paneled door that was all that stood between them and corporate nirvana on the other side.

That door was shut too, a conventional lock this time. It didn't make any difference to Sophie's lockpick gun, which took less than three seconds to fake the tumblers. Moments later she was striding down the carpeted hall between several other closed doors, toward the one at the far end. She wanted to work in an office that would provide her light from the night sky and also give her a view of the street.

Corner offices in places like this were always more spacious and comfortable. The room she entered was no exception, big and airy with an entire wall of windows looking out over the square. A massive mahogany desk dominated one side of the room, classically powerful with carved wood rather than the usual sleek modernism she expected from Gen-Xers raised on Gordon Gekko. The leather blotter in the center suggested a love of penmanship and a better, vanished age that offset the unobtrusive flat-screen monitor beside it. A big leather wingbacked desk chair completed that image.

The other side of the room was equally old-school oldmoney English stereotype, with a big leather Chesterfield couch and matching wingbacked armchairs grouped around a handsome leather-inlaid table, also carved from mahogany. It was obviously the wood of money, old and new. A row of dark, polished bookcases lined the wall behind it, filled with thick, gilt-lettered leather volumes. It gave the impression of age and wisdom, like the quarters of an old barrister or a school headmaster, the message being you can trust the man who is king of this particular castle.

It was all an illusion, of course. You could trust him about as far as you could throw him—and that was preferably out the window given the state of the financial markets.

But it was quiet, comfortable, had a computer terminal, and overlooked the entrance, which was all she wanted from the space.

Sophie pulled out the chair and squatted down beside it, studying the computer tower tucked away there. No added bells and whistles to the casing. She pulled a small, flat battery pack from her bag, then nudged the tower forward and to one side so she could see its back panel well enough to get at the power cord. She switched it out for the short cable from the battery pack then hit the power button on the front of the tower.

Even though she'd known it would work, it was a relief to see the power light blink on, and hear the deep chime of the system booting up.

She settled into the desk chair and watched the screen come to life, the same company logo popping up in a small window that demanded a name and password. She didn't have either.

What she had was better. She leaned forward and slid a thumb drive into one of the open USB slots on the tower's front.The drive lit up as it accessed the stored program, running through the permutations until the dots began to appear like magic within the password window.

The *Enter* key darkened as if pressed and the entire window vanished. The logo was replaced by a tropical sunset and a row of file folders. Sophie ignored them—she wasn't interested in this company. The only thing she cared about was its access to the broader building system.

She right-clicked up to the *Servers* header, accessed the drop-down menu, and selected *LSE*. The new window showed a series of drives and databases, each with its own acronym. It could have been written in Mandarin for all she knew; fortunately, she didn't need to be able to interpret all of the various files and subfolders.

The thumb drive was still in place. Sophie opened it and selected one of the other files there—the one she'd copied onto it before fleeing Paris. A simple black terminal window appeared, and programming code began to scroll across it as the blunt white letters raced to fill the blank black space too rapidly to read.

The program, a spider designed to crawl through the tangled web of the mainframes' file structure to the core files she needed, was fast. It took about sixty seconds to return its results.

Sixty seconds felt like an eternity. And even then, if it worked, it wasn't guaranteed to stop them. The best she could hope was that it would slow them down.

A flicker of motion caught her eye. She half-turned toward the big plate-glass window, then froze before instinctively pulling back, but it was too late by then.

A dark figure rushed across the plaza.

Whoever it was, they weren't alone. Their body language betrayed that. They moved with speed, head down, checking left and right, then behind, without looking straight ahead. They were maintaining their position, a rear scout, making sure no one was on their six.

Five seconds later—still not enough time to burn up the endless minute she needed for the program to finish its task—she felt rather than heard the concussion of an explosive grenade reverberate up through the building from below. They'd blown out one of the front doors. No subtlety. They didn't care if she knew they were coming for her. They were that arrogant or that good.

She turned back to the screen. The terminal window was no longer scrolling through new lines of code.

"Come on, come on," she urged, hitting *Enter*. She watched as the cursor on the bottom blinked, then steadied.

*Program Executed.*

She closed the window and the program, then yanked her thumb drive out of the tower. She killed the power, disconnecting the battery pack to shut the system down. It was only a matter of seconds, but each one was precious.

She stuffed the battery back into her go bag and dashed out of the office and down the hall. She needed to get the hell out of there. The next few minutes were crucial.

Sophie stopped at the frosted glass of the company's front door. She had two choices, and she knew whichever one she picked was going to be the wrong one: make a break for the exit and hope to get past the security team making their way up to her floor; or hide out here and hope they passed her by, giving her the chance to duck out behind them.

Without knowing how the team functioned, she could only think what she'd do in their place—sweep the building bottom to top, locking down each floor as she went, eyes on every stairwell, no way into or out of the building uncovered. Everything depended on how many men they had at their disposal.

There was a chance they weren't here for her, rather that they were here to do exactly what she had, find an empty office and break into the dormant system. Just because it was

London didn't make it immune—these people had plans, and those plans included adjusting the city and ushering it into the new world right alongside New York and the other traditional power bases of the global economy. So, yes, there was a chance, but it was so slim she couldn't count on it unless she wanted to risk winding up in a body bag.

Sophie eased the frosted glass door open and peeked into the central foyer. She was careful to stay back, making sure her shadow wouldn't stretch as far as the lobby floor below. Without the light sources to betray her, she was good. The foyer was completely glassed in. Even so, she could hear people moving about down there.

"Right, we know she's in here," the voice carried up from below. "Divide into Alpha, Bravo, Charlie teams. Take each stairwell, work your way up bottom to top, sweep each floor. Anyone gets in the way, end them. Jenson, find a spot and get plugged in. If we're lucky she hasn't had a chance to completely screw things up yet. The rest of you, stay sharp. This isn't a recovery mission, gentlemen. She doesn't get out of here alive."

# CHAPTER TWENTY

"**OUR MEN HAVE ISOLATED THE TRAITOR**," the voice on the other end of the line said.

"Is she dead yet?"

"No, but it is only a matter of time."

"I don't want to hear about how clever you are, and I most certainly don't need a blow-by-blow description of the hunt. The only thing I want is photographic evidence that the bitch is dead. Understood?"

"Yes, Mr. Alom."

"Good. That wasn't too difficult, was it?"

"No, Mr. Alom."

"Now listen carefully, we have reason to believe there is a new player on the field, brought in by Miss Keane and operating in New York. As of yet we haven't worked out who, precisely, he is, or what role she hopes he will play, beyond being a random integer inserted into the equation. It is possible they have been colluding for some time. That makes him unpredictable. I do not like unpredictable things. Hunhau is currently dealing with this inconvenience, but it behooves us to be aware that she may have reached out to others since arriving in London. Miss Keane is nothing if not industrious. You don't get to live this long in her game without being good at what you do."

"Understood."

"Xbalanque is on her way in from Berlin to support your action."

"Unnecessary, we have everything under control here."

"I'm quite sure you do, Cabrakan, but it is better to be safe than sorry, as the old adage goes. I would much prefer overkill to no kill at all."

There was an insulted silence on the other end of the line.

"Twenty-three hundred hours Zulu time, Ixtab and Kauil will make their move."

"We will be ready, Mr. Alom."

"I am relying upon you."

"Can I ask you a question?"

"You just did."

Again, prickly silence. The assassin gathered himself, knowing this was dangerous ground. "Do you believe any of this shit you're peddling? I mean . . . all these names, this Mayan gods crap, it's all for the cameras, isn't it? You don't really believe this stuff, do you? Like the Scientologists, right? You know it's all a pile of bullshit?"

"Let me be quite clear about this: what I know and what I believe are not your concern."

"I just mean . . . it's ridiculous, isn't it? It's the kind of thing that has conspiracy theorists pissing in their pants."

"I take it you do not believe?"

"You take that right."

"And still you fight for our cause?"

"The money's right."

"Ah, yes, the money. What about faith?"

"I have no faith. I don't believe in anything I do not know to be provably true. You cannot sell me on your religion because without faith it falls apart, and faith means believing in something you can't possibly know."

"Quite the philosopher, for an assassin."

"I spend a lot of time alone with my thoughts," the killer said without any irony.

"And if I were to tell you that we have proof?"

"Of these old gods of yours? I wouldn't believe you. I'd be crazy to."

"Indeed. But surely you cannot deny that there are things in this world we do not understand."

"And those gray places are where your gods lie?"

"Not my gods, no, my answers."

"Answers?"

"There are no gods, my friend, not old, not new. There are no great old ones in the stars looking down. The sum of all, the only thing scattered among the dust, is knowledge. There is no magic. There is no *power*. There is no supernatural. It is all about knowledge. With knowledge you can shape the world. How you come about that knowledge is irrelevant. How you present it to the masses, what dog-and-pony show you decide to put on, doesn't matter. All that matters is the knowledge itself and how you exploit it. So yes, where you see gods, I see answers. How do you think I knew to plan and then to act?"

"You knew it was going to happen?"

"I knew it was going to happen," Mr. Alom affirmed. "And that, my friend, is magic."

"How did you know? How could you know when the rest of the world didn't?"

"Market research."

"Bullshit."

"Careful, young man. I do not appreciate being spoken to with such obvious disrespect."

"You're not being straight with me."

"Oh, but I am. I have given you the answers you are looking for. That you do not understand them is not down to my shortcomings, but rather your own. It is all business at the end of the day."

"What the fuck *are* you people?"

"The winners," the voice said. "And that makes us the ones who write the history of the world."

# CHAPTER TWENTY-ONE

NSIDE, JAKE WAS CONFRONTED BY ANOTHER PROBLEM: locating the actual relays. The basement made the most sense.

He was in a hallway that ran the full length of the building, front to back, like something out of *The Shining*'s Overlook Hotel, only without the hallucinatory carpet. The corridor just went on and on. To his left was a door, presumably into the shop at the front of the building. Past that was the elevator bank, three sets of heavy brass doors with the same sort of stylized wheat design embossed on them as the building's exterior carvings. Past that he saw a row of mailboxes. And beyond that, at the far end of the passageway, were two more doors.

He walked toward them.

The first one had a company name on it, and the number 1c.

The last door didn't have a number or a name.

*Jack fucking pot,* Jake thought, and moved quickly.

Some do-gooder would have called the gunshots in to the cops. That would have made the clock start ticking. Soon this place would be a hot zone. A black guy caught breaking-and-entering in the vicinity of a pile of dead bodies in the back of a silver minivan? Case closed, judge.

The door was unlocked and opened onto a flight of plain concrete stairs that headed down into darkness. It wasn't the kind of place you wanted to get stuck when the fecal matter exploded all over the fan.

There was emergency strip lighting hooked up to a battery system the killer's men had presumably put in place.

He shut the door behind him. It was quiet. The air was musty, as if it was breathed less than other air, older, which could account for the peculiar acridness to it—a sharp, bitter, metallic tang that tasted of electricity.

The stairs ended at another steel fire door. The bolt had been cut using an arc welder. There was nothing subtle about the break-in. They obviously didn't care if anyone noticed it after the lights came back on, much like the killing in the stock exchange itself. They weren't worried about cleaning up after themselves. What did that say about their operation?

Jake eased the door open, making sure it didn't topple inward in the process. Beyond it, he saw the glow from several computer monitors.

He closed the door behind him, and before he could turn around someone wrapped an arm around his neck and clamped their other hand over his jaw. One savage jerk would break his neck.

Jake responded instinctively. His muscles tensed. He grabbed at his attacker's forearm and twisted it hard, dropping his shoulder so the guy rode his hip as he flipped him onto his back. He came down hard on the bare concrete floor. There was no finesse to the move, or to his downed attacker's response. The bastard didn't know when to quit. He lashed out with a kick that Jake barely avoided, then clambered to his feet, safely out of range of Jake's clubbing fists. The haunting light of the computer screens transformed him into a wraithlike black shadow.

Jake looked around for something he could use as a weapon. Aside from the computer screens there wasn't much of anything close to hand. Judging by the air currents, this relay station was *big*, possibly even the entire height and width of the building.

Jake focused back on the dark shape moving toward him. There was no stealth this time. No element of surprise. The guy was bigger than Jake. Meatier.

Feet, hands, it didn't matter; this did not look to be a fair fight. Jake kicked out, landing a crunching blow somewhere close to the guy's hip.

But the guy was *fast*. Before Jake could pull his leg back and get his balance, his attacker grabbed his ankle with his left hand and delivered a jarring punch to Jake's kneecap, then yanked up on his foot and sent him sprawling.

The pain was blinding. Jake barely felt the impact from the floor. He tried to push himself up, but his leg gave out beneath him.

"*Fucker!*" It was a war cry. Purely primal. Filled with rage.

The shadow man moved in to finish him off.

Jake lashed out with a clubbing fist, but swung hopelessly wide. It was deliberate. He wanted his attacker to think he was dealing with someone who couldn't handle himself. He wanted any advantage he could get, even if it was just being underestimated. "*Come on!*" Jake bellowed.

His attacker didn't say a word.

Jake swung wildly again, this time overreaching so he appeared to be off balance. As the heavy lunged forward, Jake

I
N
F
A
M
O
U
S

launched three punches to the face, followed by a leg sweep, knocking the man back on his heels, putting him on his ass. He wouldn't underestimate Jake again.

The downed man grunted.

Jake couldn't give him the time to get up and shake off the effects of his fists. He rushed in, kicking out at the guy's head, then levered himself upright. His booted foot slammed into the fallen man's jaw, lifting him six inches off the concrete floor before he fell back, the only sound beyond the crack of his skull on the ground the soft exhalation that escaped his lips. A tiny whimper. It didn't sound good, but Jake didn't care. Survival of the fittest. He hadn't started this and he knew full well his attacker wouldn't shed a tear if their roles were reversed.

Jake winced as he put weight on his knee. A stabbing pain lanced through his damaged nerve endings. He moved tentatively, hobbling toward the bank of screens. It could take his weight, so he didn't think it was broken. Just battered like the rest of him.

He heard someone else moving around in the darkness—too heavy for rats. He tried to place the sound in the secret geography of the darkness—only to reel from a sudden hammer blow to his right temple that took the world out from under him.

Jake swung wildly with his right arm, hitting something. He couldn't tell what, or even how hard.

It earned a grunt of pain and a shuffle of feet.

That bought him a second, but he had no kind of hold on the world. His vision swam and the darkness didn't help. He had nothing visual to fix on. He tried to use the light from the screens but he wasn't sure he could take much more of this. He needed to end it fast. He raised a hand to his head, touching the soft skin where the second attacker had slammed his fist, and swayed slightly as pain flashed across his eyes.

His opponent took the bait and rushed forward. Too late, Jake saw the glint of a blade in his hand. His attacker slashed rather than stabbed; left, right, left, in three blisteringly fast arcs. Jake felt the bite of the blade through his clothes as he threw himself backward, desperately trying to get out of the way before his guts were unravelling like a bloody yo-yo.

The man came at him again, slashing wildly. Jake ducked inside the backhand of the swing, and threw both fists, bringing them down on either side of his attacker's temples, every ounce of desperate strength behind them. It was a massive, crushing blow.

The lights went out in his attacker's eyes and the knife clattered to the floor.

Jake kicked it away. He didn't need to, the guy was out cold. He wanted to slump down onto the ground himself, but as he turned away from the second attacker, he saw where the knife had stopped spinning—a few feet from where the first man was slowly trying to rise again.

"Why the fuck don't you just stay down?" Jake said, ready to take another beating.

The guy stumbled as he tried to stand, but managed to retrieve the knife without falling. He shouted something at Jake, who didn't understand a word of it.

Before Jake could move, the man brought the knife down hard, slamming it into his stomach and twisting, opening himself up.

Jake just stood there, stunned, as the guy dropped to the ground.

Dead.

What the fuck was going on?

He checked the other guy, hoping he might spill a few answers when he woke up. Jake was shit out of luck, but then, so was the other guy: a sliver of bone had broken free of his temple and speared through his frontal lobe. He wouldn't be talking again.

# CHAPTER TWENTY-TWO

"SOPHIE!" THE SHOUT ECHOED UP THROUGH THE EMPTY SPACE, reverberating through the glass walls around the vast foyer. "Sophie Keane! We know you're in here!"

Sophie stayed where she was, pushing back even harder against the wall of the hallway, as if it might open up to welcome her.

She was two steps away from the interior balcony rail that circled the foyer. Her heart raced. Her mind was faster.

She ran through her options, discarding them. Head down there? Madness. The team leader wasn't an idiot. He'd stationed men to intercept her if she made a break for it. The second floor would have been a smarter choice than the third; she could have broken a window, clambered out the walkway roof, swung down, and been on the ground before they had a clue what was going on. Third floor, the drop to the walkway could be damaging if not fatal. It didn't even have to be broken bones. A turned ankle would be the death of her. It was too big a risk. Up? Head for the roof? Or just keep moving floor to floor and hope to get behind their line and confuse them?

"Don't make this more difficult than it needs to be, Sophie," the man below continued, repeating her name. Keeping it familiar. He remembered his training. It was exactly what she would have done in his place. "Come on down. Let's be civilized about this. Talk. It's good to talk to me. No one else has to get hurt."

*No one else, only me*, she thought. It was a clever choice of words. He wasn't lying, and he made it sound like he was doing her a favor. She knew better than that. The only difference is she'd never have risked being overheard if she had issued the kill order a few moments before. He'd learn the hard way.

She couldn't go down, it was suicide. She couldn't stay where she was, it was only a matter of time before they reached her floor next. Which, like the old song, meant the only way was up. The instant she decided that, Sophie was on the move.

She crossed the nine steps to the door between her and the nearest fire exit onto the emergency stairwell, yanking it open. Without power there wasn't an alarm, only the echo of booted feet rushing up to her position.

She shut the door again. That was one dead end, and her options were rapidly diminishing. She moved quickly down the hall, looking for a second set of stairs.

She passed the first pair of double doors because they led to the stairwell closest to the foyer, where Cabrakan had deployed his kill squad. She needed to move deeper into the building. It was a warren of stairways and elevator shafts. There was no way they had the manpower to cover every one of them, or every entrance and exit—unless they had snipers positioned outside with perfect vantage points over the building's four walls. That was unlikely, given the short notice, and didn't bear thinking about. One problem at a time. Right now, all she had to do was get to a secondary stairwell before the hit squad reached this floor.

She raced down the glass-walled interior, using the moonlight peeking through to guide her toward the other side, ignoring the first bank of elevators she came to, and the door marked *EMERGENCY EXIT* beside it. Too close to the main foyer. She needed to get to the other side of the building if she was going to have a chance. And she needed to get there fast.

Up ahead she saw another fire door. She didn't slow down; she hit the door hard, banking on the hydraulic arm to stop it from slamming into the wall behind it.

She was greeted by echoing silence and pitch-blackness as she let the door close behind her. She retrieved a small flashlight from her bag and shone it down the stairwell, tempted, but started climbing, moving as fast as she could. There was no hope of stealth—concrete and steel reflected sound. Yet unless the enemy had already breached the stairwell, staying completely motionless and listening, they wouldn't hear her ascent.

But now she had a new problem: she didn't have an exit strategy planned for when she hit the top floor. She was operating on pure instinct, putting as much distance between herself and the kill team as she could. There was no pretending the unit had been deployed for any other purpose than to find and eliminate her. That sharpened her thinking. But no amount of sharp thinking was going to be enough. She needed to know where she was going. Running blind would get her killed. She needed a plan in place.

She ransacked her mind for images of this building, anything she'd seen since coming in that might be of use, anything

I
N
F
A
M
O
U
S

she remembered from the past about its layout. Anything that might save her life. Tripping any of the security sensors wouldn't help, nor would setting the sprinklers off or summoning the guards. She knew what would happen to them if they tried to come between predator and prey.

The fifth floor had a terrace, which was really the top of the fourth where it jutted out farther. But that terrace faced Paternoster Square, which meant it was isolated. There was a lower office block across the square from the far end of the terrace, though the two buildings were more than a hundred feet apart. There was no way to bridge the gap between them.

Atop the fifth floor was a second terrace, also facing out onto the square, but this time it overlooked the monument in the middle. Again, a dead end unless she learned how to fly. The sixth floor was smaller than the fifth by more than half, since most of the fifth's roof was exposed and open, though part of it was taken up by ducts and air-conditioning units. Still nowhere reachable from there.

But the top floor had a sloping roof around a central square that was used as a helipad in emergencies. The nearest building, off to the side, was maybe forty feet away, its roof a little lower than the stock exchange's.

She was thinking fast, and not liking the direction her thoughts were heading: forty feet was still one hell of a jump. Even with enough space to run and sufficient motivation, she'd be looking at damn near breaking the world record to make it, even with a tail wind and the downward trajectory.

But it beat the alternative.

Barely.

So, roof it was. She climbed all the way to the top, double-time. Not exactly silent running, but she needed to be aware. Someone could enter the stairwell at any time.

When she reached the fifth floor she heard something. It took her a second to focus on it: a loud whirring noise overhead.

For a second she actually froze, staring up in disbelief. A helicopter bringing in a second kill team? They wanted her that badly?

It was flattering, in a perverse kind of way: they'd broken their own rules of engagement by releasing a chopper when the world was without power. They couldn't have imagined it would go unnoticed, even in the chaos. So, someone had decided eliminating her was worth tipping their hand. *Alom.* He had that kind of power and the arrogance to accompany it. But even he wasn't stupid enough to think he was un-touchable, was he?

She felt the building shudder as the helicopter touched down. The noise of the rotors increased exponentially, the sec-ond kill squad already pouring out of it. They'd take the stairs and start working their way down, meeting up with the first team in the middle and trapping her between them.

She couldn't go up. She couldn't go down. She was fucked.

She tried to picture the building's exterior, needing to find an alternative exit point. She refused to just lay down and wait for death to come find her. That just wasn't her. Nine stories, a covered walkway below, terrace midway, and an open square at the top. There were deeply recessed win-dows all around, and a flagpole jutting from the northern-most corner facing out onto the square.

Was that level with the fifth floor or the fourth? Was it even there?

Fifth. Had to be. She was risking her life on it. She knew it was crazy, but she didn't have a choice.

Sophie kicked open the door and rushed out into the fifth-floor hallway, expecting to be greeted by a hail of bullets. Without any better ideas, she raced down the hallway toward the corner office. Time was more important than caution now. They surely had enough equipment to pinpoint her exact location in the building. If they didn't know where she was, they would soon enough.

Keep moving. Make them work.

She reached the door and she didn't bother with the lockpick gun this time. She kicked it down, right foot against the lock plate. The trick was to allow the force to keep driving through the door, not to pull back as the shock of impact hit.

The door flew inward with a loud splintering as the wood around the lock plate twisted and tore. Sophie slammed the door shut behind her and toppled a huge glass display case in front of it. The barricade would only buy her a few seconds more.

She glanced around. This was another company's office suite, almost identical in its drabness to the one she'd borrowed on the third floor. At the end of the little inner hall was the door to the corner office. She started toward it, but then stopped. First things first. Looking around, she spotted a smaller door to one side.

It wasn't locked and there was no nameplate. It was a utility closet, overflowing with mops and brooms and cleaning supplies, and behind them, office supplies, reams of copier paper, coffee filters, rubber bands, and pens. And there, coiled at the bottom beneath the sturdy industrial shelves, she found a heavy-duty extension cord, its thick cable scarred from long use. There was an outlet beside it. Judging by the coils, it was maybe fifty feet long. Which was perfect for what she had in mind.

Snatching up the extension cord, she made for the corner office. The view from its window was spectacular, and uniquely London with the rich and diverse architecture of hundreds of years' worth of civilization all in one small place. There were people gathering down below, drawn, no doubt, by the helicopter.

The room's other window interested Sophie more. Through it she saw the flagpole that speared toward the adjacent building.

She swept the room quickly, looking for something to smash the glass. On one of the bookcases she found a handsome award of marble and glass given to the office's resident for something or the other. Sophie grabbed it, turned, and, running toward the window, hurled it with all of her strength.

The entire sheet of double-paned glass shattered, jagged shards exploding outward though a shower of small chips burst inward as well, causing her to turn her head away and shield her eyes with her arms and hands. There was no disguising her location now. She kicked away barbs of glass that clung to the frame until there was nothing but empty space where the window had been.

Stepping up onto the window ledge, she gauged the distance between her and the flagpole. Maybe twenty feet. More than she would have liked, and at least thirty feet to the next building. Too close for comfort.

She unwound the extension cord, hefting one end of it, once, twice.

It wasn't going to work, it wasn't heavy enough.

"Shit. Shitshitshitshit." She wished she hadn't thrown that award through the window. It had been a terminal maneuver, no going back. And she needed to go back.

She scanned her surroundings for anything else that

might work. There were a few other awards, but they were all plaques, glass and metal, with no real weight to them. She wanted something she could use like a grappling hook.

This office, though more modern than the one downstairs, still had a few old-fashioned touches, including the old-school banker's lamp with its heavy green glass shade. That might just work.

She grabbed the solid brass lamp from the desk. It was good and heavy, with a big round base.

Sophie slammed the lampshade against the desktop, shattering the green glass and the twin bulbs that nestled within it. She yanked the lamp's cord free and knotted the extension cord's end firmly around the base. Going back to the broken window, she swung her makeshift grappling hook. It had a good solid heft to it now, and plenty of bits to catch on the cord.

She tried to ignore the not-so-distant sounds of pursuit behind her. At least one member of the kill team had arrived on the fifth floor, but he hadn't breached the outer office yet. It was only a matter of time though. Time that could be counted out in seconds, not minutes.

She was going to have to gauge the angle and distance perfectly. The throw couldn't be too weak. Or too strong. And she only had one shot. Get it wrong and there'd be no time left for a second try.

She lifted the lamp-weighted cord, swung it in a quick circle like a lasso, and hurled it forward, holding her breath as it sailed out, arcing upward, *just* under the flagpole, then wrapping tight around it. The lamp's own weight caused it to circle the pole once, twice, three times and knot itself into the cord that trailed behind it.

Sophie gave it a quick, experimental tug, then a second one.

It held.

But that was no guarantee it would take her weight.

A splintering sound alarmingly close convinced her she had no choice but to find out.

They were through the outer office door.

Grabbing the bottom end of the cord and wrapping it around her fist, Sophie took a deep breath. Without giving herself time to think about it, she ran forward, right to the lip of the window—and jumped.

The air caught at her, tugging at her hair, clothes, and bag. As she fell, a scream ripped from her lungs when she felt her stomach drop. The ground rushed up to meet her as the cord's slack disappeared rapidly. She barely had the presence of mind to clutch it even more tightly right before it snapped taut, and suddenly she stopped falling and was swinging across the space between the buildings, arcing back upward.

It took every ounce of her willpower at the apex of the swing to unwrap her hands and let go. The cord fell back away, but Sophie's momentum carried her forward, still arcing up.

The pale stone wall of the neighboring building loomed like a giant sledgehammer ready to crush her. She felt herself slow, falling again, safety tantalizingly close, but there was nothing for her hands to catch ahold of before she fell away.

And then, agonizingly, she wasn't falling anymore.

She lay on her back, peering up at the sky.

The lower roof had broken her fall.

It hurt so much she was sure for one sickening moment that the fall had broken her spine too. Sophie lay there, gasping, the pain excruciating. But she loved every damned searing second of it because it meant she wasn't dead.

She could see the extension cord hanging limp from the

flagpole an impossible distance away. Beyond that, the first of the kill squad, carrying full assault gear, stormed into the room she'd just vacated. They broke left and right, sweeping the office, then stopped, staring at the destruction and putting the pieces together. The squad's leader stood in the broken window, probably expecting to see her lying in a whorish sprawl, dead in the square. It took him a moment to look upward and catch the inconceivable sight of his quarry stretched out on a rooftop over fifty feet away. Safe.

Sophie had maybe a second or two before he started shooting. She hauled herself to her feet, crying out in pain as she rose, and stumbled around the corner of the building, following the roof away from the square and out of sight.

It *hurt* to move. Something was definitely broken in there.

Sophie gritted her teeth against the pain, knowing it would be so much worse once the adrenaline and shock wore off. Right now the chemicals flooding through her system were the only things keeping her going. It was amazing how the human body could force the impossible out of itself in extremis.

She found a latched door at the far end of the roof where a wall of opaque window tiles descended to meet the terrace. She still had her go bag slung over her shoulder. Her lockpick gun made quick work of the mechanism—five pumps of the trigger and the door opened to allow access to a darkened hallway.

Moving as fast as she could, she found a stairway and descended all the way to the ground floor. The crash of breaking glass warned her that the kill squad had already reached this building. That was fine. That was good.

She figured they'd probably only left one man stationed in Paternoster Square, eyes on the stock exchange lobby, and one man in the lobby. Two men could only cover the main exit. This was a big building, with lots of emergency exits. It didn't take her long to find one that would allow her to slip out the side of the building.

A couple of minutes later she'd disappeared into the crowd that had gathered in the main square to stare up at the helipad and the broken window where Cabrakan still stood clutching his assault rifle.

She saw two of the kill team trying to force their way through the crowd. They hadn't spotted her. She eased between a couple of gawkers, then stepped around a huddle of men in suits. It was noisy. People were talking over each other, trying to make sense of what was happening. This was London, a city plagued by terror attacks for decades. It wasn't panic that spread through the crowd so much as outrage. It took Sophie a minute to thread through the throng to the square's far side. She slipped out of the press of bodies and disappeared into the streets beyond.

It was over.

She'd done what she'd set out to accomplish and she'd come out alive—that was a win on both fronts.

Now on to the next step.

She still had a lot to do.

# CHAPTER TWENTY-THREE

JAKE DIDN'T THINK ABOUT THE TWO BODIES less than five feet away. They weren't a threat anymore, which meant they weren't worth wasting time on. He didn't plan on sticking around down there long enough for them to become a problem.

He stripped them of weapons, getting his hands on a long, nasty-looking dagger. It was made out of some kind of highly polished black rock or ceramic. The handle had been carved to look like a strange little totem pole. Jake wiped it on the dead man's combat trousers, then unbuckled the knife belt and strapped it to his own thigh. He slid the blade into it. He found another knife over by the door where it had come to rest after he'd kicked it away in the fight. It was a standard combat knife with a long, single-edged blade and a leather-wrapped handle. Jake grabbed it and went over to the second dead man.

He rifled through the corpse's pockets, but didn't find a wallet or any ID. What he did find was a Maglite. Unsurprising, given that this was basically a stealth op. Whoever these guys were, they weren't stupid enough to carry identification with them.

There was a cheap burner cell phone. No contacts in the list, no recent numbers stored that he could see.

He didn't want to root around too much inside the device in case some kind of mercy call might give his location away.

A glint of metal caught his eye as he rose from his crouch. Jake froze, half reaching out instinctively for the source of the reflection.

It was a small metal pin on the dead man's collar, a golden circle with a weird-looking core to it, like an iris, he realized, taking it carefully from the guy's lapel. Both of the dead men wore the same pin, so it wasn't just some odd little piece of jewelry, it was something more fundamental than that. He'd seen action and hung out with military men all of his life, so he knew what a tag was when he saw it, even if it was shiny gold rather than daubed in paint on weeping brick.

He dropped one of the pins into his pocket. Right now, he needed to figure out what they'd been doing down here. He could worry about what sort of creepy cult they were part of later.

Jake pushed himself back up to his feet. His knee hurt like hell from the pounding it had taken. He limped back toward the row of monitors. There were seven computers set up against the far well—one for each of the dead men outside, he realized. Thick wire housings emerged from the floor beside those machines, and smaller lines ran back from there to the computers themselves. They were the only things in the room: seven computer terminals and two dead guys. *Not exactly Scandinavian design, but it's pretty fucking minimal*, he thought bleakly as he approached the first terminal.

Jake woke the system but couldn't tell exactly what he was looking at on the screen: spikes of energy readings? The computer seemed to be monitoring a trunk line, checking signal strength and bandwidth and current information payload, and from what he could see there was precious little activity on any of them. But there was some.

When he checked the other stations, they were all more or less the same, running constant diagnostics on the trunk lines, scanning to make sure each one was operational and keeping track of how much data was being pulled across.

And that was it.

Nothing remotely nefarious. No hint of sabotage or domestic terrorism or even just a line of suspicious code.

Everything looked squeaky fucking clean, which stank.

Jake dropped heavily into one of the chairs. He leaned forward, resting his forearms on the desk in front of him. *So what's the point? What's the endgame if these computers are doing exactly what they're supposed to do?* That didn't make sense. Why break in? Why leave sentries to make sure everything ran smoothly if you hadn't done *something*?

Which meant they must have done something, surely?

It wasn't worth breaking in to make sure the relay station was working. Too much risk for too little reward. He needed to think about rewards. What could you stand to lose if the trunk lines failed?

Getting up again, he hobbled over to the nearest trunk line and studied it carefully, training the flashlight over every inch of its housing. He couldn't see any obvious breaches, not even a scar in the casing, which meant they hadn't tried cracking it open. No physical tampering with the lines left only the computers.

He went back to a terminal and navigated his way

around the diagnostic program, but again, everything looked *exactly* the way it should.

Until Jake saw it—the anomaly between the time and the volume control.

It took him a second to realize what it meant: there had been something there before, or there was something there now that was hidden.

Sure enough, he found an active connection in a hidden new terminal window. There was a short menu, including things like, *Throttle Bandwidth*, *Static Burst*, *Resume*, and, more ominously, *Block*. This Trojan, working away in the background, appeared to offer the terminal's user an override on the main system, effectively giving them control of the trunk lines, including the ability to shut them down.

This had never been about destroying the trunk lines— it had been about control. And now they basically had it. Seven deaths at this location—nine if you included the ones at his hand—and they may have taken over all transatlantic communications. That was a price he was sure they'd been happy to pay.

Shame he'd turned up. They might have gotten away with it.

He right-clicked through the menu options again until he found the one he wanted: *Deactivate*. Jake highlighted the option, but stopped short of making it a reality. The moment he killed the Trojan those guys would lose their back door into the trunk lines, but they'd also know about it pretty much immediately. That being the case, they'd rain down fire on this place like a biblical plague. He needed to be smarter than that. If he could be.

The first few notes of Mike Oldfield's "Tubular Bells" scared the living crap out of him. Laughing at himself, Jake reached for his phone. Using *The Exorcist*'s theme song for his ring tone had been a bit of joke, but sometimes it went off at the absolutely worst times imaginable, bringing back a flood of associated memories.

He saw the blocked number notification.

Ryan.

"What you got for me?" Jake said as he answered.

"Been digging, like you asked." Ryan's tone was considerably more somber than on the last call. "We're talking about some fucked-up shit, bro. This ain't good. I kinda wish you hadn't called."

Jake was nodding even though there was no way the other man could see it. "I know. Least I'm beginning to understand. So, talk to me." Jake turned away from the monitor, keeping an eye on the door while they spoke.

"You were right, they were fucking around with those computers. My first thought was how weird it was they were even on, what with the power outages—I mean, nothing else in that entire building is working apart from that bank of machines. Ain't no coincidence there, right? Gotta be a point to it. I figured maybe they hacked into some accounts, transferred funds or stocks or some shit." Jake was still nodding, that made sense. It was the same direction his mind had been working. "But that ain't it, man. They haven't dicked with that stuff at all. I mean, not a dime."

That didn't make sense. "So what did they do?"

"Two things. I almost missed the second one, clever motherfuckers. First, they set up a lag—a time delay—a three second stutter, basically meaning anything you do, it takes three seconds to register in the system. A fuck of a lot can happen in three seconds if you're a computer. Your average computer these days can do one hundred and fifty million million floating point operations per second. If you know what you're doing, that's basically enough time to make your computer psychic. From the outside looking in, it can see into the future because it's really the past. Three seconds worth of it. Think Malaysian Airlines—news breaks that the Russians have taken out a second plane, those stocks are tanking, but your machine's now got a three-second head start on the trades. You don't take a hit. You get to dump stuff clean. It's better than insider trading. It's fucking genius, kiddo. Three seconds is an eternity with the kind of processing power they're pulling down. That was the second thing, the one I almost missed. The first? They'd slipped in a Trojan that opened a back door right into the heart of the system, giving them control of pretty much everything from anywhere in the world. Couple that with the delay, and you've got a serious breach."

"It's the same here," Jake said.

"Where's here?"

"International relay station. All the trunk lines run through here. They've got a Trojan in here that essentially controls the flow of traffic down the line."

"He who controls the spice controls the world."

"What?"

"Nothing, dude. Thinking aloud. Looking at their setup here, I figure they can monitor the whole stock exchange through this hack. And they've got a three-second delay between it and the real world in terms of functionality. That means they can block trades or alter them on the fly—whatever they want, it's all there to be fucked with and the fucking's good, y'know? It's all just bits and bytes."

"Can you disconnect it?"

"Wish I could," Ryan answered. "But it's rooted in deep.

I'd have to strip everything down just to get at it. And if they're good enough to do that, they're good enough to have some shit-hot security around their hack. Put it this way: I love you like a brother, man, but I sure as hell don't want whoever's behind this tracing *anything* back to me."

"No worries. I owe you one."

"It's all good," Ryan replied. "Listen, I gotta bounce."

"Later," Jake said, and hung up. He turned back to face the screen, tapping the edge of his cell phone against his forehead, thinking. *So these guys take down Fort Hamilton first. Stage one. Then they go after the stock exchange. Stage two. Now they've taken control of the trunk lines. Stage three. Two questions: why, and what's next?*

Why was obvious, on the most basic level: to take control.

Hitting the fort had sidelined the military, at least locally, so no help was forthcoming from that quarter until the choppers and whatever else brought in backup. That was smart. The stock exchange meant they now controlled the money— not a bank, which has all kinds of security to prevent break- ins and robberies, but something a lot safer and more insidi- ous and far-reaching in its influence. It was also the fastest way to turn a profit if they could see into the future when they placed their bets. The trunk lines meant communica- tions, particularly with anyone overseas. The only thing left was transportation. This was the logical stage four. Transpor- tation networks.

This was a huge one, and it made sense: they could control the money and the chatter, as long as there wasn't a military presence, but more soldiers could be flown in. And plenty of New Yorkers could get out, running to someplace safe, rats deserting the sinking city to let those left behind clean up the mess.

Which meant stage four: shut down all the ways in and out of the city.

The airports would be first.

But you couldn't just hit them in isolation, you'd have to go after the trains as well. And the roads too, to be safe, but the complete snarl of abandoned vehicles had turned Manhattan into an atrophying corpse, the arteries clogged with gas guzzlers going nowhere, so even if the Army tried to bus in reinforcements they'd have to use tanks to bulldoze their way through the streets. It all took time—the one thing they didn't have.

Logically, there were six primary targets: Penn Station, Grand Central, Port Authority, LaGuardia, JFK, and Newark Airport.

But there was only one of him. He could call Ryan back, get some extra feet on the ground. That would cross one off the list, but it meant he would still have to cover five.

That was a problem.

# CHAPTER TWENTY-FOUR

"**H**EY, CHRISTIAN! DO YOU HAVE A MINUTE?"
Christian Eikner glanced up, his frown turning into a begrudging smile as he realized who was interrupting him. "For you, always." He waved a hand at the others he'd been talking to and broke away from their little group, stepping toward her. "Been awhile, how're you doing, Finn?"

"You know how it is, all work and no play makes Finn a dull chica." She shook her head, shrugged, then smiled. "You?"

Christian rubbed a hand over his head. She wasn't sure if he was basically saying he'd lost a few more hairs, or if he was trying to flatten out the few errant ones that remained.

He was a nice guy, and regularly joked that Bruce Willis and Patrick Stewart had made him cool. She'd never had the heart to tell him not even an industrial freezer could make him cool. Cool just wasn't in his DNA.

"Not too bad, but as you can imagine, we're a little busy trying to keep the lights on everywhere," he said with that self-deprecating grin of his. She looked over his shoulder to where his coworkers were waiting impatiently for him to be done flirting. He seemed to sense the daggers being aimed at his back. "So, what's up?"

"I have a question and I figure you're the one person I know who could answer it."

"I always like questions I can answer. Fire away."

She wasn't sure of any other way to say this, she wasn't even sure what, exactly, she was thinking, but it seemed to make sense in a crazy way and she just wanted him to tell her she was wrong so she could drop it. "This is going to sound nuts, but do you think there's been a shift in the magnetic poles?" He looked at her, and for a moment she expected him to laugh. He didn't. She pushed on: "I'm thinking about the blackouts, obviously, but the animals too, the birds falling from the sky, the stampedes from Yellowstone, the dogs, the shoals of fish. The end-of-the-world stuff. All of it." She had his full attention.

"I'm going to ask you a question in return, Finn: where did you hear about this?" His usual easy-going, affably shy demeanor vanished. He seemed . . . what? Angry?

His friends were staring. One of them started toward the two of them.

*Great, an audience.*

"I remembered something I heard in a lecture," she explained quickly, trying to marshal her thoughts into some semblance of order. "This history professor was talking about significant natural events and how they've shaped our world and our culture. It was about the nature of societal collapse—how things didn't have to be asteroids from the sky and huge extinction events to end a society as we define it."

"And that got you thinking about polar shifts?"

"During part of the lecture he mentioned the last polar shift, which was, what, maybe forty thousand years ago? Sometime during the last glacial period?" Christian nodded, confirming her time line. "But one of the things I remember most vividly was how he said early man would have been confused by the change in animal behavior, but because civilization as we know it was basically in its infancy, they would have adapted to the change fairly quickly, whereas if something like that happened as recently as twenty thousand years ago, when civilizations were much more developed, entire societies could've fallen." Again Christian nodded, but not so much confirming she was headed in the right direction, more like he was encouraging her to go on. "So, anyway, it struck me . . . the blackout, the sheer scale of it, is way too big to be some sort of global terrorism at play, so it's got to be natural, right? Because something *has* screwed with electronics. I'm not a physicist, but couldn't something like a polar shift explain what's happening out there?"

"Not exactly," Christian said, "but you're not entirely wrong, either. Definitely on the right track." He turned to his friends, who were now loosely surrounding them. "Gents, I'd like to introduce you to Finn Walsh, a friend from Art and Archaeology." He gave her a sheepish smile. "You're not going to believe this, but we were actually just discussing the possibility of a polar shift when you saw us. We were busy congratulating ourselves about being the first to come up with the theory, so obviously when you mentioned the exact same thing my first thought was panic. I mean, the last thing we want is somebody stealing our thunder, so to speak." A couple of the others laughed. Finn rolled her eyes.

"A bad-weather joke from the meteorology department? Why am I not surprised?" But she focused on the rest of what he'd said. "You think it was a polar shift?"

There were a couple of nods from the group.

"We think so, yeah," a tall, thin woman with a long rope of red-blond hair answered. "But obviously most of our equipment got fried so we've got no way of being sure. We're trying to cobble some stuff together so we can run a few tests."

"Okay, stupid-question time: if that's what happened, what can we do?" She got a lot of blank looks in response. "Let me rephrase that: is there *anything* we can do? Or do we just have to get used to the fact that north is south?"

Christian shook his head. "What's going on is a natural process and once we're past the initial stages things should settle down."

"The lights will come back on?"

"Pretty much. Obviously a lot of stuff's been damaged, but . . ." He shrugged as if to say that was better than nothing. His coworkers were already returning to their discussion about how to get their equipment functioning.

"Do me a favor. If you find anything out, let me know, okay?"

"I will. Definitely," he promised.

His smile was sweet. Pity she wasn't into good guys.

She left him to it, head full of questions, and moved back down the stairs and across the campus toward Schermerhorn.

Back on her floor, Finn was already thinking about the iconography of one particular symbol which she'd just seen painted on a wall as she'd crossed the campus. She was about to go back for a second look when someone called her name. She turned to see Debbie Caulfield waving her over to the break room. Debbie was short and round and could have been called dumpy, but she usually made up for it with a dazzling smile. She didn't look happy. She looked frightened.

"What's up?" Finn asked, detouring to join her in the break room. "You okay? You don't look it."

The shorter woman nodded. "Yeah." She blinked a couple of times. For a moment Finn thought she was going to cry.

"What is it, Deb?"

"I . . . before . . . I was attacked."

"What happened?"

The woman was shaking. "I saw someone coming out of your office. I thought he was a friend of yours, but when I said hi he slammed me into the wall and bolted."

"Oh Jesus . . . you're okay, right?"

"Shaken up, but mainly it's just wounded pride."

Finn nodded, taking her hand. "He's no friend of mine, believe me." She recounted her own run-in with the stranger. "It looked like someone had messed with my computer. I guess you just confirmed it. We should call the cops."

"Campus security? Fat lot of good those idiots are." Debbie managed a wan smile.

"No, the real cops."

"And tell them what? That someone shoved me into a wall? I can just imagine how that'll play with them given what's going on out there."

She had a point. The cops wouldn't prioritize a break-in on campus where nothing appeared to be missing. They'd say it was a job for the clowns at campus security to clean up. She didn't trust those bozos to organize an orgy in a brothel.

Bozos in brothels brought her thoughts around in a creepy sort of way to sex, which in turn brought her back to Jake. He still hadn't called back. She hoped he would, soon. She had a lot to tell him.

# CHAPTER TWENTY-FIVE

H E WAS IN WAY OVER HIS HEAD.
He needed someone to help him see beyond the accu-
mulation of portents and weird shit that pointed toward
some sort of fire-and-brimstone Armageddon, because that
wasn't what was really going on.

The first person that came to mind was the last person
he actually *wanted* to speak to.

She picked up on the second ring. "Finn Walsh, Art and
Archaeology."

"Hey." He paused a second, not really sure how intimate
you were supposed to sound with a woman who'd no doubt
made voodoo dolls to stick pins in your cock. "It's Jake."

"Thank god! Are you okay? Where are you?"

"Yeah, I'm good. It's been a really weird day. *Really*
weird. I was going to call, but . . ." He let it hang.

"Tell me about it."

He took her literally and did exactly that, got it all off
his chest, the whole story, from hearing about Fort Hamilton to the guys who'd blown up the Times Square station,

the graffiti he kept seeing, the men dead men at the stock exchange, and the fight in the relay station. Including the bodies that were maybe an hour from going into rigor, eyes wide open but glazed over and the blood staining the cement beneath them. All of it. He even told her about Sophie's call that started the whole thing off, and how that had led him to Harry, and eventually back into her life.

"I don't even know how to respond to that," she said after he'd finished. There was no humor in her voice. Shock.

He knew how she felt. He'd lived through it and he still didn't know how the hell he was supposed to be reacting to these things. He was just focused on going forward.

"Weird doesn't even begin to cover it," she went on. "They must have known this was going to happen. They couldn't react this fast otherwise. And the gas masks. They must have known somehow." And then she told him the little she'd figured out about the polar shifts and how that would have disrupted the earth's magnetic fields, how birds needed those to fly and how that disruption could account for a lot of the end-of-the-world portents they'd been seeing. He listened, taking it all in, without interrupting her.

Jake let that information settle in. "This is a purely natural process? Are the poles going to shift back again anytime soon?"

"Not for several thousand years," she said.

"Right. Okay. So. They knew," he said. "I don't know how they knew, but they did. They knew the poles were going to shift, and they knew what it would do to the electronics when they did, and they were in place to act fast. That takes serious resources." He was thinking fast, trying to process it all.

"You really think these guys are trying to take control of

the city? I mean, if they're already that powerful why would they need to move against an entire system that's already set up for them to profit?" Which was a good question. "That's what it sounds like, doesn't it? Security, finances, communications? It's like they're going to war." She broke off, but before he could say anything she added, "The roads are already screwed up, but it's got to be transportation next, doesn't it?"

He shouldn't have been surprised. She was sharp. She might not be a soldier, or have that kind of background, but she understood strategy and was more than capable of connecting the dots.

He nodded. "They already blew the Times Square station—that's enough to bring the subway to a halt for twenty-four hours, easily, and just the threat of more bombs, saran gas, anything like that, one more explosion and it'll be down completely. But that's internal, it's all on the island. If we're thinking like military minds, they'd want to cut off external access to Manhattan until they've finished whatever it is they're doing."

"Airports and trains? LaGuardia," she said immediately. "And JFK. And, oh fuck me . . . Penn. Grand Central. Port Authority. Oh god, can you imagine how many people are there now?"

He could. He'd been thinking about nothing else since the notion had first occurred to him back at the relay station. "And Newark, it's too close to leave untouched. They can't risk it, it's like leaving the back door open. But yeah, we're on the same page. It's what I'd do if I were heading up a military op." He shook his head. "Thing is, these guys are good. They're efficient. Their strike teams are working to a timetable, no room for error, so they're already in place in at least one of those sites. There's no way I can stop all of them."

"You could call the cops," she suggested, but the problem was the cops were too busy with immediate threats to worry about some perceived one, and he had no real evidence to support his claims apart from a stack of corpses. And those would only lead to the wrong kinds of questions first. The kind he really didn't have a good answer for. Who was going to believe stories about shadowy figures going around trying to subvert the city's essential systems? It was straight out of *Conspiracy Theories for Dummies*.

"They're not going to listen," he said.

"You were in the Army, right? What about your old CO? There must be someone you could call who'd remember you. Give them your name rank and number so they know you're legit, then tell them what you've stumbled onto?"

"Might work," he admitted, but in truth he couldn't see himself getting beyond a switchboard somewhere and then being consigned to the crank calls department of Couldn't Give a Fuck HQ. It wasn't as if he was some Purple Heart hero. "I'm gonna head to Penn Station," he told her. Of all the targets this one was closest. "I've got to do something."

"What about if we phone in bomb threats or something? Try to get people out of there even if we can't get there ourselves?"

"Maybe. But that's just going to cause an extra layer of chaos. That sort of disruption helps the terrorists"—that was how he was thinking of them now. Organized, dangerous, domestic.

"If shutting the places down is their only aim, maybe, but it hasn't been before, has it? It's been about infiltrating the systems to upload some sort of Trojan horse . . ."

He wasn't sure. She could be right: if they controlled the shutdown, maybe they could use it in their favor.

"I can check on Port Authority," Finn offered. This was unexpected. She was the bookish type, not a field agent. "It's not that far," she added. Which wasn't exactly true. Port Authority was down at 42nd and Eighth, several miles below Columbia.

He rubbed his free hand over his face. "These guys aren't fooling around. They've killed their own men. They won't think twice about putting one in your head if you get in the way."

"I'm not stupid, Jake," she said with no anger or sarcasm. "But think about it, the guys you went up against earlier, they're going to have circulated your description now, aren't they? Their gangs . . . units . . . are going to be watching for *you*. Nobody's going to be looking for me. I'm just going to be another face in the crowd. That's the ultimate camouflage."

She was selling it hard, but Jake wasn't buying.

He didn't like it.

Scratch that. He *hated* it. He couldn't ask her to put herself deliberately in harm's way. But he wasn't asking, was he? And her argument was good. The more intel they had on all this, the better.

"If I say no you're just going to do it anyway, aren't you?" he said.

"You know me so well."

"Okay, fine," he agreed finally. "But watch yourself. I'm serious. If it even looks like they're on to you, get the fuck out of there. You've got my number now. Use it. I don't want anything to happen to you."

"Not on your watch?" He could hear the smile in her voice. "Roger that, sir." She wasn't exactly good with the military parlance, but the effort made him smile too. "You be careful yourself, soldier. And we'll touch base later. See if we've learned anything. Now let's go kick some bad-guy butt."

"I'm serious. Don't take any risks."

"Yes sir!"

Shaking his head, he hung up and pocketed his phone. There wasn't anything else he could do here.

No, that wasn't true. He leaned over the row of computer terminals and, one by one, deactivated the Trojan they'd installed, hopefully robbing them of their stranglehold on the phone lines.

He was about to delete the remote access program when he had a better idea.

He moved through the root directories into the security settings, and sure enough, there was a password protecting the program. Passwords were a problem. He glanced over his shoulder at the corpses. Nope, they definitely weren't going to tell him.

But he didn't *need* to know it.

Actually, it was better if he didn't.

He selected the *Enter New Password* option, and unsurprisingly it offered him a window with three blanks spaces—the first one for the existing password, the second for the new password, and the third to confirm it.

Jake entered a random string of letters in the first space, just hammering the keys, and typed *qwerty123* in the next two, then hit *Return*.

*Password incorrect.*

*Of course it is*, he thought, and smiled as he repeated the process. The same warning appeared. Then he did it again. Three for three.

Once more and this time the message was different.

*Unauthorized access detected. System lockdown in effect. Please contact your system administrator to override and restore access.*

*That should make things a bit more interesting*, he thought. *Now, none of us can get in.* Which wasn't strictly true. They could send another team in, but that would require on-site access, and with a bit of luck the only guys with the expertise to hack the system were in the minivan outside very dead. That was the risk of cleaning up as you went—if you had to go back and retrace your footsteps without the experts you'd wasted the first time around, things got a whole lot more difficult the second time.

He repeated the lockdown on the other terminals. It took less than two minutes to make sure no one was getting back into them easily.

He stepped over the dead men and made his way back toward the light.

# CHAPTER TWENTY-SIX ·····

**W**HAT THE FUCK DO I DO NOW? That was the million-dollar question.

Unfortunately, Sophie only had about a buck fifty in change, which was nowhere near enough to buy an answer. She sat in a crowded all-night café, which she'd chosen because she'd seen the reassuring glow of a *We're Open!* sign in the window. Power was starting to return to some neighborhoods, as she knew it would. The promise of warm coffee, tea, and company had attracted quite a crowd. Outside, normality was reasserting itself. That was the personality of London summed up in a few short words. No matter how extraordinary the crisis, the ordinary was only ever a few hours away. These people had lived through extraordinary times more than once, be it IRA bombs or the 7/7 terror attacks, the Blitz. They had a history of stiff upper lips.

The silhouette of an angelic statue filled half of the plate-glass window. A prewar double-decker bus rumbled down the street. It looked like it had been rescued from a museum but that hadn't stopped dozens of people from cramming into it. The bus was heading back into the city. It didn't matter to the people onboard that they wouldn't be able to do anything when they got there, it was important that they simply turned up, that they showed they weren't beaten.

The huge digital sign wrapping around Piccadilly Circus was blank. Eros was surrounded by scaffolding.

There was familiar graffiti sprayed on the boards. The Hidden's symbols served a purpose—they'd paid off a bunch of young artists, banking on their misguided sense of social justice, and were using these kids to create the feel of territorial warfare, adding to the element of confusion and uncertainty amid the populace while The Hidden took control, adjusting the place.

Which made her a thorn in their side.

She knew them.

She knew how they communicated, the frequencies they used, and how they'd shielded their technology in preparation for the polar shift; she knew how they thought, how they'd planned, and, ultimately, what their endgame was. Control. These were men who were more interested in the ability to influence the world markets than they were in ephemeral things like greed or power. Both of those were transitory. They knew what was coming. It wasn't just about systemic racism, it was about class warfare. It was about how the poor were held back simply because it suited these men to do so. Places like Ferguson, Missouri were going to be a tipping point in the struggle against racial injustice in the way that the Kent State shootings back in 1970 should have been, in the way that the Jackson State shootings ten days later should have been—but back then there had been no national outcry because the nation wasn't mobilized. It wasn't connected. Not like now. Now a simple tweet could summon forces to fight side-by-side in a full-scale riot. And it wasn't just black oppression, it was Latino subjugation, it was the haves against the have-nots with all the economic influence to make sure those ghettos never cleaned up and those kids never had a chance at a better life. They didn't want an educated populace, they wanted a frightened one, and they had their mouthpieces in place to make sure people were frightened, with the rabid right-wing press spouting hate and lies with an Ebola-level of infection that rippled through communities.

Fifty million Americans were poor.

Fifty million voters.

And yet the 1 percent kept their choke hold on the economy and the power that came with it, distracting those fifty million poor voters with hot-button issues like immigration and abortion and gun control. Manipulating the masses with television, feeding its drug to the nation.

And that was how The Hidden removed something as basic as reasonable choice from democracy—they had no intention of toning down the lies their networks vomited up. They served a cruder purpose. They weren't meant to be believed. People *knew* the TV lied, but what they didn't know was how they could make good decisions if the only thing telling them what was happening in their world was corrupt. And as long as they stood in line for 6,000-percent loans they couldn't afford to pay back without taking another 60,000-percent one, things would never change.

They didn't need to strip the poor of the right to vote. Tell enough lies, pump enough hate into their homes, and they'd do exactly what you wanted anyway.

There was no American Dream.

There hadn't been one since the greed of the nineties

turned into the cannibalism of the subprime mortgage collapse and the banking collapse and every other fiscal nightmare these people had brought upon themselves in their hunger to feed off the poor. Now there was inflation, now there were credit bubbles and fiscal black holes and honest-to-God poverty of the kind that should only exist in the third world.

That was their doing. That was what they wanted. That's what it came down to. Eat the poor. All fifty million of them. Keep them in the ghettos with no hope of doing anything other than looking at the shiny hubcaps of the cars rolling by.

They didn't need Viagra, these parasites, they'd got a permanent hard-on and were fucking each and every poor bastard out there, bent double over a barrel of oil and dollar bills.

One man couldn't fight them. Fifty million, the people they were really frightened of, *they* could. But without a voice, without a way of communicating their truths, they were just as screwed as they had always been.

The real enemies, made up of politicians, legislators, and businessmen with power worth hoarding, hid in the shadows, drawn together. A secret society of movers and shakers that had the power to change the world beyond all recognition fed the fires of hatred while people laughed as Kareem Abdul-Jabbar tried to highlight the idiocy of more white people believing in ghosts than they did in racism. An African American president hadn't meant the end of hate, it just meant the rich and powerful had to be more devious with how they manipulated people.

The helicopter and two kill teams had been enough to convince her they were looking to solve the particular problem she posed with brute force. A bullet to the head.

Which was about the going rate for fucking up their plans at the stock exchange. She'd just cost them a not-so-small fortune, but worse than that, she'd made it obvious she'd tampered with stuff, creating a false paper trail that led right back to them. She'd told the entire world they were there. That was the only way to really hurt them; they hated exposure. They lived in the darkness for a reason.

It was all about pushback now.

And who was there to fight back? Who would stand in their way, assuming they'd succeeded in destroying Fort Hamilton and isolating Manhattan. That would give them all the time in the world to adjust the city, reshaping it in their image while the government scrambled to respond.

She'd tried to tell Jake, but had he understood her message?

She would have killed to know what was happening in New York, but international communication was pretty much dead with the satellites screwed up. It would take a long time before things returned to normal. They knew that, it was what they were banking on. That was why they'd acted now. Ever since they'd uncovered the second Mayan calendar and realized the implications of its prediction of a polar shift, and what that meant for the technological world that civilization had built itself on as the magnetic fields went haywire, everything these men had done was about preparing for the shift and how to best exploit it in terms of controlling the wealth of the world.

So, even if Jake had understood what she'd tried to tell him, how long could he last in the line of fire? Because he would, wouldn't he? He'd put himself right in the line of fire without even thinking about it, even if he didn't have a clue who or what he was up against in The Hidden.

They were ghosts.

Bogeymen.

They moved in the darkness.

Until twenty-four hours ago they'd been the silent power brokers, the kingmakers, more urban myth than monster under the stairs, like the Bilderberg Group, the Illuminati, and every other secret society imagined to be out there by the tinfoil-hat brigade—but that had all changed overnight.

She had to assume she was in this alone.

Which meant giving up on doing the impossible, focusing on what one woman could actually do.

Not that she was exactly normal. In some ways, maybe, but she could kill a man at forty paces in a dozen different ways, and that number increased as the distance between them diminished. That was why they'd recruited her in the first place—her combat training plus off-the-chart intelligence scores, her Vassar background. The whole package.

She had no idea how she'd gotten here, making the transition from fiercely patriotic soldier to a corporate assassin. It would have been too easy to say it was all about the money. But something inside her was broken. They'd recognized that. They played on it when they brought her into the fold.

She'd been first approached by a woman much like herself, similar age, similar background, similar education and experience, who had sounded her out about the ills of society and her own belief system before leaving her with a business card with a number printed on it and urging her to call. That call had changed her life. Yes, the money had been good. Private security was always good. They had a job for someone with her particular skill set, demanding a degree of independence, they said, which made her laugh and translate to *Does not play well with others*. They didn't argue with that. The job was in Kosovo, an in-and-out mission where the Army couldn't go. Some rich diplomat's kid had been kidnapped. They needed someone on the ground to run things and bring the kid home alive. There was nothing, they said, that they could do to help her, no resources they could offer to make her job easier. She brought the boy home. Next they sent her in to what had been Soviet Russia, again with no backup and no resources to call on, again seemingly chasing shadows. This time it was a computer outpost in the middle of a very grim landscape they needed taking down because, supposedly, the software engineers working there were on the brink of developing a dark net that would run beneath the Internet, a place where all sorts of illicit trade and trafficking could flourish. That wasn't it, of course. They were hackers who'd found a way into the deepest darkest secrets of one of Switzerland's most prestigious banks and there were some very rich men who wanted those secrets to remain buried deep. And on and on it went—Greece, Italy, back to the Hindu Kush, Israel, anywhere they needed her.

Somewhere along the line the jobs changed and it soon became obvious she was nothing more than a corporate as-sassin, killing for the Almighty Dollar. She told herself it was no different to being a mercenary and cashing a paycheck for fighting in Kabul. For a while she was even good at lying to herself.

But it couldn't last.

There was a line.

There was always a line, a point where youthful ideals and grown-up bitterness met; the question was what hap-pened then, because it was one thing to sign up to do their dirty work—it was exciting, it felt like she was doing some *good*—but quite another to actually take a step back and think about what you were being asked to do. And that was exactly what she'd done, realizing she'd hit the point of no return when they were asking her to kidnap kids in Eastern Europe and bring their blood home to feed on it.

She took a sip of coffee, still barely able to process what they'd asked her to do, and hating the fact that she'd done it.

They weren't vampires. Not literally. They wanted the blood for transfusions. Desperate measures and unethical science had come together in a clinic in Bern where no questions were asked if your money was green enough. The young blood was meant to rejuvenate the aging process in their brain tissue and muscles. These people wanted to live forever. What was the point of wealth and power when you were pushing up daisies? The whole process was ghoulish. She didn't know how it worked, but there was no denying the results. She'd seen them with her own eyes. Dementia in one of their number had been first stemmed then reversed. Now he was giving orders again. A new man. He called himself Alom. That wasn't his real name. He was known, and beloved by millions, a face from the silver screen they trusted and had lined up to see on Sunday-morning matinees. If only they knew what he was really like. It had been his idea to use the names of Mayan gods and goddesses in their communications, a curious affectation, obviously intended to be some sort of tribute to the calendar that had opened this brave new world to them.

They couldn't understand her qualms—and argued she'd done much worse for them, which of course she had. But these were children. The results, no matter how miraculous, didn't justify the means.

They couldn't. Ever.

They were asking her to steal kids, not just their blood.

She wasn't giving them back, either. Done, they were discarded.

And that was her line. That was the thing she couldn't do. Not if she wanted to keep her soul intact.

What they hadn't expected was that she'd turn on them rather than cross it.

They'd made her.

She knew their secrets.

She was an enemy they'd trained.

And now she was hunting them.

# CHAPTER TWENTY-SEVEN

JAKE SHOULDERED HIS WAY DOWN THE STEPS leading into Penn Station. With the power still out, he'd hoped the station would be empty, or at least near empty. He couldn't have been more wrong—the place was a heaving mass of humanity, most of which smelled as though it hadn't showered for a week.

It wasn't pretty.

He pushed through the crowd.

There was no natural light once inside. Backup generators powered everything. Striplights that made everyone look like wraiths half draped in shadow.

The stairs were jammed even more than usual, and there was absolutely no order to the flow of bodies. No one was managing more than a few steps at a time with the rest of the herd. He didn't have time for that.

He didn't know what he was looking for. It wasn't like they were going to have big neon signs over their heads that proclaimed: *Bad guys.*

But the last two times he'd come across them, they'd

been entering abandoned buildings. The only other time, they'd been tagging the station, and he wasn't even sure that counted. That didn't fit the pattern. That was too low-level. Like a distraction from the bigger picture. It didn't feel right. Penn was far from abandoned; commuters waiting for the first train out of here and the homeless and dispossessed seeking shelter made it feel like Times Square on New Year's Eve.

Penn was familiar. In times of crisis didn't people look for the familiar? For known quantities? Things they could trust? Penn Station was a New York institution, not glitzy and touristy like Times Square. There was light, sure, and it was a practical place, a workhorse, solid and reliable—just like New Yorkers pictured themselves. It didn't hurt that it had a lot of open space for people to congregate in, which made it a good focal point for meeting up. Most of the people here were taking refuge rather than waiting for a train, and that made it tough to spot the terrorist hiding in the mix somewhere.

He used his height and bulk to force his way through the crowd down the long hall, past the Duane Reade and other shops, trying to look everywhere at once, heading toward the ticket booths and platform entries. There was nothing to suggest he wasn't just chasing shadows. There wasn't a central computer system like at the stock exchange or the relay station.

At least, not out in the open.

There had to be one, though, he realized—back behind the ticketing booths somewhere. They were all terminals based off a central hub, like the subway. There'd be a control room back there somewhere making sure all the junctions, tracks, and trains interchanged smoothly. Without it, the whole system would devolve into chaos.

*That* was where these guys would go.

And that changed what he was looking for—the system was off-limits to nonpersonnel, meaning they could hide in plain sight if they were in uniform. All they'd have to do was get back there and they'd have time and privacy.

It also meant that any Amtrak or NJ Transit guys manning the terminals would be an obstacle, and he knew how they dealt with obstacles. But they couldn't just shoot someone here and shove the body under the tracks. That would cause panic. That wasn't exactly working from the shadows. It wasn't their style.

He didn't sense any panic, only a murmur of how-much-longer-is-this-going-to-last rippling through the crowd.

He rounded the circular Amtrak waiting area. Beneath the big electronic billboard that hung in the middle of the ceiling, crowds of people talked, ate, and some even slept. The billboard flickered like a flattened strobe light. Every single train listed on the board had the word *CANCELED* beside it. Without that you'd never know there was anything wrong with the world.

*New Yorkers at their best. They're like the cockroaches of the human world. They can weather just about anything,* he thought, proud of his people.

He headed across to the Amtrak ticket windows. They were set off to the side, behind several pillars each holding timetables and schedules. There was a maze of chromed stands funneling traffic toward the windows, though nobody was waiting in line right now.

Jake bypassed the maze without risking the wrath of New Yorkers. The ticket windows were behind clear bulletproof plastic—a very definite sign of the times. It wasn't a problem though. He made his way to the end of the row, past the last window, to an equally transparent door.

Trying to make it look like he belonged there—after all, he was hiding behind an MTA logo, not everyone would spot the difference or think he shouldn't be there—Jake tried the doorknob. It turned easily, so he didn't have to sweat the electronic card swipe beside the knob. Chalk one up in favor of the blackout. The generators were obviously only powering bare-bones functionality like lights and heat. Jake pushed the door open.

Nobody called out. No one challenged him.

He looked across to where five officers, all of them in riot gear, manned the little police kiosk at the front of the room. A part of him was tempted to go over there and tell them what was going on, or at least what he thought was going on, and let them lead the charge. They could handle themselves. They had the look of ex-military about them, which meant good instincts and proper training. Here were a bunch of guys much better equipped to handle this shit than Finn was, and yet he knew he was going through that door alone.

It wasn't some kind of misplaced heroism. He might not be the city's last chance, but he was certainly one of her best. If he told the cops what he knew, the only way it was going to play out was with them taking him in. He'd have to answer questions. They wouldn't just turn him loose with a slap on the ass and say, *Go take down some bad guys, dude.* And that would mean he'd failed. He wasn't going to let these murderers win. Not now.

He'd come this far, what were a few more steps?

He went through the glass door. There was a narrow hall that allowed access to each of the booths. There was one more door, directly across from where he stood. It was the only one that was the same solid, reassuring blue as the walls around it. The card swipe beside this door wasn't lit and the knob turned when he tried it. So much for million-dollar security.

Jake gave it a gentle push, then walked into the back end of Amtrak's Penn Station operation. It had the same generic feel as seemingly every office block in the world: white walls, cramped cubicles, and bland tan carpeting. Most of the lights were out, bar a single emergency strip at the far end of the room. The computer screens were all dark.

He could hear voices. Nearby. Not happy.

"I don't get it. The algorithm's not working."

Jake moved toward the voices, careful not to make a noise.

"Fuck it, just give me another one."

"It should work," another voice replied. "Did you remember to—?"

"Of course I did! I'm not a fucking moron. Just give me another one."

"Fine. Here. Try not to mess this one up."

"You're such a motherfucker."

"*Quiet*, both of you!" a third voice cut across the squabble. "And hurry up, we're on the clock!" So there were at least three of them. Jake wasn't surprised. Two would have been better; one would have been best. With a bit of luck he'd even the odds out quickly.

Jake crept forward as his eyes adjusted to the semi-gloom. He flinched involuntarily when a swath of bright light suddenly appeared ahead, then dropped into a crouch, blinking as he tried to adjust his eyes to it. He half-shielded his face with a hand. After a few seconds he could squint and see blurs. Another few seconds and he could just about make out the light source: one of the screens was live in a cubicle the next cluster over.

It was the source of the voices.

Keeping low, Jake edged over to the cube's far wall, then lowered himself even more, risking a glance around the partition wall. He didn't like what he saw. There were five of them, not three. Two sat at desks, hunched over the keyboards while lines of code scrolled by on both screens. A third guy leaned on the backs of both chairs, jabbing a finger at one of the monitors. The boss. Jake wondered how they'd feel about taking his orders if they knew how the rest of the staff had been treated.

The guy jabbed a fat finger at the screen again, losing patience with his crew. Behind him, with their backs to Jake, the last two men both wore dark, well-tailored clothes. They didn't look like they were here to get their hands dirty. Both, he saw, from the way their jackets rode, had holsters at the base of their spines.

One of them twisted to say something but the words didn't carry to Jake. Something else caught his attention, a small golden glint at the man's collar. A pin like the one he'd taken from the dead guy. Jake reevaluated his take on who was in charge here. These guys were. And they were the only ones obviously armed. It was only one body different from how he'd imagined it going down.

Time to shake things up a bit.

First, he needed to neutralize the guns.

He thought for a moment about going back out to get the cops—a wall of body armor would be useful to hide behind. It wasn't five-on-one, he realized, it was only two-on-one. Think of it that way and it wasn't so bad, though there wasn't much in the cube he could use to go up against a couple of guns.

He thought about sticking the pin on his lapel and walking up to them. He could fake it, say he'd been sent to see how things were progressing, and take them out before they realized he wasn't one of them. As a plan, it was pretty thin, but it had its merits: there weren't too many moving parts to fuck up. But then again, it only needed one thing to go wrong.

Twenty feet from where he hunkered down, he saw a fire extinguisher in a wall case. That could work. He ghosted over to it, lifting the heavy red canister from its brackets. Nice and solid. Capable of doing some serious damage. That gave him an alternative to the knife, something that meant he didn't have to get right up close and personal to have an impact.

He crept back to the cube again, listening for the slightest change in sounds.

They were still fixated on the screens. All five of them with their backs to Jake. That should have made things a lot easier, but it didn't.

It made the inevitable next step harder because he didn't want to *kill* them. He wanted answers. Dead men didn't talk. Combat wasn't always face-to-face, but the majority of the time it was, whether it was fighting enemy soldiers on Baghdad Highway or going toe-to-toe with drunks in a bar. Those people all knew he was coming, and were engaging him with the same intent. It was about meting out punishment, disabling an enemy combatant as quickly and efficiently as possible.

This was different.

Three men here could be victims.

They didn't have to be the same stone-cold killers the guys with the gold pins were. But that didn't mean they wouldn't fight like a bitch if he stepped out from behind the cube and said, *Hey, honey, I'm home.* After all, even if they were relatively innocent victims here, they weren't going to be happy to see him.

Jake took a series of deep breaths, bringing his body under control. He stood up straight, breaking cover. Two long strides took him to within arms' reach of both gunmen.

The one on the left lost life's lottery. Jake smashed the bottom edge of the fire extinguisher into the base of the man's skull and dropped him like a stone. The dull thud of the impact was followed a heartbeat later by the slump of the body hitting the floor, and the other four turned to stare at Jake, trying to work out what the source of this new threat was, only for him to raise the extinguisher above his head and loose a primal roar as he charged the other gunman.

There was a split second in it; it all came down to the agonizing silence between one heartbeat and the next.

The gunman reached for his weapon.

Jake's was in his hand.

That was the difference. He swung the extinguisher as hard as he could, all of his raw anger, fear, and desperation behind it, whipping the heavy metal cylinder around in a tight, level arc. The meat of it hit the gunman square in the right arm, above the elbow, as he managed to turn slightly into the blow, protecting himself. He was right-handed and the gun went spinning from his hand as the pain reflex sprung his fingers open.

Jake didn't hesitate.

He had one chance.

He stepped in close, bringing the fire extinguisher up in a savage arc. It seemed to happen so slowly. The gunman's head rose, meeting the extinguisher halfway; it took him square in the jaw and he went down spitting blood.

Jake followed up with a vicious kick to the head.

The guy wasn't getting up in a hurry.

Two down. Three to go.

Three, who hopefully wouldn't fight too hard.

Then a shot rang out, its silenced report brutal in the confines of the room.

Jake stared at the hackers in surprise.

They stared right back at him, just as confused. Then there were two, as one of them, the one standing, slumped forward, losing his grip on a chair back as a red rose blossomed in the middle of his shirt. A second gunshot brought another's hand up to clutch stupidly at his throat as the skin started flapping while he sucked in the last air he'd ever breathe, and then he fell, blood leaking out around his fingers.

Jake spun around.

There, behind him, the first gunman, blood dripping down the side of his face, was back on his feet, gun-hand wavering as he tried to take aim. His eyes locked on Jake.

*Fuck.* The guy had a head made of granite.

There wasn't time or space to swing the extinguisher again, so Jake dropped it, lunging forward to close the distance.

The gunman got off two more shots before Jake cannoned into him.

Neither hit.

He reached out with both hands, one clamping down on the gunman's upper arm, the other slamming palmfirst into his gun-hand. The sudden impact shoved the man's hand to the side. Jake continued the motion, pushing on the gun itself now, forcing it around until the barrel pointed inward, at the gunman's own chest. It went off, the guy's finger clenching the trigger out of sheer surprise. There was a look, not pain, not fear, not even death, that crossed the gunman's eyes as he realized he'd just killed himself. Satisfaction?

The gun slipped from his lifeless fingers as he fell to the floor. This time he wouldn't be getting back up.

Jake spun around, scanning the room. The other men were all on the ground. He hadn't seen the third guy go down. He must have taken one of those last two shots Jake thought were misses. He wasn't going to cry over it.

They knew what they were getting into, or at least who they were getting into bed with. They should have done their due diligence. And to be brutally blunt about it, if he hadn't gotten involved their life expectancy was only a couple of minutes more, so in short it sucked to be them, but it wasn't his doing.

There was one guy down who hadn't been shot, though he had taken two pretty savage blows to the head, so he wasn't going to be in a good place even if he lived. Jake crouched beside him and checked for a pulse. Faint and thready, but faint and thready was a lot better than nonexistent. Jake pulled his sleeve down, grabbed the man's gun, and tossed it into the nearest trash can. He'd thought about taking it for a split second.

There were two problems with guns: one, they escalated things; the less obvious problem was what happened if you got caught with it. He had no idea what kind of shit the piece had been used in, how many open cases it could link him to. So no guns. He'd done okay without one so far.

He turned his attention back to the injured man, frisking him. He removed a ceramic knife from the guy's boot and a switchblade from his pocket. He ditched both of them before slapping the guy across the face.

"Wakey wakey, pretty boy." Jake shook the man by the shoulder. "Come on, back to the land of the living." He slapped the guy again.

He stirred slightly, wincing.

"That's it. Open your eyes."

He slapped him again, not as hard this time, and earned a groggy groan before the guy squinted, blinked, and finally did as he was told, opening his eyes.

"Welcome back."

He gave no reaction to the sight of Jake's face right up in his.

"You're the last man standing," Jake told him. "Or last man lying, I guess. So why don't you and me have a little chat? I've got a few questions for you. For starters, and most importantly, what the actual fuck is going on?" He reached down for the guy's throat, closing a hand around it, his fingers digging in. That was when he noticed the gold pin with its weird eye design. "Who are you guys, anyway? Freemasons? Scientologists? Some weird fucked-up cult shit like that?"

The man glared at him and muttered something, but it was under his breath.

"Try that again. Talk to me, big guy, tell me all your secrets."

The man wriggled beneath him, like he was trying to break free, and as Jake backhanded another slap across his face, he thrust out his jaw to take it and bit down hard.

In the silence of the back room, Jake distinctly heard something go *pop*. Something inside his prisoner's mouth. He realized what it meant a second too late to do anything about it, but that didn't stop him from grabbing the guy's chin and trying to force his jaw apart.

But the guy just lay there, a froth of foam bubbling between smiling lips and streaming from his nose, before he shuddered and his eyes rolled back into his skull. He stopped breathing altogether a few seconds later.

"Fuck! Just . . . fuck! Fuck!" Jake yelled at the dead man, slamming a clenched fist down on its chest. "I only wanted a couple of answers . . . Jesus . . . Was that *really* worth killing yourself over?"

The dead man had thought so.

So had the guys who'd given him that golden iris pin on his lapel and whatever other death-before-dishonor crap they'd fed him.

Cyanide capsules hidden in fake teeth? It was straight out of James Bond.

# CHAPTER TWENTY-EIGHT

F INN PUSHED THROUGH THE PAIR OF NOT-SO-AUTOMATIC DOORS that lined the front of Port Authority. The chill of the coming winter night crept in with her.

*Okay,* she thought, *if I wanted to cause maximum chaos, where would I start?*

This was unlike her. She couldn't quite remember why she'd volunteered to chase shadows with Jake. She wasn't even with him. She was out here on her own and the shadows she was chasing had guns. She was trying to impress him. He was a glorified goddamn electrician, he should have been the one trying to impress *her*. It was all ass-backward.

She paused at the second set of doors that opened into the terminal's central hall. *He shows up after a year and suddenly I'm acting like he's the last man on earth and my hormones are off the chart. Get a grip on yourself, woman.* She shook her head.

No time for remonstrations. She could beat herself up later. Right now, she needed to ditch the pseudo self-analysis and concentrate on the task at hand: looking for the bad guys. She could figure everything else out later. Assuming she didn't get herself shot first.

She focused on her surroundings.

Port Authority didn't change. It was always the same wretched hive of humanity, a little darker with most of the lights out, but the soaring central space with its wide columns and sturdy inner balconies managed to make the gathered horde look inconsequential. Even at its most crowded, the building felt airy and open.

Tonight, it was as crowded as she'd ever seen it. Everywhere she looked there were people wrapped up against the elements: some walked, some stood and leaned, some talked huddled around candles, some crouched or kneeled or sat, some full-out sprawled on the worn tiles. A few actually slept in corners or huddled up against columns.

She couldn't help but wonder how bad their homes were that they'd rather be here in a glorified bus station. Then she realized that for some, if not most of them, it had nothing to do with the state of their homes. It was about seeing other people, about knowing you weren't alone. And in Port Authority, you were never alone.

These were strange days.

They had been ever since the first dogs had howled and the first bullets of that deluge of rain had fallen. No wonder people were calling it the end of the world. Now, plunged into darkness, it was as if everything they'd ever known was slowly coming undone. They weren't equipped for this. They weren't made to forage and fend for themselves. Their survival skills involved forming lines in Walmart and using credit cards to gather what they'd hunted down. At best they were lethal with coupons.

On one of the far walls she noticed a spray of graffiti.

Any other day she'd have completely ignored it as just one more piece of senseless vandalism, but there was something eerily familiar about the swirls of the pattern—she'd been staring at the same thing for hours that morning. Only then it had been below the waterline, way down south off the coast of Cuba, carved into the walls of an impossible pyramid fifty thousand years ago. She'd never seen it before today. Now here it was again on the wall of Port Authority.

It stopped her dead in her tracks, causing a couple of people to grunt and complain as they nearly walked into her back.

She didn't move for a full minute, unsure what to make of it.

How could it be here? Coincidence?

She was shaking her head, telling herself no, it couldn't be a coincidence, when she remembered something Jake had mentioned about the guys he'd chased at Times Square: they'd been spraying graffiti on the subway wall.

They were here somewhere. She looked around, still not sure what she was looking for. They were hardly going to be wearing night-vision goggles and gas masks.

They'd need privacy to hack into the systems and a terminal with the right kind of access. It wasn't like they could just surf into the system from the free Wi-Fi at Cinnabon or Au Bon Pain.

And with that realization the entire mission changed. She wasn't looking for a bunch of terrorists anymore, she was looking for their access point to the system.

Finn stepped to the side to avoid more grunts and complaints, and leaned against the wall. She scanned the faces of everyone that passed her. She needed to think. She was supposed to be good at that. *What do you know about Port Authority? List it. Everything. Go!*

She closed her eyes and started ransacking her memories, looking for something she could use, anything, some clue to point her in the right direction. It didn't matter how big or seemingly small.

She'd lost count of how many times she'd been through here, how many buses she'd ridden out to New Jersey or upstate or down to DC or even to Atlantic City. She knew the station well enough to navigate through it, knew where the bathrooms and escalators were, where to go for coffee, where to get snacks, where to get a little real food too. But she'd never tried looking at it from the perspective of someone intent upon doing harm.

*Come on, woman. Think. Think!*

And then she had it.

Upstairs.

She headed straight down the hall, past the Hudson News kiosk to the two long escalators framing Au Bon Pain. The escalators weren't working, and a few people were sprawled across the bottom steps. The buses weren't running and most of the shops were closed. That meant it was quiet up there. Quiet and full of doors that led into the guts of Port Authority, passageways like arteries that kept vital services running.

Taking a deep breath, she stepped over the people at the bottom and started up.

It took her two minutes to rise up through the levels.

She brushed her hair back from where sweat matted it to her neck. She had too many layers on. She teased the scarf down from her chin and looked around, reorienting herself: a shoe repair place, a jewelry stall, a Café Metro, a florist, and beyond those, the one place that always seemed to be a little haven of peace and quiet—because the one thing you didn't do in New York was piss off the cops right in their own backyard.

She strode off in that direction, ignoring the row of old homeless guys.

One of them called out, asking her for money. She just kept on walking as he flashed her a gap-toothed grin. "Send me a postcard, beautiful," he cackled.

She shuddered, moving another step farther away from him, which brought her closer to a derelict whose teeth had all rotted away. His beard contained the remnants of his last few meals.

None of the bums followed her; habit kept them away from where she was headed. It was ingrained in them, another layer of filth coating their skin: stay clear of the cops if you want to take advantage of the heating, the benches, and the bathrooms. Don't cross them and they won't toss you out on your ass.

Port Authority was a carefully balanced ecosystem.

All the levels from bottom to top were essential to its continued harmonious existence. Bears did indeed shit in the woods. The pope was Catholic. Port Authority was full of the kind of people and practices the city had been trying to stamp out since the seventies, but as long as they were careful and didn't flaunt themselves on the steps of a police station, blind eyes were turned.

She walked through the last real blind spot before she reached the cop shop. The hall consisted of unadorned red-brick walls and a pale square-tiled floor. Nothing flashy, no ostentation. It was purely functional, a large, unassuming space with floor-to-ceiling opaque glass windows all around.

And a small sign overhead read, *Operations Control Center.*

She stood outside the door, staring at the façade, and

licked her lips. Her heart was hammering. What if there were still cops inside? She needed an excuse. The best she could come up with was ignorance, pretend she was lost and frightened and looking for help. If that didn't work she could tell them Jake thought they were at risk. But that only worked if those guys weren't already in there.

She took a deep breath, let it out, brushed her hair back, took another deep breath, delaying the inevitable. *It's just a door. You can do this. All you've got to do is open a door. Like Pandora opened a box,* she thought bitterly, wishing she was back in her office.

When she reached for the knob, a hand clamped down on her shoulder before she could turn it.

"And where do you think you're going, miss?" The voice was deep and resonant. Intimidating.

She turned to face the speaker. He couldn't have been less intimidating if he'd tried. He was short, barely taller than her, and looked like he'd been living up here for a few weeks, his oversized army coat ragged, his frayed jeans falling apart, his shoes bursting at the seams, his fingerless gloves a sooty gray that had nothing to do with their original color.

But the pistol tucked into his waistband was all the intimidation he needed.

His stubble was carefully cultivated, and even if his hair looked like it hadn't been washed in a few days, the natural oils kept it thick and glossy. His eyes were dark, sharp, and cold.

He wasn't panhandling for loose change.

# CHAPTER TWENTY-NINE

A VICIOUS EXPLOSION BOOMED OUT ACROSS LONDON, dragging Sophie from her thoughts.

She pushed herself up from her seat, rushing toward the door. Most of the café's other patrons did the same, crowding around the double glass doors that served as the outer wall.

She went out into the street. And stopped, staring.

A tongue of flame writhed above the buildings, lighting up the night sky. A thick column of dark smoke rose above it, choking the fingers of flame.

People pointed, murmurs of disquiet rippling through the crowd as they came to the logical conclusion: looters. The city had had its fair share of disenfranchised plaguing the streets, smashing up shops, tearing down fences. Fire was a natural extrapolation of that violence. She knew better. Looking at the fire rise, she knew she had to move.

She started to make her way toward the flames, but only got as far as the median strip in the middle of the road, then stopped on the white line, surrounded by other confused people staring up at the burning sky.

She was already too late to influence events there—the fire was raging, she wasn't a firefighter, she wouldn't be able to do anything even if she could get close to the source. She'd just be another face in the crowd, gawking, kept at a distance by the authorities as they scrambled to prevent the flames from spreading.

Worse, she'd be trapped if anyone spotted her.

She went back inside the café as others streamed out to look. She ran over to the counter, flipped on the flat-screen television mounted above it. Normally running a constant cycle of ads for lattes, low-fat mochaccinos, low-carb salads, and other healthy alternatives, it had shut down along with everything else. But since the power was back on, if the TV was working again . . .

If there was news broadcasting . . .

It would be a huge step toward the world returning to some semblance of normality.

The standby light at the screen's lower edge illuminated, then the black screen resolved into the image of a serious-looking man in a suit shuffling papers at a news desk.

Exactly what she needed.

A couple of people from outside had noticed the television and peered up at the screen.

Sophie found the remote and hit the volume as the man glanced up, saw that the camera was on, and smiled. It was a reassuring smile, promising everyone that no matter how desperate things appeared, it was going to be okay. He was a terrible liar.

"Welcome back," he said, his voice rich and deep. He was an image of perfect calm, no hint of the sheer scale of disasters that had gripped the world over the last day. It was all about perception. If he appeared panicked, people would feed off it. By being calm he was telling the world that this too shall pass. "Reports are coming in that suggest a large-scale explosion in the vicinity of London's financial district. This is unconfirmed at the moment, but it is believed that a bomb has exploded within the stock exchange. Emergency services are on the scene, and investigators are en route. There are no reports of casualties yet, as the building had been closed due to the power outages across the city. We'll keep you up-to-date as we learn more. As of now no group has claimed the attack, but the Metropolitan Police are advising people to stay away from the area if possible, and the country's threat level has moved up from Substantial to a current level of Severe."

The only level above that, Critical, she knew, meant they were expecting an imminent nuclear strike.

If only they knew . . .

Sophie turned away from the program and sank back into her chair. The stock exchange, gone? She couldn't quite believe it, despite the evidence of her own eyes.

She should have anticipated it—it was a radical move, but one thing she knew about these people: they weren't afraid of making a mess. If they couldn't buy it they'd break it.

She'd forced their hand by manipulating the computer systems to deny them access. By doing that she'd given them no choice, they'd resorted to extreme measures. If they couldn't have the place, no one could. Simple as that. And a terror strike wasn't something that could be easily traced back to them; if it could then a lot of other "trouble" across the world would already have been laid at their doorstep.

No, to the world at large it would be another senseless act of violence.

There was familiarity in terror these days. That helped them to hide, using their money and influence to spread the fear. That was where their real power lay.

They stood behind well-known political figures, lobbying their opinions with cash, shaping them with threats. They bankrolled certain extreme interests, making sure the funding was there to keep chaos on the bubble, but never enough to undermine their financial interests. No one wanted the money markets to crash until just the right moment; it had been carefully manipulated, timed to perfection.

Sophie stared down at her cooling coffee, wrapping her hands around the mug.

Victory turned to defeat so easily. She'd blocked them and their response had been massive and brutal.

She was frightened for the first time. Genuinely, bone-deep scared. Not for herself. Her fate was already sealed and had been since she'd said no to them. No, she was frightened for all the others who were going to be hurt because of her. She was even frightened for Jake.

It was easy to think of these people as collateral damage. But they were more than that to their daughters, sons; they were brothers, lovers, husbands, wives. They had faces, they'd had lives. Until those lives had come into orbit with hers. And then, at that point, that unknowable place, they'd ceased to matter and become collateral damage.

But she had to fight.

The Hidden couldn't be left to win unopposed. Not when she knew what they wanted out of this.

Sophie needed to take care of something while she still could. She pulled out her phone and dialed the number from memory.

It was in the hands of the gods now. She'd get a signal or

she wouldn't. If she was going to die, then she was going to die trying to end this.

# CHAPTER THIRTY

*FROM THE SUBLIME TO THE ABSOFUCKINLUTELY RIDICULOUS,* Jake thought. He stood deep in the bowels of Penn Station, staring down at the five bodies. Five dead men. He'd only killed one of them—and even that was a stretch given he hadn't actually pulled the trigger—but all of them dead *because* of him. Because he was here. Because he had gotten involved.

There wasn't any remorse or guilt on his part, purely frustration. Dead men tell no tales, as the old line went. He was rapidly running out of people to ask, and was ticking off the list of places to look just as quickly.

He thought of Finn. He'd been too far underground to receive calls, and the radio silence was unnerving.

You couldn't run a good op without contact. But she wasn't a solider.

Was she still there? Was she in trouble?

He knew he should go check on her. Port Authority wasn't all that far. Eight blocks up. Less than ten minutes' walk. Jake headed for the door back out onto the concourse.

A minute later he was easing his way through the glass

door and onto the customer side of things. Life was going on with the same alarming lack of purpose. Nobody was pointing at him, and nobody was screaming. No one even noticed him emerge from the control room. Which meant the sound of the gunshots hadn't traveled. Good. There was nothing to be gained by mass hysteria. Right now what he needed was a good dose of normality.

Not that there was anything normal about New York right now.

Jake paused long enough to scan the room, reorienting himself, and then turned to make his way toward the northernmost exit.

He froze, staring up at a huge bank of monitors mounted on the wall in the Amtrak lounge. Through the glass wall separating them he could see one of the screens clearly enough to read the ticker across the bottom. The screen was dominated by an image of smoking rubble that had once been a building. The yellow bar of the scrolling caption read: *London Stock Exchange in Terror Attack . . .*

Jake watched it roll through three times before he was absolutely sure what it said. Strikes on the world's two primary financial centers in the same day?

He ran out into the central waiting area, doubling around into the Amtrak lounge. The guard didn't even glance up at him. She was too busy watching her little TV set, which showed the same footage, but hers had sound.

"*. . . on the scene today,*" a reporter was saying, "*as the city of London was the site of a devastating explosion. Investigators have determined that this was a deliberate attack of terror. The speculation is that the lack of power and failure of usual security measures made the financial hub too tempting a target to pass up. We are reminded of Osama bin Laden's final entreaty to his followers to rise up against the nodes of* *economy, that there is no greater way to hurt the United Kingdom than to neutralize its economic heart. Police are currently searching for this woman"*—a face appeared on the screen. She had changed, but still had the same strong, almost sharp cheekbones, the pointed chin, the small, sharp nose that turned up at the end into as close to a chisel bit as bone would allow. The hair was shorter than he remembered, but still just as wild. He used to love tangling his fingers in it and pulling her against him—*"in connection with the explosion. If you see her, please contact the authorities at once. Do not approach her as she is to be considered armed and extremely dangerous."*

Sophie did indeed look dangerous, Jake thought, staring at her face numbly. But then, she always had. She looked older, tired. But yes, still dangerous.

*What the fuck's going on, Sophie? What the fuck are you involved in?*

Two big questions.

There were smaller ones too, like how there was power here. Did that mean the world was coming back online?

Jake peered at his ex-girlfriend's face for the first time in more than a decade, unable to shake her cryptic phone message. *I'm not who you think I am.* That was one thing, the other was the fact that she'd warned him. Warned him and apologized. She never apologized for anything. But that wasn't what he was thinking about now. Now his mind was focused on the last warning she'd given him. *You're going to hear stuff about me. Bad stuff.* She was involved, there was no doubt about that, but was she a victim or was she one of them?

The Sophie he knew wasn't a victim, ever. But it had been a long time since he'd last seen her. There was a lot of living done between the pair of them. They weren't the kids they had been. He couldn't even remember the naïve idealist he'd been in more than abstract terms, combat zones had beaten that kid out of him. But he remembered her nature. She hadn't been a terrorist; she'd been fiercely patriotic. He just couldn't imagine her turning against her country.

*I'm not who you think I am.*

*Then who are you? What do you do for them? Apart from blow up the London Stock Exchange*, he thought bitterly.

Control. That's what everything else had been about so far. Control. And if these people couldn't control it, the next best thing was to destroy it, right?

Was that what had happened?

They'd tried to take London and failed so they'd left nothing behind.

New York, London, and Tokyo—that was the third one. Only three world stock exchanges, and one had been hacked and another blown up within the space of a day. The same day that the lights went out across the world.

Did that mean Tokyo was next? Was that what was happening?

Was the newsreader right and bin Laden's prophecy was finally coming to pass? He tried to remember exactly what Sophie had said in her message, but all he could remember was an overall sense of: *It's bad, very bad, and about to get a whole lot worse.* Which wasn't far from the mark.

She'd obviously known about all this, there was no getting around that, and whether she'd blown up the London Stock Exchange or been framed for it, he needed to talk to her.

*I'm not who you think I am.*

*Right*, he thought, *like you won't be fighting them, trying to make things as difficult as possible. I don't know you at all.*

She was the key. She knew what was happening. More

importantly, she knew why. He wanted answers. She had them.

*What is it about the end of the world and women I've slept with?*

"Mr. Carter?"

Jake stopped.

"Excuse me, Mr. Carter?"

He saw a group of men off to the side of the waiting lounge. They stood in the shadows cast by the curving wall. They were watching him. One of them nodded as he looked their way. He knew the man. He'd seen him before today, a couple of times, without realizing he'd seen him. He'd been on the train at Times Square, but he'd been wearing a cop uniform then.

Jake walked over to them. "You've got me at a disadvantage." He stopped ten feet away: close enough to be heard without shouting, far enough to be well out of knife range. He didn't recognize the other two men, and yet, he sort of did in a way that he couldn't place, like he'd seen them before, in the background, but never really registered their presence.

All three wore business suits, dark slacks and dark button-downs and dark ties with long black trench coats over them. Men in black. Everything about the way they so desperately tried to blend in with the city screamed feds. All three looked slick, professional, but not exceptional, not memorable.

Then he remembered where he'd seen the second man: walking toward Wall Street. He'd led Jake straight into the New York Stock Exchange where this entire nightmare he was currently living began.

"That was you, wasn't it? Down at the stock exchange this morning?" He knew he was right, even though the man neither confirmed nor denied the allegation.

Instead, the guy came back with a question of his own: "Are you planning to stop The Hidden?"

He had no idea what that meant.

"And in English?"

The questioner's hair was touched with silver. He had a small, neat goatee that was streaked as well. There was a lapel pin on his coat, too small for Jake to make out the details, but it was silver and triangular, not gold, so it didn't match the one in his pocket. So what was this? Some really exclusive turf war where people with more money than sense were fighting for control of his city?

*You can hardly call it a war if only one of the factions is running around killing people.*

"Don't be coy, Mr. Carter."

"I'm not being coy. I have no clue what you're talking about."

"You aren't a very convincing liar. All I want to know is, are you trying to stop them or are you helping them? Think carefully about your answer. It's the most important question anyone has asked you in your life. Believe me."

The threat was implicit.

He took the gold pin from his pocket and held it in his clenched fist. "I've never heard of any Hidden people, apart from the mole men." His gaze drifted off toward the tracks. Probably not the best time to make a joke. "But assuming you mean these guys," he opened his hand to reveal the pin, "then yeah, I'm gonna stop them. Me and my army of one."

His questioner nodded, as did his companions behind him. "Good." He smiled. It wasn't any kind of smile Jake was comfortable being on the receiving end of. "That was the correct answer. Unfortunately, you are wasting time running around chasing shadows. The fight isn't out here, no matter how it might appear. If you want to influence the out-come of this fight you need to get dirty, and that means slay-ing the dragon in its den." There was a trash can up against the wall behind the men, just a standard city-issue bin. The man glanced over his shoulder and nodded. The third mem-ber of the trio reached into his jacket and pulled something out that Jake couldn't quite see. It was small and bright; he placed it atop the can.

"How much have you managed to piece together for yourself?" the watcher from the stock exchange slaying asked him.

Jake figured he had nothing to lose. "Some. It's all about money, it's not terrorism, whatever people are being led to think. It's about money and power."

"Leverage," the man agreed. "Control. With the right quantities of both you can convince people to do whatever you want, including slowly poisoning themselves. If I were to tell you that every day people willingly ingest a poison that was refused FDA approval thirty years ago, because it was proven to cause memory loss, seizures, vision loss, and cancer, to exacerbate and mimic the symptoms of conditions such as Alzheimer's and depression while the poisoning af-fects the dopamine system of the brain causing addiction, what would you say?" It was a rhetorical question, the guy didn't give him a chance to answer. "You'd tell me to get the hell out of here, I'm sure. We are talking about a deadly neurotoxic drug masquerading as an additive that interacts poorly with all antidepressants, L-DOPA, Coumadin, hor-mones, insulin, cardiac medications, and the like, and yet it's in circulation because of the kind of influence we are up against. The day of President Reagan's inauguration, his very first act in power was to ensure that this poison found a way through the safeguards of the FDA, appointing a new director to replace the original one who had stood in its way, and when the five-man committee looked like they were *still* going to refuse to rubber stamp the poison as fit for human consumption, he added a sixth man to put the vote into deadlock, allowing his hand-picked director to cast the tie-breaking vote in favor of poisoning the world for profit. The man who did that was then rewarded with a fat contract with the public relations firm who represented Monsanto, who are currently poisoning our food supply with genetic modifiers. But that's not the takeaway here, the takeaway is how far up the chain their influence goes, Mr. Carter. They were able to apply pressure on POTUS and get him to directly interfere with the process, overlooking the scuttled grand jury investigation of the company with a vested interest in the getting the poison into food, to overcome the recommendations of the Bressler Report, to ignore the PBOI's recommendations and pretend this toxin did not chronically sicken and kill thousands of lab animals."

Jake didn't know what to say.

"How's that Diet Coke looking to you now, Mr. Carter?" the man asked, nodding toward a kid tipping up a plastic bottle and downing the last of the black liquid inside.

"If you can force POTUS's hand, you have real power. These people have real power—beyond lobbyists and interest groups. They have the power to create political movements and get the very people they're subjugating to do their dirty work. Look at the Tea Party, a supposed grassroots movement of passionate, well-meaning people who think they are fighting elite power, fighting for the change they were promised by Obama that they are so sure he failed to deliver. But it's not grassroots. There is no mass mobilization, it's all

About the money behind it, and the irony that they are being stirred into action by the very interests they believe they are confronting. That so-called movement was established and guided with the help of money from billionaires and big business. They lavish money on advocacy groups that are instrumental in turning politicians away from environmental laws, social spending, taxing the rich, and distributing wealth. The only freedom they want is for corporations to trample the poor into the dirt while they profit. If there's a way to do this without getting your own hands dirty, leaving no trace you've been there even in this digital age, then that is the perfect storm . . . So now you know."

"Why? Why, if they've already got this kind of power, why would they risk everything by moving now? By doing this?"

"Much wants more, Mr. Carter, and ever it was thus. There is no loyalty, there is only the bottom line, and here we are talking in the billions, the greatest robbery ever known to man, unseen, unremarked on, but quite remarkable."

"That can't be enough. It just can't . . . People are dying out here. It's the end of the world as we know it and they're looking to make a fast buck? I'm not buying it. Not when they already have the kind of influence it takes to bend a president to their will. It's just . . . these are real people we're talking about, not just numbers on a balance sheet."

"It matters not. You are thinking like . . . well, like part of society. A man on the inside. These people are on the outside. Think of the world as a snow globe. No matter how much you shake it up, the flakes always fall. The chaos can be pretty for a while, but in the end you are always left with order. The chaos will return the next time someone shakes the globe, but eventually life will return to what it was. A certain type of people exploit the chaos so they have more control during the order."

"Okay, I get that, but it doesn't explain how they could know about the polar shift, what was going to happen, and prepare to exploit it like this."

"On the contrary, it absolutely explains it. Everything is for sale, even when you are facing an extinction event."

With that, the three of them simply turned and walked away without another word, which in the grand scheme of things was profoundly creepy. Jake's mind was reeling. He realized he'd have been happier if it had been terrorists. He knew how to fight al-Qaeda. How did you go toe-to-toe with the 1 Percent? Because that was what he was being asked to do, wasn't he? You couldn't fight that kind of power. It just wasn't possible.

He missed yesterday when things had been simple and all he'd been worried about was pulling a double shift.

He watched them go.

There was no point in running after them. He'd entered a world of poison pills secreted in porcelain teeth. They wouldn't give up any answers they weren't absolutely prepared to. The only thing he could do was see what little gift they'd left him on top of the trash can.

It was a business card.

Jake picked it up. It was made of good thick card stock, smooth rather than rough, and a gleaming, pristine white. One side was blank, although Jake detected irregularities in the surface as his finger ran over it. Some kind of textured embossing? He held it to the light. There was no indication of any hidden message within. On the other side was an address handwritten in pen. It was up near 91st Street, on the West Side of Manhattan.

He had no idea how the fuck he was supposed to slay a dragon, but he was pretty sure he'd just been handed the address to its den.

And he knew their name now—even if it sounded like something you'd more likely call a super-villain than a sect trying to bring down civilization—which was more than he'd known an hour ago.

He couldn't decide if he was more screwed because he was going face-to-face with the dragon or because he was the bait.

# CHAPTER THIRTY-ONE

"**M**IND IF I JOIN YOU?"

Sophie pocketed her phone. She had no idea if the call would make a difference. A lot depended on Jake Carter. She was banking on him being the same guy he'd been back then in the once-upon-a-time part of the fairy tale. Because the Jake she knew would make a difference.

She started to push back her chair to stand when she realized there was a woman looking expectantly at the empty chair across from her. She blocked Sophie's path to the door.

"No need, it's all yours, I'm done," Sophie replied, then saw the small circular gold pin on the woman's expensively tailored lapel. The symbol was unmistakable, hiding who she was—what she was a part of—in plain sight.

That pin changed everything.

Sophie scanned the room, trying to locate her backup. There was no way one of the top brass would come out alone. Sophie couldn't see anyone, which was so much worse than knowing exactly where the crosshairs were pointing at her from.

She turned her attention to the woman in front of her. She was tall, almost six feet, giving her a real reach advantage if it came down to an old-fashioned fistfight. Her deportment was good, straight back, well balanced. She had the quiet confidence of someone who knew they could handle themselves if things turned nasty. Her hands were empty, but her jacket had large pockets that could have hidden an arsenal. Her eyes were so dark there was no distinction between pupil and iris, just deep black wells. They were cold, careful, cautious, and completely unconcerned.

They were the eyes of a killer.

"Xbalanque," she said, putting two and two together. They'd lost faith with Cabrakan after the stock exchange debacle. She was looking at the cavalry.

"Sit down, please. Let's try to be civil about this, we're both women of the world." The woman inclined her head toward the seat Sophie had just vacated. "This doesn't have to get ugly. I've heard so much about you, Sophie. You're something of a legend from where I'm standing. I hope you'll do me the honor of breaking bread before we end this?"

Sophie didn't have a lot of choice. With no idea where the assassin's backup was, the odds of her making it out of the coffee shop alive diminished rapidly. She could turn it into a combat zone, create enough confusion to disappear, but the tables were too close together, and in the last couple of minutes too many people had clustered around the screen watching the news bulletin. There was no easy way out of the front door.

Of course, she could always pull a Han Solo and shoot first. It seriously crossed her mind. Her pistol was in her coat's front pocket. She wouldn't try to draw it, just shoot through the lining. It would save a couple of seconds, but if

Xbalanque was as good as her reputation, those couple of seconds might just make all the difference.

She nodded, trying to appear gracious, and sat.

Xbalanque joined her at the table, and to the rest of the world they looked like old friends catching up.

Sophie felt like she was looking in a mirror—not one that reflected the outside appearance, one that went beyond looks and reflected the inner you. Mannerisms, training, instinct, and the deeper, darker parts of her soul. This woman was her ten years ago. Fiercely loyal to The Hidden, just as she'd been, eager to prove herself to her paymasters, just as Sophie had been, willing to do anything to advance herself within the cause, exactly as Sophie had been right up until she hadn't been. No doubt Xbalanque had her own line. Would she lose her soul and cross it?

"So," Sophie said after a few seconds of silence had stretched between them, "we're sitting, there's no bread. Tell me, all bullshit aside, what are you hoping to get out of this?"

"I'm here to offer you an olive branch, Sophie. I've been asked to bring you back into the fold. I'd like to make that happen. I really would, but my orders were ambiguous."

"Of course they were. It's called plausible deniability. You'll get used to it."

The assassin's lips curled into a hungry smile. "No one said you needed to be breathing when I brought you home."

"I should be flattered, I suppose."

"I would be."

"You know what they're doing, don't you? They must have told you," she tried reason, testing just how much of the woman's soul was intact. She had to. She needed to give the girl a chance to do the right thing. "You know how many people it'll hurt. You know the kind of suffering we're talking here. It's inhuman. We can't let that happen—we can't just sit by and watch this city, every city, burn while they adjust it."

"You've mistaken me for someone who gives a shit . . . This isn't my problem," the other woman replied. "I've got a job to do."

"No. If you're the new me, you're better than that. I am. I have a brain. I know how to think. I know when something is fundamentally evil."

"You're broken. That's why I'm here."

Sophie shook her head, doing her best to keep her voice level. "This is blind obedience you're offering them, the callous disregard for anything and everything, it's got a name. It's not a pretty name. There's nothing noble about it. It's nihilism. The love of nothing and the desire to return to that nothing. Do you recognize that? Do you think you can absolve yourself of any guilt by saying you're following orders? If you do genuinely believe that, let me be the first to disabuse you of that notion, you know, being as how I was you before you were. You make a conscious decision every time you accept a job. You make a conscious decision every time you pull the trigger."

The other woman sighed. "Fine. I make a choice. Are you happy now?" She waved over one of the staff and ordered a hot tea, then glanced at Sophie. "What can I get you?"

"Nothing else for me, thanks." Sophie wasn't comfortable with the whole old-friends routine. But a cup of steaming hot tea in her replacement's face could prove decisive. "Actually, make mine a chai, thanks."

The waitress nodded and left them to it.

"So, you're here to kill me?" It came out a little more

brazenly than she'd intended, but Sophie felt like laying down a gauntlet. She'd always had a problem with people telling her how something was going to happen. No respect for authority, as the old school reports used to say. She just felt the need to prove them wrong.

Xbalanque simply nodded. "You're not walking out of here, Sophie. It ends here. You know that. Don't make it any more unpleasant than it needs to be. Death comes to us all. Today I'm better than you. Tomorrow it could be my turn. That's just the circle of life." She reached into her coat.

Sophie tensed, expecting a gun, wondering when the damned waitress would return with her hot chai. But it wasn't a gun; the woman pulled out a silver hip flask. It had The Hidden's mark lightly embossed across it, just shallow enough that you might not notice the markings in dim light.

"Think of it as kindness. I'm letting you decide how this ends." She set the flask down on the table between them. "The flask represents a choice. You like choices, right? So, you can either take the easy way"—she tapped the flask— "or, to use a terrible cliché, the hard way." Again she smiled, and it felt real.

"Don't tell me—you'd recommend the easy way?"

"Oh, fuck no, I want you to go for it," she grinned. "I want you to try to live, it's so much more fun that way. There's no enjoyment in it if you just sip from the poisoned chalice, now, is there?"

The flask no doubt held vodka or whiskey, laced with a fast-acting, relatively painless poison. She'd used similar herself. It didn't leave any clear trace evidence behind for the autopsy, its effects mirroring the natural causes of a violent heart attack.

"Ah, the arrogance of youth. I remember that."

"You sound like an old woman."

"In this life, I am. You'll come to understand that if you're lucky. I'm surprised though, I expected them to want me to suffer for turning against them." She was stalling for time, waiting for that damned chai to arrive.

"Oh, they do want you to suffer," Xbalanque answered sweetly. "Mr. Alom gave me explicit instructions to hurt you as much as possible before the end. I'm the one making you the offer. Call it a professional courtesy."

Sophie studied the flask carefully, then slowly reached out for it.

"You know . . . I didn't think you'd do it," Xbalanque said, almost disappointed, as Sophie unscrewed the silver cap.

She raised the flask to her lips as if to toast her companion and, when the other woman's posture relaxed, drank deep but didn't swallow. She spat the laced vodka into Xbalanque's eyes.

The woman was on her feet in a heartbeat. She shoved her chair back, its legs scraping loudly on the café's tiled floor as she roared at Sophie. Her face contorted in pain and she tipped the table up, sending Sophie's empty cup crashing to the floor. The bite of the poison had already turned the soft skin around her eyes an angry red as it burrowed into her system, absorbed by her skin. "You absolute fucking *bitch*!"

Sophie didn't waste time on words. She tried to push her way past the screaming woman, when a shadow crossed her path. Before she could react she felt a sharp stinging pain in the side of her neck.

"Well that was an anticlimax," the other woman said, the needle in her hand disappearing back into her coat pocket. Her eyes burned red as if she'd been crying. "You couldn't just give up, could you? You had to go and make a mess. I don't know if I even have the strength to clean it up. But who cares? People will remember our little dance, and I'm not even sure it matters if they recognize your face when they see it on the news later." She touched her cheek. "I don't even know if I'll be around to take the shit for screwing up. So much for trying to be nice."

Sophie had cleaned up plenty of times, wiping down tables and chairs, any surfaces she'd come into contact with, to remove fingerprints and DNA traces that might have been left behind. Then there was the visual stuff, scrubbing the footage from the video cameras and disposing of the body, most likely playing the concerned friend, or just calling an ambulance to have the corpse collected and save all the heavy lifting.

The only problem was Sophie didn't want to go gently into that endless winter night.

She had no intention of sticking to the script. She was dying anyway.

They only amassed power by being hidden.

She had a few seconds to bring them out into the light, and hope that her words would go viral.

She grabbed her replacement by the scruff of the neck and yelled, "*What have you done to me?*" into her face. Every single conversation in the little café stopped. All heads turned.

"That was a needle! You stabbed me with a fucking *needle*. What did you do? Poison me? Did you poison me?" She clutched at her neck again, making sure people saw exactly what she was doing. It was theater. Her skin felt sticky under her fingers. There was blood. Good. She deliberately smeared it to make the puncture wound more obvious. Everyone was staring at them.

"Don't be stupid, Soph, you're imagining things," the other woman said softly, both hands out and clearly empty now. "Come on, let's get you out of here. I'm sorry, everyone, she's off her meds. I'm really sorry."

"Funny woman. Do you want to explain how you just blew up the stock exchange?" Sophie demanded. "How about the sabotage of the Channel Tunnel, the Underground, the airports? Tell them, whoever you are, tell them why you came here to kill me. Let's speak frankly, no more lies. Tell them about The Hidden. Tell them what's happening. Confession is good for the soul, Xbalanque. We're both going to meet our makers, let's find absolution in the truth."

The assassin looked worried. Her face showed red vines in her cheeks, like an alcoholic.

Sophie knew what it meant: the poison was working its way into her system too. Two for the price of one. Sophie grabbed the other woman's wrist.

People were paying attention. Even if they didn't understand what it was they were hearing, they were going to remember it.

"You're delusional," Xbalanque argued, but there was no conviction to it. She tried to break free of Sophie's grasp, but Sophie wasn't letting go.

"We'll see. We're going nowhere. We're going to stand here until we're dead. Oh yes, I can see the red vines under your skin. That's why I spat in your eyes, they're not just gateways to the soul. Our deaths will convince everyone who's telling the truth." She turned to face the baristas behind the counter, the waitress steaming the chai she'd never drink. "They call themselves The Hidden, but really they're just some very rich men and women who are frightened of you, and because they're frightened of you they are trying to take control of everything that you could ever use to rise up against them." She didn't need to shout; the place was deathly quiet. Even the killer had settled down and was now just sitting there glaring at her. "That's what they do. You've seen their marks painted on the walls, those hieroglyphs on the walls at Piccadilly and everywhere else, they're secret symbols, but they're not passing messages, they paid street artists to put down those markers, they mean this territory is theirs. They want it to feel like there are groups, gangs, rising up around you, that the streets aren't safe, so you'll turn to them to make you feel safe. But that's a lie. It's not about that. It's everything they pretend it isn't. It's a Mayan ritual. They are invoking the old gods. Why do you think you're without power?"

She knew she sounded like a nutcase but there was so much she wanted to say and she could feel her throat closing up, each word more difficult to utter than the last.

"That's how they operate." She clutched at her temples. "You need to open your eyes and look around you! These people have been amassing power for years, taking it from you while you willingly hand it over. You might as well call them Pied Pipers . . . Just look at what they do. First through control of the media."

She needed to get this out, and hope that the security footage had sound. If it didn't, then hope that someone walked out of there, told a friend what they'd just heard, who would tell a friend, who would tell a friend, so the truth would go viral.

"They make sure you hear what they *want* you to hear, think what they want you to think. They own you body and soul, APR locked in without you even realizing. It's all about money and power. Control. They've taken communication networks, satellites, and cell phone networks. They own the utilities you consume, they even own the fucking money in your pocket. That's the magic here. Control those things, you control *everything*."

She was rambling, losing them. She needed to make them understand what was at stake but it was getting harder and harder to focus on the words and what she wanted to say. She needed to unmask them. Xbalanque stood stock still, gaping at her.

"It's not just tracking cell phones and knowing where everyone is. It's not just about monitoring e-mails or buying habits or anything else . . . It's about how if you can see the hidden symmetry, if you can piece different parts of the puzzle together, you can predict the future. If you can do that, even a few seconds ahead of anyone else, you can own the world. Think about it: a guy comes out of the doctor's and makes a call to an oncologist's office, but before the call's even connected, and without access to his medical records, a system set up to match those two numbers will know he's got cancer. But it goes beyond that. They know his insurance company and if it's going to take a hit, they know his job, everything about him and his buying habits, his house and the amount left on his mortgage, and all they need to know to turn this guy's life upside is the telephone number he called. They can sort the rest out, and they can work out how to *profit* from it." She couldn't tell if they were following her, if she was being clear with what she was saying now. "There are no secrets in the modern world. Knowledge. That's how you control the people who stand in your way." She was breathless, sweating. "But I've got news for you." She looked toward the lens of the CCTV in the corner. "You can't control everyone. It's too much. No amount of Mayan rituals and mumbo jumbo will help you. There's always one person who will say, *Fuck you, I won't do what you tell me,* and this time that's me." She looked away from the camera toward a mother wrestling with a newborn in a pink shawl, trying to settle the baby down. "That's why they've killed me. Because I've stopped doing their dirty work. Because I'm standing up to them." She peered at the diners, each and every one of them. "Look at me. Remember my face. Remember what I'm saying here." And then she gazed back at Xbalanque. "And now they've lost you, so who else will do their dirty work? Who else will kill the people who stand between them and what they want?" She grinned at the other woman, and knew she looked insane.

"There's always someone else," Xbalanque said. "We're not indispensable." She stepped in close, like a lover, seeming to embrace her. "Let's talk about this outside, Sophie, people don't need to hear us airing our dirty laundry."

But Sophie wasn't going anywhere. She dug deep into the reserves of her rapidly dwindling strength and rammed her fist into the other woman's stomach, doubling her up in pain. When her head came up another dozen red vines had cracked across the brittle skin. "You *murdered* me. That's more than fucking laundry."

She landed another punch before one of the diners moved to intervene.

Any sense of strategy or combat technique was gone. She didn't have the time or strength, she just wanted to hurt this woman in as public and memorable a way as possible. There'd be no brushing her murder under the carpet. If she'd known even a single one of her old paymaster's names she'd have been yelling them at the top of her lungs right now. All she could do was shout, "Remember these names:

Alom, Ah Puch, Hunhau, Ixtab, Ah Uuc Ticab, Camazotz, Kinich Ahau, Kinich Kakmo! Remember them! These are the people running the world!" It wouldn't help. No one would remember them, and even if they did, what had she given them? A list of dead gods and goddesses? She hadn't said half of what she wanted to say, but it didn't matter, they wouldn't remember it. It all just sounded like the ravings of a lunatic.

Any semblance of family squabble disappeared when Xbalanque pulled a knife. The move was too quick and she was too close for Sophie to deflect it in her weakened state.

Sophie felt the blade enter her side, a searing sensation that shot deep into her belly. The assassin dragged the knife sideways, making damned sure it *hurt* as she pulled it back out as well, leaving a gaping wound across Sophie's torso. The gash soaked her shirt and coat in blood as the life pumped out of her.

Sophie gasped, gritting her teeth against the sheer agony of death and the flood of poison as she came undone. Her vision was dark around the edges. She tried to hold herself up, but fell forward on the table, toppling it with a crash, and onto the floor. She didn't feel it. She couldn't feel anything anymore, there was so much pain it had simply ceased to register.

Xbalanque leaned down over her, the red vines like thick stubby fingers clawing at her face. "I wish you hadn't made me do that."

"I didn't *make* you do anything," Sophie said. "You had a *choice*. You could have just stood here . . . and died . . . with me. Now they . . . *know*. Are you going . . . to kill . . . them . . . all?" She smiled, or tried to, but she was having trouble getting her mouth to work properly. She could taste the blood welling up in her throat. She was going to drown in it before she bled out.

"Yes," Xbalanque said. "Every fucking last one of them, and it's your fault." She spat blood with each word.

"You won't have time," Sophie said, as darkness rushed in to envelope her. She felt warmth and a blessed numbness wash over her. She would be long dead before Jake picked up her message. She had done everything she could. Now it was up to him.

# CHAPTER THIRTY-TWO

"JESUS SHIT!"

Finn knew she should stay calm, try to reason with him, look for a way out, something, but with him standing right there, so close she could taste the peppermint on his breath, his cold eyes staring into hers, and the gun in his hand, panic was the only thing she could do.

The sheer vehemence of her reaction startled him. He reeled back from her outburst as if he expected her to hit him.

And, suddenly, she knew exactly what to do.

"We're gonna die in here! We're gonna die! Help me! Help me! I don't wanna die!" she wailed as loud as she could, banging her fists against his chest. "I don't wanna die!" It wouldn't win her any Oscars, but it did what it was meant to do. He grabbed her wrists to keep her from hitting him again, and backed away at the same time, keeping a good three feet of space between them.

"Take it easy, lady," he said, his tone completely different now. All traces of the gruff homeless guy were gone, as were those crazy staring killer eyes. "Let's just calm down, okay?

Nice and easy does it. No one's going to kill you. It's okay."
He looked like the very definition of Joe Average and talked
to her the same way he'd talk to an anxious pet. She half-
expected him to stroke her hair.

"Calm down?" she screamed, pushing herself right up
into his face. She was beginning to enjoy herself. "How can
I calm down? Don't you know what's happening here? Don't
you get it? Don't you understand? The storms, the dogs, the
birds falling from the sky . . . All the lights are out! There's
no power anywhere in the city . . . in the *world*! Look out
there, the streets are dark and cold, there are dogs and worse
prowling around looking for food . . . Without the generator,
we'd be left in the dark. They won't last forever. Then what?
You know what it is? Do you? Do you? I'll tell you what it is,
it's the end of the world!" And she let herself sag a bit as she
started to sob.

She was overselling the whole hysterical-woman act. It
was far too cheesy to be believable. No one in their right
mind was going to buy it. And yet, this guy totally did.

He dropped her wrists like they were burning hot, and
put a little more space between them, mumbling something
under his breath. Then dipped his hand into a filthy pocket
and offered her a handkerchief. A clean white linen one.

For a second she didn't know what she was supposed to
do with it, then she took it from him and rubbed her nose
and eyes and chin with it before blowing her snotty nose into
it, leaving it sticky and gross. She tried offering it back to
him, still crying, amazed that the tears were suddenly real.
She'd tapped hidden reserves of thespian talent.

"No, no, it's fine. You hang on to it," he said, still keeping
a safe distance between them. The last thing he wanted to do
was have her suddenly move in for a reassuring hug. It was

almost enough to make her drop the act and burst out laughing; tough-guy killer passing himself off as a bum freaked out by a few crocodile tears.

But she didn't let on.

Instead she slouched forward a little and then swayed to the side until she found herself leaning against the command center's wall. She slowly slid down it until she was a crumpled heap at its base, just a few feet away from the door she really wanted to go through.

The man stayed where he was, seemingly not sure if he should comfort her or just put her out of her misery. In the end, it wasn't his choice to make.

"What the hell's going on out here?" The voice preceded the groan of the command center's door opening. A man appeared and he didn't look pleased. He had a darker complexion than the fake hobo, with long shaggy hair that hung in thick greasy clumps around his dirt-smudged face. He wore tattered clothing that was held together by the grime crusted into it, but had that same alertness about him as his partner. That, and a very similar-looking gun.

"Nothing, man, nothing, it's all good," the first guy said, crossing the hall in a hurry to stand by the partially open door so she couldn't see in. "Just some crazy broad. It's all good."

The second guy grunted, pissed, but pushed the door the rest of the way open and exited the command center. He didn't look toward her once. It must have been the weirdest fancy dress party of all time in there, she thought, as two more men emerged after him, both dressed down to look like they lived on the streets. It was a good way to go unnoticed up here. People didn't see the homeless in New York, they just ebbed and flowed like so much flotsam in the river of the American Dream. The third man turned a curious eye on Finn before dismissing her as irrelevant and turning his attention to the second hobo.

"Let's go," he said after the door slid shut behind the last man.

All four of them walked back down the hall. They barely even acknowledge she existed, which was just fine by her. Even able to study them now, she wasn't sure she'd be able to recognize them in a lineup without all of the crap they were covered in. It was an effective disguise.

Finn waited until she was sure they were gone before she stopped sobbing. She blew her nose again on the borrowed handkerchief and sat up, brushing a few errant strands of hair out of her face.

She looked around—no sign of the men. She couldn't hear the dull echo of approaching footsteps either.

She was alone in the hall. It had worked.

The question now was whether she could reverse whatever it was they'd done. She thought about calling Jake, but she wasn't in trouble. He was a line of last resort.

She pushed herself to her feet and tried the door again. This time no one stopped her.

Inside, the Operations Control Center for all of Port Authority was unimpressive, except for the fact that it appeared to have power. There were a handful of desks set around the room's outer wall, each with a couple of monitors and a battered desk chair in front of it. She wasn't sure if the room was shielded, if the men had brought in a generator, or if power was starting to return on its own accord, but across the far wall was an entire array of fully functioning flat-screen displays. The flickering from them cast the room in an eerie glow. The nine screens alternated views of various locations within the Port Authority complex. She saw one fixed on the hallway just outside where she'd run afoul of the hobo. Finn kept half an eye on it as she walked over to one of the desks and hit the space bar on the keyboard to wake the computer.

She didn't want to think about what would happen to her if those guys came back. She focused on the monitor instead. It showed what looked like an Excel spreadsheet, all number-and-letter combinations and blinking lines. It was a timetable, she realized after a few seconds of confusion. That made sense. The control center kept track of when each bus was scheduled to arrive and depart, and determined which bay they should use so that there wasn't a backup or a collision on the tight ramps.

Right now everything was on hold, hence the blinking lines instead of times. What she didn't know was how that could help the four men she'd seen leave. What good did it do them to interfere with a schedule that would be updated manually the minute things returned to normal?

There was absolutely nothing beneficial about hacking into a manual system that would change every single day of the week. Unless they'd put in a way to override the updates.

She clicked around, looking for options, and found one under *Preferences*. When she followed the chain of commands she was offered a *Remote Access* option. The box had been checked, an IP address entered. So that was it. They had reset the system so they could log in remotely and change the schedule any time they liked. It wasn't exactly the crime of the century.

How had it gone from looking at glyphs carved into an ancient wall to trying to bring down a complex public transport computer system in less than twenty-four hours?

She shook her head. No point attempting to make sense of it.

When she tried clicking off the remote access, a pop-up demanded her authorization. She hit *Return*. It told her: *You do not have authorization to alter these settings*. Which was rich, all things considered. Since she didn't know the passwords to get in, she needed an alternative.

Finn sank into a chair, planted her elbows on the desk, and stared at the screen. Her gaze flicked back to the rack of nine screens on the wall, making sure the men weren't coming back. Not that she expected them to—they'd gotten what they wanted.

She needed to think. There had to be *something* she could do, even if it was as simple as turn it off and turn it on again, the regular sysop joke in college. Whenever anything went wrong that was always the first response: have you tried restarting it?

She didn't think it would work here. But if she couldn't figure something out, when the buses started running again they'd have full control.

Finn started banging randomly on the keys. She hit multiple keys in combination, trying different configurations and mashing down like a toddler trying to control the computer by sheer brute force. Several new windows popped up as a result of her efforts, and strings of nonsense appeared in various cells here and there, but still she kept at it, hitting the keys harder and faster and earning warnings about authorization that she willfully ignored until the beeps of protest became a one-note concerto.

Finally she must have hit just the right combination—or, in this case, the wrong one—and the screen went dark. Then it turned a bright, blank blue.

The Blue Screen of Death.

She'd crashed the system.

Finn rooted around under the desk for the master power switch and shut the computers off. All of them. She counted to ten then added ten more for good luck before she flipped the switch back on. Then she waited.

She didn't dare to so much as breathe. Everything rested on this. After thirty agonizing seconds, the power lights on the various computers began to blink. The monitors woke back up next. And then, on one monitor after another, she read the same message: *System damage detected. Restore to last safe restore point? Y/N.*

*Safe restore* sounded absolutely idyllic, though of course there was nothing to say the hobos hadn't set the restore point after they'd screwed around inside the system. But she'd cross that metaphorical bridge when she came to it. Finn stabbed at the *Y* key and the computer acknowledged her choice: *Restoring default settings. Please wait.*

She watched as the screens showed the percentage that had been rebuilt. *70%, 80%, 90%, 95%, 99% . . . 100%. Default settings restored. Restarting system.*

There was a whine as the computers shut down, a sharp click and then a whir as they started back up again. And this time, once they'd warmed up, they showed the MTA logo as a startup page, with spaces for users to enter their logins and passwords.

She didn't have the passwords, so she had no idea if she'd done it, but hopefully standard settings didn't include the remote access patch they'd put in. They could always come back and repeat the process, but Jake had been fairly sure they were running on a detailed—tight—time line. Anything that messed with that bought precious minutes or hours for normality to reassert itself outside.

She could do one more thing to make it even more difficult for them to get back in. She rooted through the desks, looking for what she needed: a long wire paperclip. After she'd closed the door behind her, she inserted it into the lock and gave the slim piece of metal a vicious twist so that it snapped in half—half still between her fingers, the rest embedded in the lock. They wouldn't be able to pick the lock, and breaking the door down would attract attention. Attention seemed like the last thing these guys wanted. Of course, the MTA wouldn't be able to get back in either until a locksmith had undone the damage she'd caused.

Finn smiled to herself as she tossed the broken paperclip aside and walked away.

She'd done it. She'd had to improvise, and she'd broken her promise to Jake not to get too close, but she'd done it. She'd not only found them, she'd thwarted their plan. She was a regular Nancy fucking Drew, she thought to herself, grinning as she exited Port Authority.

Now it was down to Jake.

She wanted to check in with him, see how things were going at Penn and if he needed her to go somewhere else. She was fired up. She really wanted to tell him how she'd fooled the fake hobo and screwed with their hack, but without knowing what was happening where he was, she had no way of knowing if a call would betray him.

She'd just have to wait for him to check in with her.

*He's a soldier*, she thought. *He can handle himself.*

As she walked back out into the cold of the winter, she saw the first few flakes of snow drifting down. It was the absolutely last thing the city needed. Snow.

Up ahead she saw a group of men in uniform. Soldiers. The cavalry had arrived.

# CHAPTER THIRTY-THREE

"ZACCIMI IS DEAD," THE ASSASSIN SAID.

"She lost the rights to that name when she turned against us," Mr. Alom countered. "Sophie Keane is dead. Well done. Cabrakan has covered our tracks in London; though the explosion may draw more attention than we would have liked, it will effectively purge our presence from the financial district. Today is a good day."

"Not really. She killed me."

He paused a beat, as though trying to process her last few words. "I don't understand."

"Poison. I have minutes, maybe fifteen if I'm lucky, before it stops my heart. It's already hard to focus and think."

"Antidote?"

"Too late. The race is run."

"You have served us well, Xbalanque. May the lords of death find use for your unique talents."

She remained silent.

"Was there something else?"

The assassin said nothing.

"I do not like silence. What is it?"

"Before she died, she exposed us."

"How?"

"She named you, she unloaded everything she knew in public."

"Who did she talk to? I need to know everything. Be very clear in your account, soldier."

"She grandstanded in a café. Fifty, sixty people inside."

"And where are you now?"

"Outside."

"Has anyone left?"

"Not that I have seen."

"Good. Contain the situation."

"I might not have the time left," she said simply. It had nothing to do with the fact that fifty more deaths would weigh heavily on her soul as she made the journey to the afterlife, or anything like that. It was purely practical. Killing fifty people took time. She didn't have the ammunition, for one, and she couldn't very well ask them all to sip poison-laced lattes. Unlike Cabrakan she had no access to explosives either—and given the black mess of the sky behind her, he'd probably used all of his.

"Then find another way. Make your last fifteen minutes with us about limiting the damage. It is too late to silence Sophie Keane, but it is not too late to make sure nothing she said leaves that café. You are industrious when it comes to death. I have faith in you."

Mr. Alom hung up.

He hadn't given her a choice.

But that didn't mean she couldn't make one anyway.

Zaccimi's words came back to her: *Do you think you can*

*absolve yourself of any guilt by saying you're following orders? . . . You*
*make a conscious decision every time you pull the trigger.*

The dead woman was right: she did make a choice. And right now she had another one to make. Yes, it was blind obedience. She understood this. But that didn't make saying no any more likely. She stood there with her hand on the door, looking at the young mother putting her baby back into the buggy.

*You make a conscious decision . . .*

She opened the door.

# CHAPTER THIRTY-FOUR

T HE ADDRESS ON THE CARD HAD LED HIM to an old brownstone. He arrived as night fell, before the storm broke.

There was nothing really remarkable about the building itself—it was one of the wider ones, with large bay windows flanking the front door, five stories tall plus a subbasement below the entrance stairs. It was made entirely of dark brown stone rather than brick, meaning it was a proper brownstone—apart from the fact that it was patrolled by obviously armed, obviously well-trained, obviously on-high-alert guards.

*Who are you people? Really. Not just some made-up name . . . Who are you?*

He watched the guards pace around the front gates. The suit at Penn had called them The Hidden. He'd also called them a dragon. A dragon, Jake saw, that was equipped with automatic rifles and God only knows what other ordinance.

Jake sat on a stoop a couple of hundred yards away, rolling a cigarette so he looked like any other guy taking a load off, and ran through the most immediate problem he faced—how to get in there.

His phone started vibrating in his pocket. He assumed it was Finn letting him know how things had gone down at Port Authority. But it wasn't her, it was an alert from his voice mail.

He dialed in, assuming it was telemarketers or some other sign that the world wasn't in fact ending and that the vermin who preyed on people were already out in force trying to sell them shit they didn't need.

He listened to the message.

It was Sophie: *"I'm not going to say I'm sorry again, Jake. You know I am. I'm banking on the hope that you'll do the right thing. Remember the girl I was, not the woman they are telling everyone I became. I'm neither. Both, I guess. But I can't get out of this now. I have to see it through to the end. I've done things I'm not proud of. Things I should never have done. And I've gotten you mixed up in all this. I've sent you out to fight Goliath and forgotten to give you any stones for your sling. You need stones. I'm going to send you something. Use it well. And try not to hate me, Jake. I'm not a bad person. I just messed up. We've all done that, haven't we?"* The message was time coded over an hour ago.

As he hung up, his phone hummed again, an incoming text message. There was an attachment. When he opened it, he saw a crazed black-and-white square like a Mondrian block painting filling the tiny screen. It was a QR code, a square barcode with information embedded inside. It was by far the most intricate one he'd ever seen. Every QR code had smaller squares in the top two corners and in the bottom left, but normally those took up almost a fifth of the total space. On this code, the squares were so small they were barely visible to the naked eye, drowning in random pixelated lines. If a normal QR code could hold a URL, this one could probably store an entire book. Or at least an e-mail, he realized.

Which meant there could be another message within Sophie's message. Secrets within secrets, Jake thought, answers hidden in plain sight. These secrets were going to have to wait a few minutes. He couldn't get at them right now anyway, since he first had to storm a barricaded building single-handed. He put his phone away.

He wasn't getting in through the front door unless he came back with some serious ordinance of his own. Even if the house had a back garden or patio, which a lot of the older brownstones did, it would be secured. Short of parachuting in, he didn't have a lot of options. He looked up at the darkening sky.

That wasn't true; there was one: below.

No one expected an attack from below. He knew this city—and especially its tunnel systems—like the back of his hand. He was basically a mole man. He spent most of his days down there, using long-forgotten access tunnels, cattle tunnels that weren't on any map, and of course the original drainage sewers that predated modern Manhattan.

His sense of spatial awareness, overlaying the map of the city below on the city streets above, was sharp, and pushing himself up from the stoop and starting down the block back toward Broadway, he realized that there was a chance, a slim one, but a chance. This was more than he'd had a few minutes ago.

When his phone vibrated again, he snatched it up thinking it was Sophie. It wasn't. It was Ryan.

The conversation was brief, Jake trying to say no, Ryan refusing to listen. It ended with Jake promising to meet up with him before he went underground, Ryan convincing him that assuming he did manage to infiltrate this secret society's ultrasecret lair, the answers he was looking for weren't going to be in a folder conveniently labeled *The Truth*. He was going to need Ryan.

Jake didn't have a counterargument.

Half an hour later they trudged along the 1 line.

They'd entered the tunnels at the 96th Street station, grateful to duck out of the swirling storm as it finally took hold. There was a raised walkway along the side for MTA workers, which saved them from splashing through sewage and detritus that accumulated down there, and meant they weren't walking directly on the wooden sleepers of the tracks either.

That didn't change the fact that it was dark, dank, and reeked of filth and putrescence. Mercifully, there were no trains.

The Maglite Jake had acquired back at the relay station offered a little light. Ryan had come equipped, bringing a second, more powerful flashlight. Yet together they barely scratched the dark surface of the world below.

They kept moving. They didn't talk, even though Ryan clearly had a thousand questions.

The subway tunnel walls were covered in graffiti—not all words and tags either. In New York, every available surface inevitably became an artist's canvas, especially where they weren't supposed to go. There were whole abandoned tunnel systems down here that were covered in so much paint they looked like the inside of a clown car, all riotous color and motion. The tags and images were sparser but still present, including a stick figure of a man running, a strange flower with a grinning evil smiley face at its center. There were eerily accurate renditions of the mayor of New York sucking an oversized cock right beside a caricature of Hillary fingering herself to a caption of *I still believe in a place called Hope.* That was as political a polemic as the underworld could offer. Equal-opportunity homemade porn. Ryan read a line out loud, *"God is nowhere. God is now here.* Trippy." His voice carried far too loudly in the darkness but Jake didn't shush him. That would have been worse.

It was a veritable gallery of street art. Some of it went back before Giuliani's reign, a time capsule back to the six-ties and seventies. Bob Marley smoked a giant reefer beside a newer painting of Kurt Cobain and Courtney with a decla-ration of *She shot the sheriff.*

Jake figured they were almost back down near 91st now. They kept on walking. The art changed to a commentary on bankers, making the obvious visual gag.

A minute later a subway platform came into view. They kept on walking. It was the old 91st Street station, which had closed nearly sixty years before when the platform at 96th was extended. Closed meant that the stairs had been re-moved and the entrances at ground level sealed. Everything else remained. The tracks still ran through the old station stop, right past the deserted platforms.

As near as Jake could guess, they had to be somewhere close to the brownstone now. They hadn't walked quite as far as the platform. "You don't have to do this," he whispered to Ryan.

"Are we gonna go through this again? Von'll kill me if I let anything happen to you. So, like it or not, you're stuck with me. Or, more accurately, I'm stuck with you."

"I'm serious."

"Deadly. Now, *shhh,* unless you want to get us caught."

They began looking around, scanning the walls with their loops of cable and nailed wooden planking. The place was a warren of maintenance tunnels, complete with exits going off in seemingly every direction imaginable apart from up. Most of those tunnels came out in public buildings or between them, but if someone had wanted a place with its own escape hatch, they could have bought property directly above one of the old entrances and incorporated it into their own building. These guys had money; they were devious and secretive.

Jake was banking on them having secured a way out. It would involve real long-term thinking, but given everything he'd seen so far, these guys were playing exactly that game, and today's events were very much the latest in a long line of well-executed moves. Buying the perfect building for their needs—months, even years in advance—didn't seem like such a stretch.

The walls here were covered in years of grime and dirt and cast-off oil, but mixed in with the dark smears and spots were slashes and swirls of brighter color. Two splashes were made by a pair of weird symbols somewhere between drawings and oddly shaped letters.

Jake paused; they looked familiar. He shone the light directly on them. They were the same scrawls that the two graffiti artists had daubed on the walls right before the place blew up with them shouting about warriors. They were remarkably similar, if not identical.

"Over here," he whispered. He ran the flashlight over the wall, ignoring the symbols themselves for a moment, instead looking for the shadows of a door. The wall was as unbroken and dirty as everything around it.

Ryan shone his own light all around the surface, letting it linger along the ground while he searched for telltale scratches. Nothing.

Frustrated, Jake kicked out, catching something that might have been a piece of burnt, twisted metal that had fallen from a train but could just as easily have been a lump of coal or a fire-blackened brick. It shattered from the force of the blow, fragments flying in a powdery explosion. Shreds of newspaper that had been stuck to the lump floated free, springing up before wafting slowly back down again.

Jake watched one of wisps of old paper drift down right by the wall, seemingly sliding halfway under it before finally settling to rest. He crouched down to study the spot where it landed. "Bring the light over here."

Sure enough, he could just make out the darker shadow of a tiny gap beneath this section of wall. Which meant it was a fake front placed carefully to hide the real wall behind it. And what would you want to hide down here?

A door.

He didn't see any obvious way to move the fake wall, but there had to be one, otherwise any door it concealed would be completely useless. They wouldn't lock and bar their emergency exit. It needed to be easily accessible. Of course, it could have been only accessible from the inside, which would make sense. Exits were about getting out, not in.

"Don't suppose you brought a fire ax, Rye?"

"It'd kinda fuck up the whole element of surprise, don't you think?"

There had to be an edge. A weakness. It couldn't be perfectly flush. Not given the nature of the ancient tunnels. Even if he couldn't see it, it had to be there.

Jake started running his hand over the wall, feeling for any dips or gaps, anything he could slide a fingernail in to work loose. Ryan kept the beam pointed toward the surface of the wall.

Jake almost missed the tiny gap. The tip of his fingernail snagged on it as his hand brushed over the space. He stopped moving, then carefully ran his fingertips back over the area, slowly. "Here," he whispered.

Ryan brought the flashlight's beam up to focus on where that finger had been as Jake lifted it out of the way. At roughly shoulder height there was a narrow gap.

It wasn't an accidental chip; the edges were neat and perfectly squared. It looked like a coin slot in a vending machine.

If this was the keyhole it was pretty clear no ordinary key was going to fit it. It had to be something only these guys would have, because they didn't want some transit worker stumbling in through their back door. Something only they would have . . .

"Keep it steady," Jake said, as he reached into his pocket and dug out the small gold pin. It went in far enough for its outer edge to line up precisely with the wall around it, no farther, earning a muted click from somewhere deep inside the hidden mechanism.

The fake wall shifted a couple of inches under his hands, creating a suddenly visible seam. Ryan wedged his fingers into that space and together they heaved it so the door could swing open. It wasn't smooth or quiet as it dragged away across the rough ground.

Jake winced as it opened onto an old, battered metal door with a submarine-style capstan lock. The door was recessed in a dirt-smeared frame, solid steel, gunmetal gray.

"Shall we?"

Jake grasped the wheel and, after a moment's resistance, felt it turn.

# CHAPTER THIRTY-FIVE

*THERE'S NO PLACE LIKE HOME*, Finn thought as she collapsed into her chair.

Of course, it wasn't really home, and out there the real world wasn't exactly Oz, but in all the ways that counted her office was now more of a home than her apartment. She spent more time in this room than anywhere else in the world and, truth be told, had experienced more damn excitement here too. Through the window, she watched the snowfall thicken as it swirled. By morning it would be knee-deep.

She caught herself grinning at the memory of Jake.

Some time very soon she was going to have to have a word with herself, because she wasn't prepared to be anyone's dirty secret or their mistake. Simple as that. He was going to have to work hard for a second chance.

She wasn't all that forgiving normally, but saving the world would be a start. Though it wouldn't bring automatic forgiveness with it.

She grinned again. *Who am I kidding?*

She'd considered heading back to her apartment for a

nanosecond—the Port Authority adventure had left her drained and shaking when the aftereffects of the adrenaline receded—but the weather made that a fool's errand. The odds were it was still without power and she didn't like the idea of pacing around the tiny one-bedroom apartment in the dark, unable to relax or do anything useful while a storm raged outside. She wasn't about to waste the evening cleaning kitchen countertops and folding laundry. She was tired, but there was no way she could sleep. So, the equation pretty much balanced on the side of work. Besides, there was an element of safety in numbers too. The campus was never deserted, even at this time of night.

"Let's see what we've got, shall we?" she said aloud, typing in her password. She opened her e-mail and web browser. It took a minute for the pages to refresh. It was still faster than it had been that morning, so maybe the Internet, and therefore by association the rest of the world, was starting to recover a little?

She had a few new e-mails, but what caught her eye was a notification that new images from the dig site had been uploaded. That surprised her. It was the most obvious sign yet that normality was beginning to get a grip. Finn grabbed a water bottle from her little fridge and twisted the cap off, taking a long swig as she navigated over to the dig's private page and opened the first of the new pictures. Then she sat back, sipping her water and watching as the gallery began to propagate on her screen.

Even as thumbnails it was obvious the new pictures were considerably better than the first batch, much sharper and cleaner. The water down there must be incredibly clear and almost without undercurrent or motion, because in most of the shots Finn had to consciously remind herself that these ruins were underwater. It was only the soft, diffuse lighting that gave it away. There wasn't a single place in all North America that looked like this, she was absolutely sure of that. Several images offered close-ups of the buildings, zoomed in on the markings carved into them.

Finn created blank pages in her imaging program and traced each symbol methodically so she could study them more easily without the distraction of the environment to lead her thoughts to any particular conclusion. By the time she was finished adding the new symbols to the file she'd already started, her vision had a blurred sleep-deprived quality, but she was absolutely certain of one thing: these markings were not Egyptian.

She'd thought that already from the initial images, but now she was sure. Everything about the images suggested they were in some way related to hieroglyphics, but at the same time they had too many dissimilarities to simply be different presentation styles. Which begged the obvious question: what *were* they?

They really did bear a strong resemblance to Olmec. Maybe Mayan? The problem was the building they were on. It was a perfect classic pyramid, a four-sided, smooth-walled triangular structure that would put the pyramid at Giza to shame. And here it was on the bottom of the ocean near Cuba. That didn't fit with any history of the world she'd ever learned.

Minimizing the shots of the ruins, Finn opened the page with all the text changes marked. Then she pulled up an Olmec glossary, an Egyptian one, and a few others, hoping that one of them would act as a key.

She completely lost track of time. The hunger in her belly was the only indication that it had past at all.

Finn pushed her chair back from her desk and stood up, stretching to the audible crack of her joints realigning. Every bit of pain was worth it because she'd finally found a match. While not perfect, it was as close as she was likely to find.

For the hundredth time she looked at the two images side by side. She'd been right first time: they were Olmec. The images on the ruins were a little sharper, more formal in their construction, but that made sense considering they had been carved into what was obviously a holy building. Carving was the business of sharp lines and clean edges. Any image could be chiseled out, but it would wind up more even, more precise in appearance, than something crafted with the smooth sweeps and flourishes of handwriting.

So what she was looking at here were Egyptian pyramids with Olmec carvings at the tip of the Bermuda Triangle. There was something absolutely impossible about the juxta-position, she knew. But it was brilliant.

These carvings were close to home, but the pyramids themselves were in a part of the world they had no busi-ness being in, making this one of the strangest discoveries Finn had ever heard of. Which meant, inevitably, she'd be questioned, doubted, and probably accused of falsifying her data to get attention. The joys of academia. None of that changed the truth of what she was looking at, though.

The images challenged the established socioanthropo-logical norms. Everything academia thought it understood about migratory populations and the reach of Egyptian cul-ture was undermined by a couple of deep-sea images. They were a game-changer.

And outside the storm worsened.

# CHAPTER THIRTY-SIX

THE DOOR OPENED INTO A DARK, NARROW TUNNEL that stretched out before them.

"After you," Ryan said.

Jake retrieved the pin before allowing the door to swing closed behind them. There were no obvious light switches, but a quick sweep of the Maglite revealed several small white ovals along one side of the wall, set a little above head height. At a guess, battery-powered emergency lights. He tapped one. It glowed slowly to life, confirming his supposition. Nice. But he wasn't about to light any more of them just yet. Better to go forward in the dark. He tapped the light again and it dimmed. He hooded the flashlight beam with a hand, keeping it aimed at the immediate ground in front of him. Ryan did likewise.

The tunnel was straight. There were no obvious bends or junctions turning off it. They walked slowly forward, placing each footfall carefully, not wanting their steps to echo ahead and announce their arrival.

It took them a surprisingly long time to come to another

capstan-locked door. This one was in much better condition than the outer door.

Jake twisted the capstan wheel; it moved freely, well oiled. Behind it, he found a staircase, leading up. He nodded to Ryan, who killed his flashlight and followed Jake as he took the steps slowly.

The risers beneath their feet were well worn in the middle, meaning at one time or another they'd been heavily trafficked. The brickwork was painted sky blue above their heads. As they reached the top they faced another door. No capstan this time. Jake paused and heard footsteps on the other side. He stood right behind the door and waited, his whole body tense, ready to slam it into whoever was unlucky enough to open it.

The door didn't open. He waited, still tense. Behind him, Ryan fidgeted. Then he heard something, a slide, and realized his partner was carrying. It was difficult to relax, even after the footsteps had faded to nothing.

"What the fuck are you doing what that?" Jake rasped.

"Protecting your pretty little ass. Someone's got to."

Jake shook his head. "Seriously not cool, my friend."

"Tell that to the first fucker who tries to ventilate your carcass."

"Do you even know how to use that thing?"

"What do you think?"

He looked Ryan in the eye. He didn't want to admit what he thought. He knew a killer's eyes—Ryan knew how to use the gun. He didn't want to know where he'd learned. He stopped trying to argue with him, and decided to open the door.

It led into a decorative hallway, straight out of a better, vanished time. It was all hardwood floors with thick brass carpet runners, and exquisite end tables showcasing priceless art. It looked every inch the exclusive old gentlemen's club, though after his encounter at Penn Station it was hard to think of the people in here as anything approaching gentlemen in anything but the most vulgar form of the word.

Jake slipped out into the hall. Ryan followed him, closing the stairwell door carefully behind them. They began to make their way down the hall, but with no real clue as to where they were going it didn't matter whether they went left or right. Jake was looking for stairs, working on the principle that anything of value or importance wasn't going to be in the basement or on the ground floor. They needed to be up near the top floor of the brownstone.

They were halfway down the hall, a few feet from a door, when it opened. A guard stepped through. The man—dressed in the uniform black and gray of almost every single flunky he'd ever encountered—was armed to the teeth. He carried a submachine gun cradled in the crook of his left arm, a holstered pistol at his belt, and a wicked knife strapped to his thigh.

Jake couldn't give him the chance to raise the alarm—or to get a shot off. Without time to think, he threw himself forward, putting himself between Ryan and the guard so he couldn't shoot even if his trigger finger itched. Forgetting combat training in favor of pure street-fighting instinct, Jake then launched himself at the guard, who turned right into the trajectory of his clubbing fist. The punch answered the riddle of what happened when an impossible force hit an immovable object. The object's head snapped back, lights out, and hit the deck cold.

"Fuck . . . one punch, man." Ryan said, voice full of admiration. "Nice."

"Take his legs," Jake said as he grabbed the guard under his arms. They carried him back toward the staircase down to the subway level.

Jake thought about dumping him in there, assuming no one would venture that way, but it was a risk. He needed to minimize the chance of someone simply stumbling onto the unconscious man or of him being able to raise the alarm when he came around. Short of slitting the guy's throat, that was going to be easier said than done.

They passed the door, looking for an alternative. The third door to the left opened onto a small storeroom. There was industrial-strength shelving filled with a survivalist horde of food, electronics, emergency gear, and other supplies meant surely to see out the apocalypse. Everything imaginable, and lots of things he'd never have considered. Jake dragged the guard into the storeroom. He found industrial tape on the shelf, and used it to bind the guy's hands and feet, then slapped a piece across his mouth. There was no way his screams were going to bring the house down. Done, he shut the door behind him.

"That should buy us a little time," he said. But just how little was little?

He started trying doors, one at a time, carefully working his way down the hall. A few were locked, nothing he could do about that. A few had voices coming from inside so he didn't bother even trying them. The place was a labyrinth.

They found the stairs and went up. They opened out into a grand foyer, with wooden balustrades and paneled walls that reeked of old money. There were leather couches and smoking paraphernalia beside an open hearth, tall glasses on the table beside the butts of smoked Cuban cigars. But there were no people.

Jake heard a noise off to the left, which he assumed must be the kitchens.

The stairs continued up. On the next landing they found the library. Well appointed, floor to ceiling with leather-bound books, no doubt priceless, like the works of art decorating the walls. In the hallway Jake saw what he was sure was Raphael's *Portrait of a Young Man*. On the wall in the library was an unmistakable van Gogh, *The Painter on the Road to Tarascon*, and in the smoking room Bellini's *Madonna and Child*. They were priceless works of art, and each had one thing in common—they were considered lost in World War II to the Nazis, presumed destroyed. Yet here they were, in this brownstone in Manhattan.

Everything has a price.

He couldn't even begin to imagine what else was hidden in this place.

They kept on looking, not sure what it was they were hoping to find, mindful always of how long they'd been inside and of every creak and groan the old building taunted them with, expecting a shout at any second to let them know their time was up.

It was as though they'd stepped back in time to some colonial plantation house. Jake felt deeply uncomfortable, sure they were the first black men to set foot inside the brownstone who weren't servants.

Then on the fifth floor he tried a door that opened onto a small, tidy little study off a reading room. There was a slick high-tech computer dominating the green leather inlay of the desk's surface.

"Now this is more like it," Ryan said, setting his gun down beside the terminal as Jake shut the door behind him. The computer was in standby mode, not full shutdown. He tried waking the machine up, but the words *Enter Access Code* popped up in the middle of the screen.

"How about a little space while I work my magic?" Ryan said, grinning. He was enjoying himself now, very much in his element.

Jake moved over to the window and looked down into the street. Life seemed so ordinary out there. Snow settled. Snow swirled. People hurried by, heads down, hurrying to get out of the storm. It was hard to imagine there was a fight for control of the city going on right now on every corner, in every waking network and computer system, every banking system, air traffic control, anything and everything he could think of. It all just looked so normal, like any other winter night. Even the streetlights were coming back on.

Behind him, Ryan rubbed at his face with one hand, staring at the display as if he could simply bludgeon it into submission with the sheer intensity of his will. He'd come prepared; this was his world. They didn't need to have a folder labeled *Secret Global Domination Plan*. They could wrap themselves in a million levels of code and cyphers and protections. But this was Ryan's domain. No matter how smart they were, he was smarter. He slipped something into one of the ports on the machine, cracked his knuckles as if about to start a piano symphony, and started typing.

"Fuck," Ryan said after a few seconds. "No, no, no, no, no."

"What is it?"

"Fuckers," Ryan grunted, his hands moving fast across the keyboard. Then he slammed his fist on the table beside him and kicked the chair away from the terminal, making a lot more noise than Jake was happy with. "The fucking code's optical."

"What? You mean like eyeball scanners?"

Ryan grunted again, looking at Jake like he had just fallen out of the moron tree and hit every branch on the way down.

*Optical.* He'd said it himself, a scanner. Not eyeballs though. Jake dug his phone back out of his pocket and scrolled through the recent messages to the last one, from Sophie, with the elaborate QR code embedded in it. She'd said it was a stone for fighting Goliath. "Like this?" he said, handing it over to Ryan.

Ryan took it from him and angled the phone up at the computer's webcam.

*Come on, Sophie, don't let me down,* Jake willed, staring at the screen while the pair of them waited for something to happen.

There was a faint but audible click as the computer seemed to accept Sophie's QR code and the regular desktop opened up for them.

"And we're in," Ryan said. There was nothing fancy about the desktop, no secret Hidden logo on the screen like he'd have expected if Tom Cruise was playing his part on the big screen. Nothing like that at all.

But Jake wasn't watching the screen anymore. There was a photograph on the bookcase, three men fishing, shaking hands over a big catch. He recognized two of the three. One was the incumbent whiter-than-white president, who'd just been sworn into office; the other was Harry Kane.

He didn't know what to do with that. It had to be a coincidence, surely. That's what two things were. It needed three things to be a pattern. But . . .

"You need to see this," Ryan said, pointing at something on the screen.

The first time Jake read it, it made no sense. The second time scared the shit out of him.

He read it three times. It had to be some sort of mistake. Wishful thinking by some seriously fucked-up mad men . . . some sort of Nietzschean superman crap.

The documents were all there, the gruesome details of their plan, an itinerary that started with blowing up Fort Hamilton, then progressing through terror after terror to the moment Jake first spotted two of their foot soldiers inside Times Square. In addition to the stock exchange, the trunk lines, Port Authority, and Penn Station, they'd targeted air traffic control and the MTA itself, meaning his worst fears had been right—they were out to conquer New York. But there was so much more to it than that, or seemed to be. It wasn't some bullet-point itinerary, it was photos, schematics, and other pieces of the sick puzzle.

"This is some heavy shit," Ryan said.

"Can you search for something for me?"

"Sure. Hit me."

"Harry Kane."

It took a couple of seconds to return a string of results revealing that Harry's name was all over this system.

Jake stared at the screen thinking: *Why?* But even before he could ask that aloud, he was asking a new question, a new name. "Sophie Keane?"

Wordlessly Ryan ran another search and turned up another set of hits. Unfortunately, the files were all locked, and the QR code wasn't offering up any more secrets. "They're running some sort of cypher, 128-bit encryption. It's tight." He pointed at something on the screen. It took Jake a second to realize it was a single file that had been returned in both searches. It was a JPEG, a photograph of Harry and Sophie, only it said *Cabrakan* and *Zaccimi*. Code names.

"Can you get into any of this stuff?"

"Given time I can get into anything. You keep a lookout, make sure we're not about to receive any visitors, I'll do my thing here. What are we looking for?"

"Proof. Something we can take to the cops. The military. Something we can use to bring these guys down."

"Ah, nothing easy then."

Jake crossed the room to the door. He wasn't sure what the connection was between Sophie and Harry. He'd sat up late at night more than once, rolling ice around a tumbler of whiskey, lamenting the one that got away, with Harry nodding along sympathetically, never once mentioning that he'd met Sophie, and yet here they were, sharing a photograph on the billionaire murdering playboy's computer servers.

One of the only things he knew for sure about these two people, he realized, was that Harry Kane was old money. His parents were filthy rich, the wealth inherited from his parents, and their parents before them, going back generations. *But just because he comes from money* . . . Jake didn't like the way his thoughts were going. Harry was a friend. He'd been a friend for a long time. He'd known the guy for the better part of fifteen years. Now, seeing his name on a file was enough for him to get the tar and feathers out?

"Okay, got something," Ryan said. "Kane's personnel file, well, what passes for one in a crazy-ass cult. Says he was recruited by Zaccimi. That's Sophie Keane. Lists his activities, places they've sent him, completed missions, that kind of thing."

"Do I want to know?"

"Probably not."

"Tell me anyway."

"Better you see it for yourself."

It felt like his entire world was being turned on its head.

He'd come here expecting to find, what? Membership rosters? Instead he was looking at a list of assassinations. And that's what they were, he was absolutely sure of it. Kills carried out by one of the men he'd always considered to be a close friend. The man he'd first turned to when he was searching for answers here. It was all in there, how he'd been approached by Zaccimi—Sophie—and how he'd been recruited. It was like he was some kind of sleeper agent for the CI-fucking-A waiting to be woken up and sent on a killing spree. "I can't read this," he said, but didn't take his eyes from the screen. There were other names and events he recognized. Things that had been reported as tragedies. Accidents. And looking at this, he knew they were anything but. "Is it the same for Sophie?" he asked, already knowing it was. *I'm not who you think I am.*

Ryan said nothing. He simply opened a series of surveillance photographs from Paris, time-stamped this morning. There was no mistaking what was going on. She'd been marked for execution. Harry Kane had been dispatched to kill her.

Jake pushed through the photos, looking for verification that she was dead, but there was nothing. There was a photo of him in there too, taken as he crossed Zuccotti Park. Toward the back of the shots he came across photos of strange drawings, all of them a lot like the markings he'd seen the two men spray across the wall in Times Square.

"Can you copy these?"

"Sure," Ryan said, dumping them onto the stick he'd plugged into the machine. "They important?"

"Everything's important right now until we know it's not."

"Roger that."

Ryan was still copying across the last couple of images when the relative silence in the room was violently broken by a loud, grating sound that filled every inch of the old brownstone. The alarm was brutal.

Their time was up.

# CHAPTER THIRTY-SEVEN

J AKE WAS ON HIS FEET AND AROUND THE DESK in a fraction of a second, Ryan two steps behind him, gun in hand.

If they didn't get out of there, it wouldn't matter that Ryan had found a way into their system.

Jake opened the door, but shut it again a split second later without managing so much as peeking around the doorjamb. Shadows moved across the hardwood floor. He wasn't stupid enough to think these guys wouldn't recognize him. They'd be all over him like a rash if they saw him. He was a marked man. He had been dragged into the middle of this by Sophie—as proven by that single photograph at Zuccotti Park.

Right now it was kill or be killed. He wasn't naïve enough to think there was a way out of this that didn't involve blood.

He had to think like them. He was in their place; this was familiar ground, they knew every inch of it. They knew all of the hiding places and escape routes. There was nowhere he could run they didn't know about, including the door out of the basement into the abandoned tunnels. In their place, he'd do a grid search, making his way down the hallways one room at a time. He tried to think.

He spotted a small flange on the doorknob and turned it carefully, locking the door. It wasn't much and it wouldn't stop them for long—they didn't need to be subtle, they could just kick the door down.

Then Jake realized he had inadvertently locked the two of them into a small inner room with no windows or other doors. He'd effectively trapped them.

"What's our goal here?" Ryan asked. "Beyond just getting out."

"Just getting out," Jake replied. "Nothing beyond that."

"Not good enough," Ryan said. "We get out of here, nothing's changed. We've got a few photos, but these guys have got their own assassins, man. All we've done is paint targets on our backs."

"Strategic withdrawal."

"Now you sound like a fucking soldier boy. We need to hurt them. Hurt them bad. But the key, the main thing we need, really need, is insurance so they don't come after us." Ryan tapped his temple with the barrel of his gun. "That's thinking."

"Right now I'm just thinking about keeping you alive."

There was a heavy lamp on the desk beside the computer, an old-fashioned brass light. Jake thought about using it as a makeshift weapon, yanking its cord free of the wall and wrapping it around his fist. It would have some heft to it. But Ryan was right—even if he hadn't used these words—he was thinking like a victim. He'd taken the ceramic knife from the guy in the relay station—he could do a lot more damage with that. If he cut them, they would bleed. He'd have to get up close, which wouldn't be easy given they were packing some serious heat. Still, he'd take a few of them with him before they cut him down. Maybe that'd buy Ryan the time he needed to get out.

"I'm gonna get you out of here, and when you do, I want you to find a woman."

"I've got a woman, unless you've forgotten," Ryan wisecracked.

"Shut up and listen. Her name is Finn Walsh. She works up at Columbia. A lecturer. She knows what's going on. Find her. Give her the USB. She needs to see those photos. Understood?"

"Show her yourself."

"Just promise me."

"Fine."

They needed another way out, but this wasn't some locked-room mystery. There was no secret panel in the wall that would pop open when Jake pulled the right book from the shelf.

He peered around the room again, which wasn't much to look at. He could just about stretch from wall to wall, touching both sides at once. Maybe with a sledgehammer he could pound his way through the wall. But there were two problems with that: one, no sledgehammer; the other, the noise. Jake slammed his hand against the wall in sheer frustration.

"What you doing? They'll hear you!"

The dull thud echoed through the compact study and into the room beyond—then stopped. Jake repeated the strike, listening to the echo. Then he heard it: the sounds of *outside*—they were muted but unmistakable. He needed to somehow get into the room next door, even if they were five stories up.

He stood with his back against the wall, staring at the

door, expecting the handle to turn at any second. The inces-
sant wailing of the alarm had spiraled to the kind of howl
that would drive the dog packs in the neighborhood wild.

They couldn't just stand there waiting for the inevitable.
He needed to do something, to be proactive, not reactive. So
far he'd been reacting to adversity, trying to fix problems as
they arose. Now he needed to *be* the problem. He needed to
take the fight to them, like Ryan had suggested.

"Give me the gun."

Ryan shook his head, but handed it over. A Beretta M9.

Jake knew the gun well. Fifteen 9mm rounds in the clip.
It had been a long time since he'd handled a weapon like
this. Right now he hoped it was like riding a bike, something
you didn't forget. It wasn't a standard M9, he realized, it
was a General Officers Model, unique to the Army and Air
Force. He didn't want to know where Ryan had gotten his
hands on it. He checked the firing pin block to make sure
it wasn't engaged, racked the slide, and moved to the door,
ready to go out shooting.

"Follow me. And don't get yourself killed."

"I'll do my best."

Jake opened the door and stepped out. There were two
men in the corridor with their backs to him. They must not
have heard him banging on the wall above the screech of the
alarm.

Jake didn't hesitate. There was no room for moralizing.
He pulled the trigger, feeling the fierce recoil of the double-
action, and put a bullet in the back of one man's spine. The
second managed to turn in time to take a bullet in the face.
The impact blew out the back of his head.

There was no hope of hiding now. Jake stepped over the
corpses, going for the door as another black-clad foot sol-

dier came charging up the wide arc of the staircase. His next shot took this guy in the kneecap, bringing him down like a felled tree, but it didn't stop the soldier from trying to put a slug though Jake's brain. Mercifully, the bullet whistled by his ear and bit into the plaster and ripped through masonboard wall. Standing over the man, Jake used another bullet to put him down.

"Cold, dude," Ryan barely breathed.

"Shut up," Jake said. He could hear more of them coming. He looked back at Ryan and gestured with two fingers toward the door.

Ryan nodded and ran for door while Jake kept him covered.

Jake stopped dead in his tracks after following Ryan through the door. He'd been expecting another quaint pseudo-Victorian gentleman's lounge. This was anything but—they had stumbled upon a modern-day technological nerve center with two men trying unsuccessfully to duck behind the terminals. Jake immediately shot them both, then closed the door behind him.

The room was deceptively large, with an array of screens against one wall that would have been fit for a Pentagon briefing room. They displayed a global map, targets and trajectories marked off and all sorts of other information he couldn't understand with icons beside names like *Xbalanque*, *Hunhau*, *Ixtab*, *Kauil*, *Cum Hau*, and others. Jake saw names two he recognized, *Cabrakan* and *Zaccimi*.

*Zaccimi* was the only name marked in red. Out of play. He didn't know what the map meant beyond the obvious. There were two banks of monitors, a dozen on each. He thought for one terrible second that he had been mistaken and that there were no windows here because it was so dark in the room, but then he saw that they were blacked out.

Ryan was over by the wall now. Jake didn't know what Ryan was doing at first, then he noticed several pipes running down the far wall. One was water, the other, definitely not. "Old building, old pipes," his friend said, by way of explanation, and started chipping away at one of them.

Jake didn't question it. Three long, quick strides and he was across the room. He grabbed the nearest chair and hurled it through one of the windows, sending thousands of shards raining down on West 91st Street below.

Jake had one thing on his mind—and that was learning how to fly, because he was going out of that window one way or another. The snow on the ground wasn't much of a safety blanket.

Ryan broke through the seal on the pipe and was rewarded with a dull *thunk* and the rasping hiss of escaping gas. He reached into his pocket and pulled out a lighter.

Jake looked at him and nodded. "Do it."

Ryan thumbed the wheel, and set the flame burning as the first gunshot rang out. He took this as his signal to jump—three steps and he hurled himself through the shattered window, Jake one step behind him, and for one excruciatingly long second he thought he'd gotten it all wrong, that there was nothing there, then he hit the wrought-iron railings of a city-mandated fire escape and rolled.

Thank God for rules and regulations. Simple as that. Some officious little prick somewhere had just saved their lives. But only for maybe another fifteen or twenty seconds if he didn't *move*.

It was a long way down. Jake fired the M9 through the window, buying them a couple seconds more, and started down, running three, four, five iron steps at a time, chasing behind Ryan until he hit the next landing, then again.

Shots rang out.

Jake aimed backward, firing wildly as he dropped another level lower. It was still a long way to the ground and he could hear someone clattering down the fire escape behind him. The snow made the iron steps treacherously slippery.

Ryan launched himself down the next set of steps, then jumped all the way to the platform below, hit the sheet of metal hard, his legs buckling beneath him, and rolled, scrambling back up to his feet even as the concussion of bullets pitted the wrought-iron platform beside his hand.

Jake followed and then kicked open the ladder, grabbing it and shimmying down as it locked into place, then dropped the last few feet to the alleyway that ran beside the building. He took aim and put a bullet into the chest of their pursuer. The shot spun the guy around, and left him sprawled across the lower levels of the fire escape.

The same cars that had clogged the street earlier were still there now, but with the snow it gave the scene an ethereal, otherworldly quality, like the surface of an industrial moon. There were hundreds upon thousands of dollars' worth of abandoned machinery in this street alone, running all the way across the heart of Manhattan, millions of dollars of useless steel.

He looked up at the brownstone. There were lights on in almost every room. In fact the only room with no lights on was the nerve center up on the top floor, where the windows that weren't shattered were blacked out. Another guard climbed through the broken window at the exact moment that a shudder coursed through the street.

Fire roared out through the black windows, engulfing the man. He fell, arms and legs ablaze like some burning angel crashing to earth, shrieks escaping from his lips. And then silence and flame, the air sucked out of the world around them.

Jake felt the explosion like a physical blow, as so much anger erupted within the old brownstone, tearing at the brick and asphalt as it ripped its way out through the walls. Then he realized he couldn't hear a thing. The rending of brick and mortar was horrific, but for Jake it was all happening in eerie silence.

He could feel the heat on his face as he stared up at the brownstone, backing up a step and then another as a ripple ran through the sturdy old walls almost as if the bricks had turned liquid. They buckled as the conflagration roared. Then the entire structure was bathed in flame, windows on all floors shattering, though the façade held its shape even as a fresh wave of fire billowed out from a second explosion deeper in the building, chasing a shock wave so fierce it took Ryan off his feet. He staggered, trying to catch his balance, stepping back off the curb. As the sheet of flame rolled out across the street, only to suck back into the building, Ryan hit the ground hard, narrowly missing an abandoned car.

But Jake wasn't looking at him. He couldn't take his eyes off the fire ripping through the building.

Everything else along the quiet residential street was unchanged save for the mound of shattered stone and wood and glass where the window frames had been, the twisted columns of the sentry boxes outside its gates where the debris had rained down. The wrought-iron gates themselves hung open, their frames mangled, beckoning toward the burning building like the gates to hell. There was no sign of the sentries themselves.

Jake simply stood there shaking his head, trying to comprehend the enormity of what had just happened. He rubbed his fingers across his rough palms, still trying to process what he'd found in there, when Ryan began to tug at him.

"We need to bounce."

Jake's hearing was beginning to return and he knew Ryan was right. Of course he was. They'd just caused untold damage to this billionaire boys' club. They couldn't exactly stand around and watch it burn. But Jake's head was ringing, and not only from the explosion. All he could think was: *Sophie? Harry? Assassins?* He couldn't even begin to comprehend the implications, and just how far back into his own life they delved. *I'm not who you think I am.*

"Von's going to kill me when she finds out the shit we're in," Ryan said, shaking his head. "I can't do this. It's not me. You have no idea how hard it was to clean my identity, to start fresh, away from the Russians. Not to be always looking over my shoulder expecting a bullet. I don't want that kind of life. Not now. Not for her." Which was his way of saying, *I wish you hadn't dragged me into this.*

"I won't tell if you don't," Jake told him, dead straight, no hit of humor in his voice. "You get the files?"

Ryan nodded.

"Good, because right now that's all that's keeping us alive."

They started walking.

And didn't look back once while the building blazed behind them, turning the night sky a bloody shade of red.

# CHAPTER THIRTY-EIGHT

THEY HEARD SIRENS THROUGH THE CLOSED WINDOWS. They'd been there less than fifteen minutes. In that time he'd told her everything.

"We couldn't go home. I didn't know where else to go . . . so we came here," Jake said, taking another swig of the ice-cold Diet Coke Finn had given him. He kept thinking about what that guy at the station had said about willingly putting poison into his body, but he drank anyway. Ryan lay on the cot beside him, legs crossed at the ankles, hands behind his head. He was pretending to be asleep. Jake still felt slight tremors that marked the aftermath of their escape.

Jake drank deep, but lowered the can quickly when he saw Finn's wide-eyed expression. "Not straight here," he assured her. "I made sure nobody was following us. Don't worry, we're safe."

"I'm not so sure about that," she muttered, then told him about the stranger who'd broken into her office earlier.

"Damn," Jake sighed. "That's my fault. I didn't even think before . . . I must have led him here. Look, we should go."

To his surprise, she shrugged it off. "Maybe not. Maybe it was Harry's doing. It doesn't matter. We're in this together. The three musketeers." She looked across at Ryan. "Well, two and a half." He smiled at that. "The only question that matters is where do we go from here? Who can we turn to? Who'll even believe us that isn't already in their pocket?"

It was the million-dollar question. *Billion*, Jake corrected himself. Where the fuck did you go when you'd just made enemies with some of the richest men in civilization? On the plus side, though, he liked the way she used the word *we*.

"Honestly? Every time we make a breakthrough and learn something, it just leads to more questions, not answers, like Sophie and Harry and where they fit into this." Jake had explained about the code names and everything else they'd found inside the brownstone. "We know these mythical rich guys are behind this, in the shadows, pulling all the strings, killing people, but we don't know who they are, we don't know any of their names, the corporations they represent, any of it. So who *can* we trust? We're just three people. They might as well own the fucking world."

"Then we take the fight *to* them," Ryan said without opening his eyes. "That's the only reason I'm still alive. I learned that much pretty fast out in Russia. Wait for them, we wind up all kinds of dead. These people aren't messing around. They're serious. And you're wrong, you do know who they are. Or at least one of them."

"Harry," Jake replied.

"If this was the streets, I'd say we needed a sit-down, organize a truce, 'cause there's no good way out of this. We can't keep running and hoping. They know who we are, they've got resources. We can't hide. Not like them."

"When did *you* get so wise?"

"Long time ago, in a galaxy far far away," the younger man said, finally sitting up. He swung his legs over the side of the cot and stood up. "Let's see what we've got, shall we? It better be good because we need to trade it for something useful, like another forty years on this planet." He held up the stick crammed with files stolen from the brownstone.

# CHAPTER THIRTY-NINE

INN STARED AT THE SCREEN. "You know what they are, don't you?" He studied her face.

She navigated through the desktop to her secure files, and the link to the dive's photos, then opened one of them. It was a pyramid, but unlike any he'd seen before. There was a peculiar quality to the light. It was too green, too blue, not nearly yellow enough. But it wasn't just that. There was an odd filminess to the pyramid and its surroundings as if the photographer had put a soft filter on the entire image. No, not a soft filter, he realized. He was seeing the entire image through a natural filter: water. He was looking at a submerged pyramid. But only part of his mind registered this.

Those symbols were a perfect match for the ones they'd stolen from the computers in the brownstone. And as best as he could recall, they were a decent match for the ones he'd been seeing in the subway.

"What am I looking at?"

"It's what I've been working on. A ruin they just discovered off the coast of Cuba," Finn explained.

"How does it fit in?"

"I was brought on board to analyze the symbols. It's what I do. I'm probably one of only a couple people in the world who can decipher them. This pyramid is literally thousands of years old. And as far as I know, nobody had seen these markings until our divers took the first photos the other day. Actually, today, if you're looking at a decent hi-res shot where you can make them out properly. It's a lost language. We haven't seen anything like it in three to five thousand years. And those files you stole have perfect copies on them."

"Okay . . ." Ryan said slowly. "Humor me here. These ruins are *thousands* of years old?" She nodded. "And they've got these symbols all over them?" Another nod. "The whole world goes dark and a group of rich guys use that to cover their tracks while they wipe out the city's entire infrastructure and replace it with their own?" A third nod. "And it just so happens these guys are using the same symbols as your drowned society? That's one hell of a coincidence right there."

Finn opened one of the images they'd taken from the brownstone. "This is definitely a message of some sort, it's got to be," she mused aloud. "The one symbol I've identified is Olmec, but this is Mayan, or as close as can be. I can translate, it'll just take me a few minutes."

"Mayan?" Jake scratched at his chin.

Finn frowned. "In a nutshell, yes. It's more complicated than that, the ruins are covered in a mix of Olmec and Mayan writing, which makes no sense . . . It's just . . . wrong. Civilizations don't blur like this. At least not the way we understand it. One might supplant another in a region, of course, but this . . . these carvings, the pyramid itself, I don't know what to make of it all."

"And you can read it?"

"With luck."

"Maybe it'd be good to know what this shit means," Ryan said. "Before we have the pow-wow? Forewarned is forearmed and all that."

Jake nodded.

Finn pulled her chair over to the desk, enlarged one of the shots, grabbed her old, battered research guides and notebooks, and got to work. It didn't take long before she clearly forgot Jake and Ryan were there. Jake liked that she could do that; it demanded a kind of focus he could appreciate. For a while there was no such thing as time, no constraints from the outside world, only a string of symbols. It was a dangerously sharp focus that skirted the border between concentrated and obsessive. Most people deliberately wore faces, and were conscious of how they looked to the outside world, worried about how others would see them. Lost like this, Finn was as good as naked. It was natural, life in extremis, facing down death, delivering it.

She started changing the pictures rapidly, and scratching down numbers. Jake couldn't take his eyes off her.

"Got it!" she exclaimed, brushing her hair out of her face. "It's a date."

"I haven't even asked you out yet," he said before he could stop himself.

A quick grin flashed across her face. "They all are. The entire city down there is covered in them, like a gigantic calendar, but this one is duplicated on the main pyramid, right at the zenith. This one's different. It's a date for the end of the world."

"That seems a bit extreme, I was thinking dinner and a movie," Jake said, earning a chuckle from Ryan.

"Smooth, Jakey."

Jake ignored him. "Anytime soon?"

"Yes, actually. This morning."

"So we know how they did it. We know how they knew," Jake said, scratching at his cheek. "But how is that even possible? I thought the polar shift was a natural event. How could someone have predicted it thousands of years ago?"

"It was natural," Finn assured them. "But it's one that scientists have been theorizing about for years. Centuries. You forget, science isn't new. It isn't something we invented in the twentieth century. A lot of ancient civilizations were incredibly advanced in certain sciences, including astronomy and geology. We're still rediscovering things they practically took for granted. The Mayans were one of those, the Olmecs too. They were able to predict eclipses and other astronomical events with a precision and accuracy we can barely match for all our computers and lasers. And now it seems they understood enough about the polar shifts to be able to calculate accurately when the next would occur."

"And our spoiled little rich kids found that prediction," Jake guessed, "and formed their boys club to exploit it for their own gain."

"They used it, certainly," she affirmed, "but I'm not so sure about finding it. There've been end-of-the-world predictions for ages. The Vatican has archives filled with hundreds of them dating back centuries, and they all tend to cluster around turn-of-the-century cataclysms and end-of-millennia disasters. The Mayans' is one of the most famous, even though it didn't really predict an end so much as a transition, from one age to the next. But this," she gestured at the images still displayed on her computer screen, "is way more detailed than anything I've seen before. I don't know how to explain it, it's like the *real* prediction, the full text, not just a calendar. It's everything. And these symbols we've been seeing, they're markers, they're mirroring the ones on the lost city. I think it's some sort of ritual celebration." She frowned, pausing for a moment. "I don't think they *found* this. I think they already had it. I think they've been observing it the whole time."

"A ritual celebration? You mean like Día de los Muertos?"

"Exactly like that. There are two days, Día de los Muertos and Día de los Inocentes, the Day of the Dead and the Day of the Innocents, where they're honoring deceased children. November 1 and November 2. These rituals are known to be nearly three thousand years old."

"Like our lost civilization?"

"Like our lost civilization. And back then, from all we know, it used to run for an entire month. August. They used to keep skulls as trophies to be displayed during the rituals to symbolize death and rebirth." She tapped the screen, at the center of the clearest image.

Jake could just about trace the lines of what was obviously a skull. "So you think they're Mayan? Isn't that all a bit . . . 2012? End-of-the-world prophecies and all that?" He hadn't even considered them being anything other than the super-rich, American, venal, greedy—the powerbrokers, the movers and shakers of the city. That they could be rooted in some long-extinct societal heritage had never crossed his mind, but it certainly provided the motivation he'd wondered about earlier. They were taking back what was once theirs. Jake considered this, then nodded.

"I don't think they're some long-lost branch of the Mayan civilization, no," Finn said. "At least not genetically. Spiritually, maybe. There's an affinity, a strong one—you only have to look at the names they've chosen for their assassins:

they're all the names of Mayan gods and goddesses, most of them associated with death in some way. This is our missing link. This is what turns a coincidence into a pattern, Jake."

"I got this off one of them," he told her, pulling the ceramic knife from the sheath on his thigh and laying it on the flat of her outstretched hand.

She was careful not to touch the blade's edge as she studied it. "It's obsidian," she said after a minute, "and chipped rather than forged, I think. The style, the materials, the decoration, it's all classic Mayan." She handed it back to him.

He handed her the gold pin he'd taken from the same guy. "What about this?"

She turned it over in her hand, studying it. "It's not. At least, the eye isn't. That's Egyptian, the Eye of Horus. It's a popular image, supposedly gives protection and health. The circle—see the markings here?" Jake and Ryan leaned in closer. There was a pattern around the eye, and it looked a lot like things Jake had seen on Mexican coins and calendars. "That's Mayan, or maybe Olmec." She frowned and clicked over to the image of the underwater ruins again. "Mayan and Egyptian together." She shook her head. "It's strange. I suppose it's not out of the question that refugees or colonists from Egypt could have wound up forming the start of the Mayan Empire. That would explain the ruins. They may have been the bridge stage, between their old culture and their new one, some of the heritage bleeding into the new, being subsumed by the locals, rather than consumed, and altered to fit their own circumstances." She was getting excited, Jake could tell. Her words came thick and fast, like she could barely keep up with her thoughts and their ramifications. "The Mayans were about the end of one thing and the start of the next, but the Egyptians, they were more about the journey, weighing the soul and proving its worth before being allowed to move on. There's a heavy element of gatekeeper-ship in their mythos, the idea that someone has to stand in judgment and decide who is worthy and who isn't." Now her eyes grew wide. "If you combine the two cultures, the way these ruins suggest, you might wind up with a people who know when this age will end and feel it's their duty to control the transition and make sure those who are worthy will survive and even prosper as the new age dawns."

"The Hidden," Jake said. "That's what the name means. They've been hidden all this time, in plain sight, watching and waiting, preparing for this day. Ready to sit in judgment and dispense their justice to the unworthy. That's why they could act so quickly—they've had years to plan this all out. Every last detail."

"All but one," she said. "They didn't count on *you*. Make the call."

# CHAPTER FORTY

THE LIMO CAME TO COLLECT THEM AT FIRST LIGHT. The driver didn't say anything as he opened the door.

"Harry," Jake said, looking at him. "Or should I call you Cabrakan?"

"You can call me whatever you like, Jake. We're old friends."

"I thought we were."

"Nothing's changed."

"Everything's changed," Jake disagreed.

The other man didn't contradict him this time.

Jake had come alone; he didn't want to drag the others any deeper in. They were also his insurance policy. If things went south he was relying on them to get the information out there somehow. All Ryan needed was a computer and he could disseminate the truth far and wide. He had connections in hacktivist groups like Anonymous, the kind of people who had an interest in getting the truth out there. Not that Jake expected anyone to listen.

"Where are we going?"

"Where you wanted to go. Mr. Alom's looking forward to meeting you."

"I wish I could say it was mutual."

They drove awhile in silence. Life hadn't returned to normal—the roads were still clogged with abandoned vehicles. Snow made it worse now. It would be weeks before it was cleared, but there were already signs of the National Guard moving in and beginning the clean-up. Jake didn't see a single dog on the drive. Harry kept to the fringes of the borough, wending his way to his destination, a riverside heliport. The cranes of the docks towered over the scene, unmoving. There was a white Sikorsky S-76C on the tarmac. The pilot was already in his chair, the rotors turning over slowly.

"After you," Harry said, pulling up on the hard stand.

"One question," Jake said, unclipping his belt.

"Shoot."

"Did you kill Sophie?"

Harry turned to face him. "Would it make any difference if I said no?"

"Yes."

"I didn't kill her. You have my word."

Jake stared at the man and realized he had no way of knowing how hollow that word was. Up until a few days ago he would have said Harry Kane was one of his few real friends in the world, now he had no idea who he was. What he did know was *what* Harry was: a killer.

"How did you get messed up in all of this, Harry?"

"You said one question, Jake. That's two."

"I'm just trying to understand."

"Then save your questions for Mr. Alom."

"What about you? Don't you ask questions anymore?"

"As few as possible. Come on, he doesn't like to be kept waiting."

They clambered out of the limo, leaving the doors open as they crossed the tarmac to the waiting helicopter. The rotors began to chop the air, the engine's whir turning into a roar. The downdraft battered them as they ducked low.

"Relax, mate," Harry said, his Englishness coming out in that single world. "If he wanted you dead, you'd be dead. We've had plenty of opportunities to kill you, believe me."

"That's not as comforting as you'd think," Jake said.

Harry laughed. "I guess not. Just remember, you asked for this. No one forced you into it."

"Again, not as comforting as you'd think."

"No offense, but I need to pat you down, make sure you don't try anything stupid. Up against the car, spread 'em," Harry said, this time putting on a piss-poor American accent.

Jake did as he was told.

As Harry's hands moved up the inside of his right thigh they found the obsidian knife. Harry stripped him of it, tossing it aside. Satisfied there were no other surprises concealed on his person, he told Jake to buckle up and try to enjoy the flight.

A minute later they were rising up over the canyons of the city.

Jake stared out of the window as they streaked south down the line of the Hudson River before banking west toward the New Jersey blight. The world looked so small down there. If he'd needed any sort of dividing line between the haves and the have-nots in this world, this journey was it. The Sikorsky was about thirteen million bucks' worth of extravagance. It was also the only thing in the sky. It rode the thermals, skimming over the rooftops of the skyscrapers before angling away toward the sea.

It took twenty minutes before the city was a thing of the past and the distant white blur on the horizon resolved into the shape of a luxury super-yacht with concave surfacing and sleek lines as well as its own onboard pool that jutted out from the transom.

The pilot brought them down smoothly onto the helipad.

A woman waited on the sundeck. She was dressed in a pencil skirt and crisp white blouse with her hair pulled back in a tight bun.

"She really is something, isn't she?" Harry said.

He wasn't wrong. The woman's lines were more impressive than the super-yacht's.

"I've seen better," Jake said.

"Of course you have. Come on then, let's get this over with, shall we?" He let Jake out first. "Miss Kinch Ahau," he said, inclining his head deferentially.

"Cabrakan," she replied. "Mr. Carter, Mr. Alom is expecting you. If you'd be so kind as to follow me?" She led them across the sundeck to a stairway that led up to a glass-fronted cabin that offered an incredible view of the sea from all aspects.

"How the 1 Percent lives," Jake said, doing his best to take it all in.

The woman opened the door without responding. The interior was the epitome of wealth over taste. Jake stood on the threshold.

"Come in, Mr. Carter," a voice said from inside. "Miss Kinch Ahau, please see to it that we are not disturbed."

"Yes sir."

"And invite Cabrakan to join us."

"Yes sir. Anything else?"

"That will be all, thank you. Close the door behind you on the way out."

She nodded and backed up a step, allowing Jake past, then closed the door.

"Sit, please. No reason we can't be civil about this, Mr. Carter."

Jake still couldn't see the speaker. There were three leather armchairs in the room. Jake took the middle one, and turned the angle slightly so it faced the room's one solid wall. It was made of rich lacquered wood, and within the grains he was sure he could make out some of the same swirls and spirals of the Mayan symbols he'd seen elsewhere. They were subtle, and he could just as easily be seeing patterns where there were none, but before he could rise and cross the room to check, a door opened on the far side of the cabin and an older man with silver hair and steel-gray eyes entered. Midseventies, Jake guessed, but in good physical condition, not bowed by the weight of years on his narrow shoulders. A regular Hugh Hefner playboy character. There was something about his face, though, that didn't look quite right. No doubt he had small scars behind his ears from where the surgeon had performed the lift. Jake rose out of habit, though stopped short of offering his hand.

"Now, this is a pretty mess we've gotten ourselves into, isn't it, Mr. Carter?"

"That's one way of putting it," Jake countered.

"So, perhaps you should tell me why you wanted this meeting. I see little benefit in it, personally, but Cabrakan made a good case for your life. You should thank him."

"I'll try to remember that. As to why I wanted to face you, apart from knowing my enemy? Short term: survival. Long term: survival."

"Indeed?"

"Look, it doesn't take a genius to know you outrank

me in society's chain of command. I'm a grunt, you're a general."

The old man offered a wry smile. "Flattery will get you everywhere, Mr. Carter. Is that the plan?"

"Something like that."

"Perhaps you'd like to explain to me why I shouldn't simply have Cabrakan throw you overboard and be done with it. You've been nothing but a thorn in my side, Mr. Carter. I am not a forgiving man. Don't make the mistake of thinking you can appeal to my better nature. You have cost me a lot of money, more than you can possibly imagine, and that is not even the worst of your crimes. You've left a trail of bodies in your wake that I am sure the authorities would be interested in, for one. But that's just being petty. You obviously view me as some kind of monster, no?"

"It has crossed my mind."

"Let me ask you a question, Mr. Carter."

"Shoot."

"Are you a patriot?"

"Of course."

Alom nodded. "As am I. I love my country, Mr. Carter. Fiercely. Everything I do, I do out of love for this great nation of ours. I watch over her."

"Like a vampire watching over big herd of human cattle."

"No, no, no, not like that at all. I look around and I see everything our fathers and our forefathers built slowly crumbling and decaying and I want to stop that. I see riots in Ferguson, Los Angeles, and Baltimore, and I feel immense pain." He held a hand flat against his heart. "I see people without hope, ground down by circumstance and failure, and I want to do something."

"Profit."

"Cynical, Mr. Carter. I want to make a difference. I want to protect everything that is great about this nation of ours."

"You make it sound like a noble cause."

"It is. I'm not the monster you are looking for. Look around you, look at a government that has its hands bound tight by conflict in both houses of Congress, that can't pass legislation to make even the least bit of difference because it's all about politics and fear. Look at how insular everything is. We don't have global leadership initiatives in place to handle things like the climate and depletion of natural resources, and they are global issues. Wouldn't you agree that our greatest debt to the world—and our greatest challenge as a species—is to build a *better* world? Aren't things like clean water, nutritious food, affordable housing, education, medical care, safe energy, access to high-tech communications and information, and freedom—aren't these things all basic human rights? A life of possibility for all?"

"Are you trying to tell me you're some sort of benevolent force sneaking around in the background trying to make everything all right?"

"I'm trying to tell you that things are not as black-and-white as you might like to believe. Everything I do, I do it for the greater good. Take what I believe to be one of humanity's greatest failings: aging. I truly believe we are within striking distance of changing everything. We already know so much about how life works, and our scientists—men and women working in clinics we fund in Switzerland—are in the process of developing a medicine that will bring aging under the same degree of control that we already have for most infectious diseases. Think of it, think of the pain and suffering caused by age-related conditions like Alzheimer's,

SUNFAIL

macular degeneration, dementia, cardiovascular disease, cancer, all of them brought under control. *That* is the greater good. *That* is what governments like ours will never bring us, because they cannot work together. So we take matters into our own hands. Money can change the world, Mr. Carter. And I make no apologies for being a very, very rich man."

"And all of this? Everything you've been doing?"

"To ensure that we can continue to protect people who need protecting."

"Is that your sales pitch?"

The old man's smile flickered for just a moment, betraying a chink in the armor, a glimpse at the man behind the mask of civility. "I am simply asking you to consider the bigger picture. Prejudice, as I am sure you can appreciate, is a killer."

"I'm just not sure I'm buying this, Mr. . . . . I'm sorry, I'm not very good at names. Until yesterday I thought he," Jake nodded out toward the deck, "was called Harry. Turns out I was wrong."

"Alom. Gabriel Alom."

"Mr. Alom. It all sounds a bit too good to be true. Self-serving."

"Let's not forget that you asked for this parlay, Mr. Carter. You have come here, into my home, carrying secrets I already know, and want to trade them for your life? But I don't see how that benefits me. If you want a secret kept, the best thing you can do is not share it. Once two people know, a secret it is impossible to keep unless one of them is dead."

"I'll be honest, that's what I expect. I came here thinking that maybe I'd get one shot, cut your throat or crush your skull, and then your goons would take me out. I came in here prepared to die. I've made my peace with it."

312

"How very noble of you. You truly are a warrior. What if I told you it doesn't have to end that way? That there's an alternative."

"I'd say I don't believe you," Jake replied. "We're both men of the world, let's keep the bullshit out of this."

The old man leaned forward and put something on the table between them. A gold pin.

"I can always use a good man like you, Mr. Carter. Especially considering the losses we have encountered recently."

"You're asking me to join you? What, just pick up where Sophie left off?"

"I'm presenting it as an alternative."

"You want me to kill for you?"

"Crude, Mr. Carter. I want you to consider how you have wasted your life since leaving the service of our country, and to consider taking it up again. We have enemies, people who don't want us to see our plans through to fruition. There are always predators and prey, Mr. Carter. And every predator is prey for some other apex hunter."

"And who preys on you? Or are you the apex predator?" Jake asked, unable to help himself.

"You can answer this yourself. Did you simply stumble upon the brownstone, or were you dispatched? And don't bother lying to me, I know Sophie reached out to them. She told them who you were and how she hoped to use you to strike at the heart of our operations here in New York. She used you. They all did."

"But you won't? Is that it?"

"Oh, no. I'll use you too. I won't lie to you, though—that's the difference."

"But who are they?"

"Department of Defense, Homeland Security, the NSA,

the FBI, the Defense Intelligence, any of them, all of them. We frighten them because we are the one thing that can deny them control as we march toward a brave new world. We are free men. We have money. Money grants power in this day and age, but more than that, it buys influence. We shape the politics of the world. We can make things happen one way or another."

"So why all this now?"

"Control costs money, Mr. Carter. That is just the way the world works. If you want to make a difference you need to have money. Lots of it. It doesn't matter whether it is New York, Paris, London, New Delhi, or Tokyo—it still costs money. If you are poor, you are a drain on society, you weaken the world rather than add to it."

"Okay. So you're not some end-of-the-world cult? This is all about money and politics?"

"Isn't it always?"

"Right. The rich get richer, the poor get poorer, and never the twain shall meet? And the deal is, I take this," he looked down at the pin, "you let me live, but I become an enemy of the United States government. I say no, you kill me. Am I missing something?"

"I won't kill you."

"Semantics," Jake said. "I'll be just as dead whether it's you who pulls the trigger or Harry."

"Then use your head, take my offer. Think of the good you can do. You say you are patriotic. Serve your country again, Mr. Carter. She needs a few good men now more than ever."

Jake stared at the tiny gold pin on the table between them, such a small, insignificant thing, and yet carrying so much weight. Picking it up would mean taking on the burden

Sophie had carried, but it would also keep Finn and Ryan alive. Was that the kind of devil's debt he was prepared to take on?

He took the memory stick out of his pocket and set it down on the table. "This is everything we took. But like you said, the only way two people can keep a secret is if one of them is dead. Take it in exchange for their lives. This is just between us. It ends here."

"Does that mean you are saying no?"

"No."

# THE BEGINNING

"**S**O THAT'S IT, THEN?" Finn asked, not quite accepting that they'd just given up. "We're good? No one's going to be waiting for me in the office one day to make me disappear?"

They were having lunch at a little café near Columbia. She'd had a morning class but was free until two. He was tired but didn't have anywhere to be now that he'd handed in his notice with the MTA. He had a new paymaster.

"We're good," Jake replied, running the back of the spoon over the latte's foamed milk. It was hard to believe it had only been a week. It already seemed like a long nightmare ago, but in those seven days so much had happened to undo the worst of it: the city had regained power, the grid coming back online after a couple of days. According to reports circulating in the mainstream media, the poles had stabilized; scientists were on the TV all the time talking about magnetic fields and shielding the earth from solar radiation. Suddenly everyone was an expert. There were still shooting stars, but people had stopped thinking they were meteors coming to wipe out humanity because the sun had failed. The blackouts were becoming fewer and farther between as things settled down. Now they were down to the weather, not the sunfail phenomenon.

Most noticeably, the birds had begun to fly again, returning to their usual migratory patterns, and the dogs weren't running wild through the streets—proof if any were needed that the animal kingdom had adapted to the change. Dogland was a thing of the past. Manhattan was back to being Manhattan.

"Any news from the dive?"

"Actually, yeah . . . I've been thinking . . ."

"Always a dangerous thing."

"Indeed." She grinned at him. "I really hate the snow and I'm due a break. Fancy a trip to Cuba? I hear the diving's really good this time of year."

Jake smiled. "I've got a confession to make." She hadn't questioned him about the gold pin on his collar. He'd told her it was a souvenir. A reminder. He hadn't told her it was the price of her safety.

"Uh-hunh?"

"You might need to teach me how to swim."

She smiled too, the tension visibly leaving her body. "I can do that."

New York's key infrastructure seemed to be functioning normally—power, transportation, communication, finance, security; there were no obvious signs of interference. All indicators seemed to suggest life around Jake was returning to normal.

Of course, that was *around* him. His life would never be normal again as long as he wore that pin on his collar. He knew they were watching him even if he couldn't see them.

That was what they did. Lurked. Clung to the shadows. Alom might claim it was all noble, but monsters never thought they were evil. And he had absolutely no doubt that Gabriel Alom was a monster.

Jake had made a deal with the devil. If he was lucky, he'd live long enough to regret it. But that was a problem for tomorrow. Right now, Finn was safe. That was his win. That was all he'd wanted when he set foot on that yacht, to keep her safe, to keep Ryan safe. He was a simple man.

A week, two, a month, just them, even if she was working, would give them a chance.

They hadn't slept together yet. He liked that word: *yet*. It was only a matter of time. He wanted to get it right. To get to know her properly. He wanted to be her friend first.

Or that was what he told himself. He didn't want to think about the fact that in saving her life he'd essentially traded his own.

"Harry's handed his notice in," Finn told him. "He's got an offer out in France."

*Paris*, Jake thought, knowing Harry had stepped up to fill Sophie's shoes, making the opening here in New York for Jake. Or should he call himself Bahlam, the Jaguar God who, so Alom told him, protected people and communities?

Yesterday he'd seen Sophie's face in a newspaper. The report explained how she had been murdered in a café in London, and how she was believed to have been behind the bombing of the stock exchange. They didn't know the truth, and they weren't interested in it, because the people paying to put the news out there were the same people who wanted to keep it hidden.

That was just the way the new world worked. He understood that now better than anyone. Sometimes in this life you had to become the thing you hated in order to protect the thing you loved. But this didn't mean you had to like it.

Jake didn't know how he was going to do it, but when he'd said "No" to Alom, he'd meant it. Two people couldn't keep a secret. He *was* going to bring Alom down. And all the others. He was smart enough to know the only way he was going to do that was from the inside. So if he needed to pretend to be their man, he'd pretend. He'd smile and grit his teeth and all the while remember Sophie and her promise that she wasn't who he thought she was. Was that how she'd started? Trying to make the world right? She'd known exactly who he was when she'd dragged him into this. He was a man who couldn't walk away. Not now. Not ever.

Jake took a sip of his latte, and reached out for Finn's hand.

She was the bridge between past and future. He was going to need her. With Finn at his side, he felt like he could take on the world.